Dan Mc Faul The Weaver

Copyright ©Danny Mc Faul 2011

All rights reserved. No part of this book may be reproduced, stored, or transmitted by any means— auditory, graphic, mechanical or electronic—without written permission of both publisher and author, except in the case of brief excerpts used in critical articles and reviews. Unauthorized reproduction of any part of this work is illegal and is punishable by law.

Formatted using Microsoft Word

Printed and bound in the United Kingdom.

Compiled

By

Dennis Linton

&

Danny McFaul

Written

By

DANNY Mc FAUL

Contents

Dedication	7
About Us	8
Our Family Tree	9
Mc Fauls from Larne	10
Preface	11
Acknowledgements	12
Map of Northern Ireland	13
The old town of Larne	14
Introduction	15
What is Genealogy	16
Mc Faul Genealogy Wish	17
Family Crest	18
Family History	19
What's in a Name	20
Heraldry & Coat of Arms	21
Clans & Septs	22
What happened before the Plantation?	23

The great potato famine	37
The Second Generation	43
The Third Generation	52
The Gribbens	61
The Fourth Generation	76
Descendants of John Gribben	100
The Fifth Generation	143
Descendants of John Kirkbride	211
The Sixth Generation	216
The Seventh Generation	242
The Eight Generation	257
The Sullivans	260
Changes in Larne	280
Kinship of Dan the Weaver	282
Marriage Report	291
Other McFaul marriages in Ulster	293
Going home to Larne	311
I Had a Dream	350

Dedication

This is a Family history book and it is about people that we have lived with and loved and there are none more loved than our parents. That is why when we say "Father And Mother I Love You" the first letter of each word spells out **FAMILY**. For this reason we would like to dedicate this Family History book to our Fathers and our Mothers.

Denis Mc Faul

1904 - 1943

Mary Ellen Sullivan

1901 – 1942

Thomas Linton

1915 – 1942

Cecelia Mc Faul

1910 – 1980

About us

Dennis Linton and I only found out recently that we were related, but we soon realized that we had enough material between us to think about a book like this. I had written and published a few books and poems previously, but this was something quite different. Dennis has quite a good knowledge of both of our Grandfathers who were brothers, as he lived with **his** grandparents during World War Two instead of being evacuated as a refugee. He lived near the Harbour area of Larne. I on the other hand was brought up in the Mill Street and Mill Lane area of the Old town. Dennis and I have not lived in Larne since we left Ireland many years ago. I have been back to visit numerous times and if I am honest, I don't like that "Carbuncle" that can be seen on the landscape on the approach to the town via the A2. I am of course referring to the blocks of flats that replaced the area where I grew up in. The houses in the Old Town needed replacing as a lot of them resembled a "Slum area" but slum or no slum that was our home and we made the best of it. Because of my childhood memories of the Old Part of the town it will always have a special place in my heart. One thing that both Dennis and I agree about is that if we had been given the same opportunities in Larne after we had left school; we would not have left in the first place. But after school in those days the weekends were long and laborious as Sunday was a time when one had nothing to do unless you were a priest or a nun, boring for young men looking forward to making something of our new life in the workplace that was just beginning. But jobs were hard to find then, decent ones anyway. We therefore followed the path of many of our fellow countrymen before us and crossed the Irish Sea to mainland Britain.

Our Family Tree

For over two centuries Larne has been home to families called McFaul. This book attempts to Chronicle one such line of a McFaul family whose roots go back to about 1815. It is not meant to be an uncovering of individual family secrets as I hope that it rather presents some family history of those who are included and I hope that I have presented it in a reader friendly manner. Compiling a family history over 200 years is not an easy task as certain information poses a problem of what to include and what to leave out. It is made slightly easier in general terms by the fact that most of the families especially in the earlier years all went to the same school and church which in themselves played a part in their social, culture and educational lives in the town of Larne. In the early 19th century, Ireland was a poor place to live in and very few people when they died had any kind of a permanent memorial in a graveyard to celebrate their life and mark their passing away. Most families were of modest means and headstones being expensive, were not often considered. Therefore our early ancestor's last resting place would have been marked only by a small cross onto which was scratched his or her name. The wind and the elements would soon erode the name away and they only lived on for a while in the memory of those who knew and loved them. But once they too passed on, the memory would then die with them forever. I have tried to learn more about them; where and when they were born, what they worked at and how they lived and died. I am grateful for the opportunity to tell my family history in my own words as where once I only had names, dates and places on pieces of paper, these names, places and events have now helped me to view our ancestors in a very different way and look upon them as very real people again.

Dan Mc Faul The Weaver

Mc Fauls From Larne

This family history book is being written and published in order that our wider family members, those who are named McFaul, or otherwise, may understand their heritage more clearly. We hope that it will be read and referred to many times by those who have an interest. It may also be used by others from several nations to connect to their roots and in doing so accept or reject the information that we have included. However we would like to point out that it is more to do with the times and conditions that pertained to the people and the social pressures of the times. It is a "Family History" as well as just a "Family Tree". There are some pieces of information and statements of fact as we see it, from a perspective of hindsight and open information. We do not wish to hurt anyone or raise issues that may be long forgotten, we are endeavouring to put forward facts with clarity and honesty. Most of all we hope that readers will gain some knowledge of the life and times of the McFauls of Larne as well as perhaps being encouraged to seek further knowledge of their own inheritance.

Dennis Linton (2011)

Preface

There is nothing very nice about the history that was imposed upon Ireland and her people for the period during which my Ancestors lived there in the late 1700s. The atrocities committed in the name of 'British justice' over the centuries have few, if any, parallel in historical records. I was born in Northern Ireland into a Roman Catholic family and raised on Irish history as opposed to English History. I hold the view that everyone knows the same history as I do about my homeland. That same history that I have read in books or what I was taught in school. But history is never simple straightforward or without controversy. History is about the past and there should only be one truth about what happened in the past. I am not a historian but most historians write their individual accounts of what has happened in the past and no doubt all equally based on the true facts as they **believe** them to have been; at the same time reflecting different interests and written from **their own** points of view. We might all agree that history is about the past but it is looked at and written about from the 'present'. The past can't change but the present and the future does and so it should. But for the most part, few of us would like to be actually living again in the days gone by. However when dealing with the question of Irish History it is a fact that instead of having advancement for the benefit of all of mankind in Northern Ireland and learning by improving; those who have Ruled and Governed in the past have been a dismal failure for centuries.

Acknowledgements

It is difficult to single out individuals to thank for their information and interest when trying to put this book together in an interesting manner. There has been so many and I could never have compiled the information alone. But the one person who has been there with me over the years to search cemeteries sometimes in pouring rain has been my daughter Bernadette McFaul. She drove me between Larne and Portstewart visiting churches and cemeteries along the way, in what were days of working from early morning until late at night searching and recording our findings on five separate occasions over the past seven years.

I value the help that was given to me by Hughie McRandal during our research in Larne in 2004. I learned that Hughie had passed away some time after I had returned to my home in England. I have also learned that the Parish Priest at that time has also passed away. I am truly grateful to both of them for their invaluable help. The staff at Larne Library, the Museum (the old Carnegie Library), The Larne Borough Council, the churches, the Police and a department at the Public Records Office in Belfast have all tried to help us with our research even when some of our information was very sketchy and last but not least the great input that my cousin Dennis Linton has contributed to the shaping and compiling of this book, my grateful thanks to them all.

Dan Mc Faul The Weaver

Map of Ulster

Larne is described as a large town by the Northern Ireland Statistics Agency as it is in the category of a population between 18,000 – 75,000 people. The population at the 2001 census was 18,228 people, so it could be described as a very small, large town, by my Irish logic. The town is situated on the north east coast of County Antrim in Northern Ireland. It is about twenty miles north of the City of Belfast.

Dan Mc Faul The Weaver

The Old Town of Larne

This map shows the Old Town of Larne before 1963 when someone decided to build that eyesore in the shape of concrete blocks of flats. What must visitors coming to the town think, it is like the War years are back again. I hope the person responsible for building them has not been paid a bonus for his big mistake.

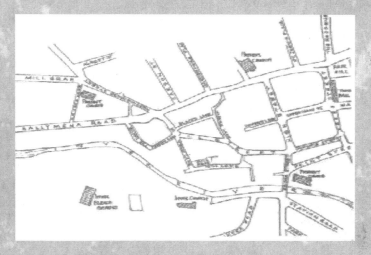

Cross Street virtually divides the new part of the town from the old town which comprised Mill Street as the main thoroughfare and a maze of other lanes. What is not shown on the map is the old Narrow Gauge Railway line that ran parallel with the Inver River. That single line track carried pulp from Ballyclare to Larne Paper Mill in Circular Road before the train was derailed in the 1950s and the wagons of pulp were deposited into the river. After this incident the track was never used again except by boys and girls like me to explore the mystery of the train that once passed us at Mill Lane every day on its way to the Paper Mill.

Introduction

Larne, small town as it is, has its own place in World History. It was where the town of Larne is now situated, that the very first settlers arrived in Ireland. They landed via the short Sea crossing from Scotland about 6000 BC and settled along the East Antrim coast.

They lived on fish and other food that they found in the area. Their tools included knives and scrappers made of flint. Gradually these settlers moved north along the coast to Magilligan Point, then Southwards to County Dublin and inland along the Bann and Lagan river valleys. Now I am not claiming that any of these people were called McFaul, or that they are amongst our ancient ancestors as they probably came from mainland Europe.

However the first record of the McFaul surname I believe was found in medieval records at Inverness in Scotland. These McFaul roots can be traced to Pictish time before the year 1100. It may be that our McFaul family ancestors arrived in Northern Ireland at the time of the Plantation of Ulster about 1607 when the counties of Antrim and Down were settled, mainly by people from the Scottish Lowlands. These settlements were the most successful of the plantation in Ireland and they helped to shape Northern Ireland to give the Province of Ulster the protestant character that it has today.

What is Genealogy?

The dictionary says it is the study of family lineage, but those of us who have delved into it can tell you that it is much more than a dictionary definition. The dictionary also says that since the 18th century it has developed into separate disciplines and listed amongst these is Family History.

Family History to me is by far the most interesting part of Genealogy. It is here that we place family members in their time period and find out how they lived, what they worked at and the living conditions at the time, putting the 'meat on the bones' of our family history I like to think.

People who tackle their genealogy and family history by galloping backwards in time just collecting dates names and places are rather like train spotters collecting train numbers who often miss their objective as the train thunders through the station at great speed. This is not the way to get the most out of our precious family history certainly not for me anyway.

However, for many reasons I cannot make comments about all the 570 plus Family Tree Member that appears in this book, but those whom I have commented on may be of interest to you and therefore help to make this book more pleasurable to read rather than just a long list of Names, Dates and Places.

Dan Mc Faul The Weaver

My Genealogy Wish

I

wish

to find

some relatives

from the past, by

searching in the sands

of **time.** And hope to find the

kin who are, this family tree of **mine.**

I wish to trace the trodden path, that once

my kin had **found.** Before it led them to, their

present resting **ground.** I wish to find the missing gap,

that seems to elude us **all.** For that is when I know I'll find,

those

who

are

called

McFaul

Family Crest

Our Family Surname of Mc Faul as far as I can ascertain does not have a Coat of Arms but it has a Family Crest as the above, at least I thought it did. I acquired this Crest from what was at the time, supposedly the largest reputable company dealing in this field in the United Kingdom. They did supply me with a Certificate of Authenticity way back in the 1970s and which I now believe is not worth the paper it is written on. It started by saying that this historyigraph (that is a fine word) was prepared for the McFaul surname on such and such a date. The crest was designed from information about the McFaul surname and its association with Heraldry.

In the language of the ancient Heralds the crest is described as follows; "Quartered: 1st, or the letter "M" sa; 2nd and 3rd az. ; a stag embowed purp.; 4th sa.; two fasces or Charged with a small golden inner shield purp. " The McFaul Family Crest is translated; etc etc.

This of course is absolute rubbish and I was not impressed. So be warned and be careful about where you look for your Family Coat of Arms.

Dan Mc Faul The Weaver

Family History

Family History is the study of our ancestors and it is commonly referred to as our ancestry or family tree. Though genealogy as a whole has been popular since biblical times, people have been inspired all over the world to learn more about their family history and Genealogy has become in many countries their number one hobby. For many people, and I am one of them, it is more of a passion than a hobby. What inspired me to find out more about my family history was when I discovered that my mother had been born in the Workhouse in Larne in 1901. My curiosity then got the better of me. "What about the rest of my ancestors"? I thought. I wanted to try to imagine what it was like to be living in that era, in one of those horrid establishments. It is after all a part of my family history and I want to publish and preserve it for my great grandchildren as it is a part of their Family History as well. I can think of no greater gift that I can offer them than a written knowledge of their family history. It may just help some mothers to answer that age old question that all children ask at some time in their young lives. *"Where did I come from Mum"?*

What's in a Name?

European surnames first occurred between the eleventh and fifteenth centuries. Prior to this, particularly during the "Dark Ages" between the fifth and eleventh centuries, people were largely illiterate. They lived in small villages, and had little need of distinction beyond their given names as everyone knew everyone else. During Biblical times people were often referred to by their given names and the locality in which they resided such as "Jesus of Nazareth." However, as populations grew, the need to identify individuals by surnames became a necessity. The majority of surnames are derived from patronymics, i.e. the forming of a surname from the father's given name such as Johnson, meaning literally "the son of John." Other methods of origin for surnames are derived from place names or geographical and occupational names. In some cases an individual was named after a bird or an animal. Fox would have been used for a person who was cunning or sly. Surnames were also derived from a person's status, such as Bachelor, Knight and Squire. Among the illiterate, individuals had and still have, little choice but to accept the mistakes of officials, who wrongly bestowed upon them new versions of the surnames that they were meant to be born with.

Heraldry & Coats of Arms

Heraldry emerged in Western Europe in the 12th century to meet the necessity of military identification. It originated from the military aristocracy as a hereditary system of identification. The term is commonly accepted as the devising, granting, and use of Coats of Arms, or armorial bearings. This type of symbolism became so popular that it was soon adopted by corporate bodies such as town governments, universities, and the church; and eventually by regiments and national states. Strictly speaking, the term heraldry has a wider significance, covering all the functions of a herald, or officer concerned with arms, genealogy, ceremonies, and precedence. A Coat of Arms was originally a light tunic i.e. (a coat extending down to the knees) decorated symbolically and worn over battle armour. The symbols served to identify the wearer (whose face might be covered by the visor of his helmet), as the member of a particular family or group. The symbols themselves eventually became known as a Coat of Arms.

Septs & Clans

In Scotland, a clan or a Sept are all families; within a certain order a clan is a family that is a legally recognized group which the head is a legally recognized chief. This group is like a company and is recognized by the law. A group that does not have a chief has no official or legal position. The Arms and the Seal of the chief are the seal of his clan, issued by Lord Lyon's letter of Patent to be used only by him to seal clan documents. The clan is the recognized personal and heritable property of the chief. He owns it and is responsible for its administration. Clan territories were the development of lands, either owned or controlled by the head of a family or the chief of the clan. Those who came to live on those lands were usually families that the chief had adopted as members of his clan. Some families that lived on these lands were not members of the clan and some Sept families, as they are known, belong to more than one clan. These families owed allegiance to the chief and showed it by wearing the chief's tartan and the crest badge of his arms that has now become the clan badge. A Sept family is only by the acceptance of the clan chief. McFaul is a Sept family of clans Mc Phail and Mc Intosh, but McFaul has more than one descendant family line; thus all the McFauls are not related to each other. Genealogical research is required to determine if a particular branch of a family was a Sept family of a Clan.

Dan Mc Faul The Weaver

What happened before the plantation?

There had been many wars in Ireland between the Irish and the English. The last one was the nine year War (1594-1603) which took place during the reign of Queen Elizabeth the First and ended with the defeat of the Gaelic chieftains. This now meant that the whole of Ireland was under English control. But in that very same year Queen Elizabeth died and as she had no children there was some controversy as to what would happen now. Elizabeth was replaced by her Scottish relative, King James of Scotland. The King of Scotland now became the king of England also. As a result the Scots were to play an important part in the plans for the plantation in Ireland. King James the First hoped that with the help of the people who came to Ulster that he would change the Province, as previous attempts at plantation had failed to do. He also hoped that the settlers from England and Scotland would be obedient to him and to his Government as he thought that Ulster needed to be 'civilized' and made to be more like England and parts of Lowland Scotland.

After being defeated by the English in the nine years war, two of the most powerful Irish chieftains, the Earl of Tyrone and the Earl of Tyrconnell left Ireland with many of their supporters in an event known as "The flight of The Earls". They boarded a ship at Rathmullan in County Donegal on 4 September 1607 hoping to sail to Spain where they would ask for help from the Spanish King to drive the English out of Ireland. Unfortunately due to storms the Earls never reached Spain. Instead they landed in France and ended up in Rome. They never returned to Ireland. The lands of these chieftains were confiscated and King James now had to decide what should be done with these territories. He eventually decided that the solution to the problem in Ulster should be to have another try at plantation. Most of the Irish people living in Ulster didn't see things this way and they resented the King interfering in their land. However the plantations did take place and brought many changes to Ulster.

The population grew rapidly as thousands of settlers arrived; many of them with their wives and children. The new people brought new names and customs to Ireland and the Protestant faith was introduced. Many people would argue that Ulster's problems really began with the plantations.

Ulster was the last Province to be brought under English control. King James hoped that the "planting" of loyal subjects would stop the threat of rebellion. Keeping law and order in Ulster was expensive and the King was also worried that if a Spanish army invaded Ireland they would find support among the Irish people.

The flight of the Earls meant that the King was now in possession of vast territories in the six counties and he could choose who should receive them. He saw a plantation as the perfect answer. By encouraging settlers from England and Scotland to move to Ulster, he hoped that the province would become richer and a richer Ulster meant a richer King because of the extra tax that would be paid. Many of the men from England and Scotland who received grants of land in Ulster sold out quickly and returned to their homelands. Some found it impossible to encourage British families to settle on their estates especially if the land they owned was remote and mountainous. Native Irish chieftains who were resentful of their changing circumstances took to the wilds as outlaws and were known as "woodkerns". Kerns were foot soldiers, lightly armed, with swords and wooden throwing darts. They represented a real threat to the more remote settlers, many of whom were wiped out in midnight raids. Despite the Woodkerns and the wolves that roamed the land at the time changes to Ulster came, evidence of this is everywhere, if we look around us. The changes manifest themselves in not only the buildings and towns, but in the very people who live in them. Many surnames are English and Scottish in origin. Inevitably many settlers and Irish married each other, so there are people today who regard themselves as Irish when they have British surnames and British when they have Irish surnames. Differences in speech and pronunciation were also introduced as a result of the plantation with the most important change being the spread of the English language. The Scottish settlers spoke Scots (also called Lallans) which continued to develop into what we now call Ulster-Scots (Ulallans). Of course new words were introduced by the Scots and even more new words were introduced through the close influence of the Irish language on the settlers. The plantation also brought a new religion to Ulster, Protestantism.

The church was ruled by bishops and archbishops, but many Scots settlers preferred a different system that was called Presbyterianism in which the ordinary people had more of a say in the running of the church. For some time there was trouble caused by the two different systems but eventually in the second half of the seventeenth century the Presbyterian Church was established as a separate denomination from the Church of Ireland.

Generation 1

From the earliest of times fibres have played a vital part in human life, not only as a means of clothing, but also as basic commodities such as wool, silk, linen and cotton, on which entire empires have been based. Without the skill to spin a thread and to weave it into cloth, textiles as we know them today would not exist. The invention of the spindle for twisting fibres into yarn was on a par with that of the wheel in terms of importance for the progress of civilization. The earliest known evidence in Ireland of woven material dates from about 1600 B.C, as pottery from that period shows signs of woven material in which the clay was placed before firing. Cloth found in a bog in County Antrim is dated from about 700 B.C. Fragments of woven fabric and weaving tools have also been found in the excavations of Viking and Medieval Dublin. So important were the skills of spinning and weaving in early Ireland that the Brehon Laws, written about 700 A.D. lay down as part of a wife's entitlement in cases of divorce, that the wife should keep her spindles, wool bags, weaver's reeds and a share of the yarn she had spun and the cloth she had woven.

At this moment in time our Ancestry Trail goes back to the year of about 1815 when one Dan McFaul was born somewhere in the Glens of Antrim I believe. Dan worked as a weaver in the mid 1800s and he had a son called Denis McFaul who was born in 1840.

Dan Mc Faul The Weaver

The Industrial Revolution had spread throughout Europe. Steam powered machines led to an increase in the number of textile factories or mills from Country to Town. As the number of factories grew people from the countryside began to move into the towns looking for better paid work. Farm workers were poorly paid and there were less jobs available working on farms because of the invention of new machines such as threshers. In addition, new workers were needed to operate the machines in mills and foundries and in many instances factory owners built houses for them. Cities filled to overflowing as rooms were rented to whole families. If there were no houses to rent people stayed in lodging houses. Belfast was the engine room that drove the wheels of the industrial revolution in Ulster.

But of course this was not all good news because housing conditions like these were the perfect breeding grounds for diseases. More than 31,000 people had died during an outbreak of cholera in 1832 and lots more were killed by typhus, smallpox and dysentery. But we must remember that Belfast was only a village in the 17th century. As Belfast grew it became a metropolis of half a million people; which at the time was approximately one third of Northern Ireland's population. Developing industries like linen, rope-making and shipbuilding doubled the size of Belfast as a town every ten years as it did many other towns throughout Europe. In Larne during 1833 there were 152 cases of cholera reported and 54 of these resulted in death. Twenty two years later in 1854 the dreaded **Cholera** returned to the area when it claimed the lives of some of its victims in Glenarm village. Popular belief is that it was brought there by a woman lodger from Ballymena who had come to the village for a Fair Day.

Whatever Era of history we talk about, *"lifestyle"* is a person's way of life. In modern times wage earners can usually determine their own lifestyle. Therefore by living in comfortable accommodation, buying nice clothes, going on holidays and driving a modern car, one could be considered to have a good lifestyle and quite obviously income is the main factor in all of this. That was not the case in the early nineteenth century Ulster when Dan the Weaver's family were making their way in life. At that time 90% of the population lived on the land. Landlord-ism, religion, famine, market forces or politics determined the lifestyle for everyone. To understand what it was like living in Dan the Weaver's time it is perhaps best done by trying to answer the question; "What were conditions like in rural Ulster between 1800-1900"?

In a nut shell, landlords monopolised the political and economic power of Ulster since the plantations in 1607 and the colonisation during the first few years of the seventeenth century. Later the landlords safeguarded their position by voting for the Act of Union in 1801 which ensured their dominance for a further 50 years. During this time the rural population had inadequate incomes, yet everyone, no matter what their religion, was compelled to pay tithes to the Church of Ireland, (and the Tithe records of these payments are another good source of Family History information).

These taxes had a devastating effect on country lifestyle and with harvest failures in 1835 and 1837 tenants had to continue paying exorbitant rents with no guarantee given. By 1842 over £6 million from rents were lost.

Non- payment in many cases meant eviction and no economy could have survived such restrictions as these. Then in 1830 the linen industry collapsed and for generations small farmers, labourers and those who rented a small cottage with or without a plot of land supplemented their incomes by working hand looms from home. The raw material was supplied to homes and weavers got paid for the finished product. Weavers that lived on uneconomical farms of 12 acres or less suffered the most. Throughout the years in Ireland the Wars seems to have helped the Ulster economy while Peacetime seemed to bring recession. This was the case after Waterloo (1815) when prices for farm produce plummeted. This caused great concern in the farming community. Also much civil unrest had spilled over from the 1798 rebellion.

However mechanisation put a sudden end to any extra income. In short, new factory looms were invented and each loom could do the work of 100 hand weavers. Consequently tens of thousands in rural Ulster lost a valuable source of income.

Life was one of hardship for most. People felt safer in their own neighbourhoods and an acceptable lifestyle was now non-existent. More tension ensued when in 1823 Daniel O'Connell formed the Catholic Association. This was the first time Catholics became properly organised and commenced agitating for reforms. Catholic Emancipation (1829) was the outcome. Around the same time the Orange Order increased its membership rapidly and had around 20,000 Yeomen in its ranks. Ulster at the time was on its knees and it was not because everyone was praying. Yet, Larne became Ireland's greatest centre for tourism after the Shore road was built between 1832 and 1842. It is about 32 miles in length and runs from Larne to Ballycastle through the Glens of Antrim. Hotels and lodging houses were built. On the Antrim Coast hotels were established in Glenarm, Carnlough, Cushendall and Cushendun.

The main reason for all this building activity was that the Antrim Coast Road was the only scenic route in Ireland where up to four horses could pull thirty passengers for over thirty miles. This was due to the lack of hills on the road that runs parallel to the sea coast for most of the way and the wealthy middle class, had incomes to spend on their lifestyle. As a consequence, the short sea route from Stranraer in Scotland to Larne, attracted many tourists from Glasgow and further afield. The Coast Road cuts through some of the darkest events in Irish history. It was planned immediately after the 1798 Rebellion, an event which led directly to the 1801 Act of Union, creating the United Kingdom of Great Britain and Ireland under one government in London. The road hugs the coast around massive headlands and great bays for over 20 miles. Its completion was overshadowed by the Great Irish Potato Famine. Thankfully the road became an escape route for a starving population from this part of Co. Antrim at that time. The road was originally called the "Grand Military Way" and was seen, especially after the 1798 Rebellion as an essential entry for the Military to move into a former inaccessible area. Today the Antrim Coast road remains one of the most unique and scenic coastal drives in the whole of Europe and I personally enjoy every moment travelling through the beautiful glens of Antrim. This boom time on the Antrim Coast had a knock on effect on peoples lifestyles as thousands of jobs were created locally which improved the local economy and the middle classes were provided with facilities to 'while away' their leisure hours. But there is a price to pay for every success and in the building of the Antrim Coast Road, magnificent feat that it was; the price in this case was a life being lost for each mile that was constructed. Dan the Weaver would have seen the time, well into the 19th century, when there was no standard time in the United Kingdom. Each town or village set its own time, with varied differences occurring between one town and the next. This never posed a major problem then, as people never moved very far from their birthplace until the advent of rail travel when people started to make frequent journeys between towns for the first time. But with so many different times in operation, railway companies found it impossible to devise a sensible timetable. In January 1848 all railway stations adopted GMT for their timetables. But Legal time remained "local time" until an Act of Parliament in 1880; when Greenwich Mean Time was adopted. GMT was adopted by an international conference in 1884 as the basis for international timekeeping.

Like many other places Larne saw much jubilation in 1862 with the arrival of the first train from nearby Carrickfergus. This was the first broad gauge passenger train to convey visitors to the town despite the many problems and setbacks that had been encountered prior to its arrival. To make this all happen land had to be claimed from the sea to make way for the broad gauge line and a new road that we now know as Circular Road. But in the nineteenth century Ulster was not a healthy place to live in, despite a gradual rise in living standards. Diseases such as typhus, smallpox, typhoid and diphtheria were rife. In 1851 an Irish dispensary service was established under the control of the Poor Law Commission. It was available to all who could not afford medical attention. There were 180 dispensaries in Ulster, each with one or more medical officers. A new class within the medical profession emerged, the general practitioner. Nevertheless there were never sufficient sick beds (so nothing has changed there). Sharing of beds was practised in workhouses which only helped spread these diseases. Inevitably thousands perished unnecessarily due to ignorance and neglect. I am always mindful when I write or read about the times and the troubles in Ireland that Dan the Weaver could have perished as a result of one of the many diseases, the sectarian strife, or the disasters that have occurred since his birth about 1815. Possibly the most horrific being the Great Potato Famine of 1847. A lot can be learned about how our ancestors live from studying old photographs of the County of Antrim; especially around the Larne area where many of our relations were born and comparing them with present day images. It helps one to visualise what it must have been like to live there at that time. It was a turbulent period of Irish history and to fully understand Irish life as it was then, it is essential to know that the Protestant landowning class created by the plantations ruled Ireland. But the British Government didn't allow them complete freedom. Restrictions were put on Irish trade and only the linen industry was encouraged, which is no surprise then that our ancestor Dan was a Weaver. If there was not a school, the children would be set to work at home from a very early age. Many Country Weavers worked at their homes, or in bad weather, worked in sheds or barns, rented from farm owners. Some also lived in thatched peasant cottages, whilst City Weavers worked in Mills. Socially they had periodic festivals that included music and dancing in the fields. Storytelling was also a pastime; and a typical village community would include a forge, a weaving cottage, a post office, and a smoke house. Though this was in the 1800s other than people's names, very little else seemed to have changed in the manner in which the people lived. People in their small villages lived very simple lives and lived mainly off the land. Their lives were uncomplicated. A typical village school size would be around thirty children and families were also much larger then. This could be a result of the high Infant Mortality rate. Many in those days lived and died having only ever travelled but a few miles from where they were born. Generally speaking the earliest Schools in Ireland were those established by Royal Charter in the 1700s and more commonly known as "Charter Schools". The provision of Catholic Education and the ability for Catholic Teachers to Teach during Penal Times was forbidden. So whilst there was no

Catholic Schools, education was often provided through illegal "Hedge Schools" so called because they were conducted in the open country side. In addition to Charter & Hedge Schools, wealthy estate owners would often build a school on their land for the education of children living on their Estate and in the local area. These schools were often open to children of all denominations. In 1782 Catholics were granted permission to teach, but it took the Stanley Education Act of 1831 before the real start of Primary School education in Ireland. This Act entitled all children, irrespective of religious denomination, to receive a free education. Despite this provision, and the establishment of National Schools in every Parish in Ireland, school attendance was poorly supported during most of the 19th Century, with the number of children attending usually in the region of 10 and 20 per class, and often fewer, especially during the Harvesting months. It was only in 1893 when Primary education was made compulsory that parents were legally obliged to send their children to school, and Inspectors were empowered to take offending parents to Court for children having poor-attendance. It is therefore unlikely that Denis and his father Dan had received any formal education. The first Christian Brothers School, like the one that I once attended in Belfast, was established in 1824 and the 19th century saw many of these schools being opened throughout Ireland. These Schools were a popular alternative to the National Schools for Catholic families, especially since the 1831 Education Act provided for all lessons to be taught in English, (as opposed to Gaelic) and English history lessons to be taught, as opposed to Irish History. The early School Registers only provided basic information on each pupil, usually a name, address and age. Though the date of leaving School, can very often be of great genealogical importance, in terms of what our

Ancestor went on to do next and can really help us progress in Family Research. Often the School teachers would write;

"Off to America" Or "Gone to help on Father's Farm" Or" Gone to College"

The School teacher would also sometimes write details of previous Schools attended together with details of where our Ancestor lived previously, which is a great help when tracing what people done, or where they lived. Some schools in the middle of the 1800s kept a logbook of entries for attendance and lessons, much like the register today. But this would not be recognisable to today's pupils who may now walk through into a reception area with a library, before making their way to one of their centrally heated classrooms. On the other hand, pupils back in the 1800s probably had to make do with one room heated with an open fire. Today's children enjoy a rounded education with the aid of computers and the Internet, as well as the opportunity to do extra-curricular activities. Back in the 1800s, the School logbook might have stated: "Reading doesn't seem to be well taught, children wrote much better on their slates." These logbooks would also possibly have recorded that a pupil was absent for reasons like; "Keeping birds off the berries and Hay making,". Or "Hop-picking not finished yet". Or "Spud planting"

Many village schools were run by just one teacher, who if they were lucky may have a senior pupil or a past pupil to assist in the running and teaching of the school or classroom. The following extract from the 1851 Census of County Antrim illustrates just how young some of the children started working. You can see also that young Patrick Mc Cambridge was working as a linen Weaver at the age of twelve, and his younger brother Thomas was Herding Cattle at the age of ten.

Z//2/UPPER TULLYKITTAGH TOWNLAND//

J/ARCHIE/MCCAMBRIDGE/HEAD/M/44//FARMER

J/MARY/MCCAMBRIDGE/WIFE/M//34/NONE/

J/MARY/MCCAMBRIDGE/DAUGHTER/U//18/WEAVER.

J/JAMES/MCCAMBRIDGE/DAUGHTER/U//15/LABOURER

J/PATRICK/MCCAMBRIDGE/SON/U/12//WEAVER/

J/THOMAS/MCCAMBRIDGE/SON/U/10//HERDING CATTLE

J/FRANCIS/MCCAMBRIDGE/SON/U/5//NONE

There is also that glaring mistake that was made by the census official when he recorded that Archie Mc Cambridge's DAUGHTER James age 15 was working as a labourer. Or maybe it was a Census transcriber who actually made the blunder.

The Irish Potato Famine

Throughout the Famine years, large quantities of native grown wheat, barley, oats and oatmeal sailed out of places such as Limerick and Waterford for England, even though local Irish were dying of starvation. This was because Irish farmers, desperate for cash, routinely sold the grain to the British in order to pay the rent on their farms and thus avoid eviction. In the first year of the Famine, deaths from starvation were kept down due to the imports of Indian corn and the survival of about half the potato crop. Poor Irish people survived the first year by selling off their livestock and pawning their meagre possessions whenever necessary, to buy food. Some borrowed money at high interest from petty money-lenders, known as "Tick" men. Throughout the summer of 1846, the people of Ireland had high hopes for a good potato harvest. But the cool moist summer weather had been ideal for the spread of the potato blight. There were only enough potatoes to feed the Irish population for a single month. Panic swept through the country. Local committees were besieged by mobs of people, demanding jobs on public works projects. Fish, although plentiful along the West Coast of Ireland, remained out of reach in waters too deep and dangerous for the little cowhide covered Irish fishing boats. Starving fishermen pawned their nets and tackle to buy food for their families. To make matters worse, the winter of 1846-47 became the worst in living memory as one blizzard after another, buried homes in snow up to their roofs. Amid this bleak winter, hundreds of thousands of desperate Irish sought work on public works relief projects. By late December 1846, 500,000 men, women and children were at work building stone roads. They built roads that went from nowhere to nowhere in remote rural areas that had no need of such roads in the first place. Many of the workers were poorly clothed, malnourished and weakened by fever some fainted or even dropped dead on the spot. The men were unable to earn enough to feed themselves let alone their families as food prices continued to rise. Corn meal now sold for three pennies a pound, three times what it had been a year earlier. As a result, children sometimes went unfed so that parents could stay healthy enough to keep working for the desperately needed cash.

Some children had become like skeletons, their features sharpened with hunger and their limbs wasted, so that little was left but bones, their hands and arms, in particular, being much emaciated, and the happy expression of infancy gone from their faces, leaving behind the anxious look of premature old age. The dead were buried without coffins just a few inches below the soil, to be gnawed at by rats and dogs. In some cabins, the dead remained for days or weeks among the living that were too weak to move the bodies outside. In other places, unmarked hillside graves came into use as big trenches were dug and bodies dumped in them and covered with quicklime. Most died not from hunger but from associated diseases such as typhus, dysentery, relapsing fever, and famine dropsy, in an era when doctors were unable to provide any cure. Highly contagious 'Black Fever,' as typhus was nicknamed since it blackened the skin, was spread by body lice and was carried from town to town by beggars and homeless paupers. Doctors, priests, nuns, and kind-hearted people who attended to the sick in their lice infested dwellings also perished. Rural Irish, known for their hospitality and kindness to strangers, never refused to let a beggar or homeless family spend the night and often unknowingly contracted typhus. At times, entire homeless families, ravaged by fever, simply lay down along the roadside and died. Landlords, desperate for cash income, now wanted to grow wheat or graze cattle and sheep on their estates. But they were prevented from doing so by the scores of tiny potato plots and dilapidated huts belonging to penniless tenants who had not paid rent for months, if not years. To save their estates from ruin, the paupers would simply have to go.

The stark realization of how difficult our Ancestors' lives were in bygone years becomes all too apparent, and although the Potato Famine destroyed many Irish families in the 19th Century, there were many other difficulties that they had to overcome. Families were large in the 1600s-1800s, as many children didn't live to see adulthood. One of the causes of death in young women was childbirth; countless numbers of our Ancestors lost family members to Cholera, Typhoid, Tuberculosis, Smallpox and other diseases that were rampant during those times. Also young men in Ireland gave their lives in the countless battles that were fought during the 19th Century and earlier. Yet, despite these and many other adversities, our Ancestors were survivors and we are all the living proof.

Dan the Weaver may well have suffered as a result of the Famine in Ireland as would his son Denis McFaul as he would have been a lad of seven or eight years old when an estimated half a million Irish were evicted from their cottages.

The famine was a defining event in the history of Ireland and of Britain. It has left deep scars. That one million people should have died in what was then part of the richest and most powerful nation in the world is something that still causes pain as we reflect on it today. Those who governed in London at the time failed their people through standing by while a crop failure turned into a massive human tragedy. We must not forget such a dreadful event. Britain in particular has benefited immeasurably from the skills and talents of Irish people, not only in areas such as music, the arts and the caring professions, but across the whole spectrum of our political and economic and social life. The actions by the Government at the time were deliberate, as it was of little consequence to them how many Irish people died.

This is the type of transatlantic ship that was transporting Famine victims from the port of Larne. These ships were supposed to be inspected for disease and any sick passengers removed to quarantine facilities. But in the spring of 1947 shipload after shipload of fevered Irish people arrived, many suffering from the effects of the crammed and unsanitary conditions aboard the ships. It was estimated that nearly half of the "below deck" passengers died during the journey or immediately after arrival.

Although there were supposed to be regulated, many of the ships were privately owned and some Captains grossly overcrowded them in order to make more money. It has been said that only the Slave ships of the previous century would have had worse conditions.

Indeed the untold story of the Great Famine in Ireland is hidden behind myths and the distortion of the truth as the plain facts are that the British allowed both communities, Protestant and Catholic to starve; while the ports of Derry, Belfast, Larne and Newry continued to export food that had been sold by farmers from both of the communities in order to pay their rent. Those who left the country to go to North America or Canada were taken there on what were called Coffin Ships many of which were not seaworthy.

This then was the harsh background that Dan the Weaver and his family members would have been born into and lived through in Ireland during the nineteenth century.

I am disappointed that as yet I have not been able to trace a pioneering Ancestor who took that bold step of leaving Ireland for America during the Famine years in the mass exodus from Ireland following the Potato Blight of 1846. Over 1 million Irish emigrants passed through Castle Gardens Immigration Station in New York between 1847-1861, all seeking to escape starvation, poverty and hardship. The majority arrived on American shores penniless. For most a farm environment in Ireland was all they would have known, where very little time and attention was paid to numeracy or literacy. This meant that their only source of employment on arrival was in the unskilled labour market (for men) and domestic service (for women). The 19th Century unskilled labour market was a dangerous one with very little pay as our Irish Ancestors helped dig America's first canals, lay the first Rail road tracks and pave New York's Streets. The Domestic Service market was no better where hard labour and long hours was met with a pittance as payment. With no savings income or employment many Irish found themselves trapped in places like New York. The Green fields of Ireland were replaced with over-crowded tenements filled with destitution, filth and disease. Before leaving Ireland our Ancestor may have complained about having to share the family home with numerous siblings, parents and grandparents. In New York they would have found themselves sharing a room with three maybe four different families. In 1862 over 6,000 families were found to be living in Cellars in New York that had no light, drainage or sanitation. The reality of emigration was that most Irish were worse off for leaving Ireland and many wanted to return home, but very few could afford to. Despite the hardships in the New World, many of our Irish Ancestors were able to claw their way out of the slums and secure a better future in the New world and in Ireland

Generation 2

1840

DENIS Mc FAUL2 (DAN1)

Denis McFaul was born in 1840.

He married Ellen McAdorey in Larne on 14 March 1864

He was described as a Sailor on his marriage certificate.

Dan Mc Faul The Weaver

This is Agnew Street where Ellen lived in one of those white houses on the left and where the Catholic schools were situated. McKenna Memorial School has gone now but it was next to the church. You can just see the church Spire on the right. The boys went to McKenna Memorial Public Elementary School (PES) and the girls went to St. Mary the convent school.

The girls were taught by nuns and I have heard a few stories of parents having to go to the schools to tell the nuns and teachers a "few home truths", after complaints from some of their children about how they were treated. The Nuns, Priests and School teachers were no saints or angels I know, I went to school there. This was to my mind because they had no proper accountability as they ran the schools and were answerable to no one else.

Dan Mc Faul The Weaver

Little is known about Dan the weaver's schooling, nor that of his son Denis, but in the 19th century, due to the Penal Laws, the elementary education of Catholics in Ireland was mainly carried out in the Hedge Schools, so called because of the custom of holding classes in the open in fine weather. During bad weather a shed was generally provided; and in Glenariff one of three caves near the pier where Denis would have sailed into and out of in his "Sailor" days provided shelter. Another of the caves was occupied by an old woman, who was the local poteen supplier. She also supported herself by knitting and spinning. She died in 1847 aged 100. A blacksmith's forge occupied the other cave.

Ellen Mc Adorey and Denis had seven children. Their first born was a son that they named Daniel after his Grandfather Dan, which was the tradition at the time. Daniel was born on November 12, 1964 and he was registered at Larne where his parents lived. Sadly young Daniel developed Scarlet fever and died on 25, June 1896 in Larne at the age of 4 years. When their son Daniel, (their second son called Daniel) was born in 1881 Denis and Ellen were living in Quay Lane which was a narrow roadway at the foot of which was a small pier where boats tied up at high tide. Some years later they also lived in Cockle Row, a row of cottages where mainly the Fishermen lived. They could bring their boats right up to Cockle Row, which was so called because of the number of Cockles found nearby.

However one of the important contributions to this book was made by Dennis Linton in the form of a document that seems to point to when our Ancestor Denis McFaul died. This document is from the Registrar's Office regarding deaths at Larne Infirmary in 1922 and it confirms the following facts. Denis died on 17 February 1922 the cause of death was debility.

It seems that Denis was residing in the Infirmary as that is what is documented as his address.

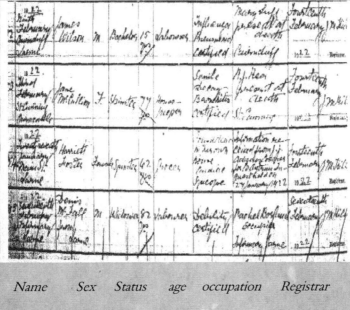

Name	Sex	Status	age	occupation	Registrar
Denis McFaul	M	widower	82	labourer	M. Killen

The Registrar, Doctor Killen was appointed as medical officer for the Larne Union Workhouse in 1872 a position that he held for more than 50 years. He signed my mother's birth certificate in 1901 when she was born and also those of her brothers Barney in 1904 and George in 1906. He also signed my father's birth certificate after his birth in 1904. He was appointed to the Larne Dispensary in 1883 and served in this capacity for 41 years.

Doctor Killen died in 1926 at the age of 80 years. He was also a very well - known and respected son and servant of Larne.

The infirmary was part of the Workhouse so sadly Denis died in the workhouse infirmary.

Dan Mc Faul The Weaver

This Marriage Certificate for Denis and Ellen has no McFaul, or McAdorey sponsors.

The names of the two sponsors are; Daniel Agnew and Mary Anne Dorris.

It is very interesting to note that when I bought this certificate at Larne it was £1.25pence and today it costs from £20 - £30.

This is Quay Lane and Cockle Row as I said; where Denis and Ellen lived when my Grandfather Daniel was born in 1881. As can be seen it was a narrow roadway at the foot of which was a small pier where boats tied up at high tide. They could bring their boats right up to Cockle Row.

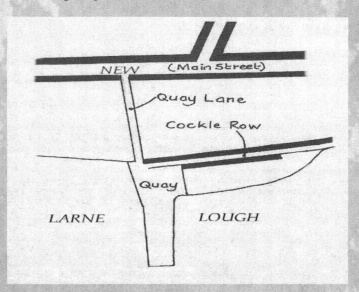

I believe that when the tides were right the fishermen in Cockle Row could set to sea from their back doors. Since those days some of the land has been reclaimed from the sea as the town continued to build and keep up with modernisation.

Generation No. 2

2. DENIS² MCFAUL *(DAN¹)* was born 1840, and died 17 Feb 1922 in Larne Infirmary. He married ELLEN MCADOREY 14 Mar 1864 in Larne. She was born 1840.

Children of DENIS MCFAUL and ELLEN MCADOREY are:

DANIEL³ MCFAUL, b. 12 Nov 1864, d. 25 Jun 1869,

DENIS MCFAUL, b. 17 Dec 1866, Larne; d. 10 Apr 1948,

ALICE MCFAUL, b. 12 Nov 1868, Larne; d. 05 Aug 1935,

JAMES MCFAUL, b. 05 Aug 1871, Larne; d. 06 Jul 1944,

ELLEN MCFAUL, b. 30 Aug 1873, Larne; d. 05 Feb 1943,

BRIDGET MCFAUL, b. 12 Dec 1878, d. 12 Apr 1951,

DANIEL MCFAUL, b. 10 Jun 1881, Larne; d. 06 Feb 1957,

In 1865 a newspaper, Larne Weekly Reporter was printed for the first time in. Plans were drawn up to construct Curran Road and a Town Hall. All the streets and lanes are to be named and houses to be numbered.

These changes followed within a short while. Lots of other changes were being made, providing much needed work for the townspeople. These were all new ideas then and what we take for granted today. Can you imagine it; Streets with no names and houses without numbers and no junk mail.

Generation No. 3

1866

DENIS Mc FAUL 3 (DENIS2 DAN1)

Son of

Denis McFaul & Ellen Mc Adorey

Was born 17 Dec 1866 in Larne, and died 10 Apr 1948 in Larne. He married MARGARET MCMULLAN 25 Aug 1888 in Larne, daughter of WILLIAM MCMULLAN. She was born 1868 in Larne, and died 24 May 1933.

This Denis worked at Larne Harbour as a Dock labourer for the greater part of his life which was a tough job in those days as the unloading of the ship's cargo was all done manually including the many Coal boats that passed through the busy port of Larne. This was an interesting time in the history of Larne as prior to this time the linen industry was mainly confined mainly to the banks of rivers where there was a constant water supply to drive wheels, which is the reason Mill Street and Mill Lane were the chosen area in Larne for the Milling industry; next to the Inver River. The invention of the steam engine opened new opportunities for the mill owners and being no longer dependent solely on water they often moved premises, or to larger towns and not just Belfast. This increased the trend of urbanisation and generally Towns grew in population.

When Denis's son Denis was born in 1903;

The Smiley Hospital was built.

1906 the Carnegie Free Library opened.

1907 a new Weaving factory opened in Glynn Road.

1911 Larne Technical School opened.

1913 the Mourne Clothing Company opened.

1913 British Portland began to make Cement.

1915 saw the construction of High Street.

The Great War 1914 – 18 started.

1919 Shipbuilding Co. opened at Curran Point.

1920 the Electricity Power station in Point Street is moved to Coastguard Road at the Curran Point.

1922 the Mourne Clothing Company moved production to Mill Street and by this time the population of the town of Larne had soared to well over 10,000.

It is worth mentioning here that the following statistics were recorded at the 2001 Census of our town of Larne;

18,228 people living in Larne.

20.9% of the population were under age 16.

21.2 % were aged 60 or over.

48.2% of the population were male.

51.8% were female.

26.2% were from catholic background.

70.7% were from a Protestant background

4.3% of the population aged between 16 and 74 were unemployed.

I suspect with the" credit crunch" today in 2009, these figures will be very much out of date, not to mention the influx of foreigners to the country from other parts of the European Community.

I look forward to seeing the 2011 population statistics for Larne.

Children of DENIS MCFAUL and MARGARET MCMULLAN

ELLEN[4] MCFAUL, b. 16 Mar 1889, Larne; d. 16 May 1945,

JANE MCFAUL, b. 19 Apr 1891, Larne; d. 17 Nov 1959,

JAMES AGNEW, 04 Aug 1930, Larne; d. 09 Jun 1967,

WM JOHN MCFAUL, b. 23 Jul 1893, Larne.

JOSEPH MCFAUL, b. 15 Jul 1896, Larne; d. 12 Nov 1944,

JEANIE RAMSEY, 27 Feb 1930, Larne.

REBECCA MCFAUL, b. 1899, Larne.

DENIS MCFAUL, b. 1903, Larne; d. 23 Nov 1950, Larne

1868

ALICE 3 Mc FAUL (DENIS 2 DAN1)

Daughter of

Denis McFaul & Ellen Mc Adorey

Alice McFaul was the first female child to be born to Denis and Ellen Mc Adorey. She being the first female would have been called Alice after her Maternal Grandmother (Dan the Weaver's wife), if the naming tradition was adhered to. Alice was born 12 Nov 1868 in Larne, and died 05 Aug 1935 in Larne. She married ALEXANDER HAYES 07 Jan 1891 in Larne.

Children of ALICE MCFAUL and ALEXANDER HAYES;

JAMES[4] HAYES, b. 1893, Larne;

d. 29 May 1933,

REBECCA HAYES, b. 1897,

The 1911 census indicates that Alice had three children born alive but only two were still alive. The other thing of note is that it states that she was married and that she was the head of household, there was no indication of her husband's whereabouts.

1871

JAMES 3 Mc FAUL (DENIS 2 DAN1)

Son of

Denis McFaul & Ellen Mc Adorey

Was born 05 Aug 1871 in Larne, and died 06 July 1944 in Larne. He married CECILIA GRIBBEN 15 Nov 1900 in Larne. She was born 1879 in Larne, and died 11 May 1944. James owned a small fishing business. He had a small boat, known as a skiff which he used to fish for herring and mackerel. James and some of his family would go with a handcart to sell their fish. Mostly their herring was sold from house to house. James used a white enamel plate to display about half a dozen herring to best advantage to catch the eye of his customers. He also sold to local shops from his cart. James was also a Harbour Pilot and worked at this over the pre-war and early war years of the 1940s. As a Harbour Pilot he would row out to vessels wishing to dock and brought these ships in through the rocks and the tricky treacherous weather in Larne Lough.

This is James in the forefront, with two of his "Last of the summer wine" friends relaxing in the town park in Larne during his retirement sometime in the late 1930 or early 1940 years. The business that James had was sold to a Mr Moore, also of Quay Street Larne some time before James died as he had Alzheimer's disease then; and it is probable that it was his wife Cecelia and the family who sold the business.

This ship that is docked at Larne Harbour in 2009 is a far cry from the days when James was working as a pilot. At least two of these huge ships enter and leave the Port of Larne approximately every four hours day and night with Lorries laden with goods and supplies from and to Fleetwood in England and Cairnryan in Scotland.

Several of James and Cecelia's children were associated with the sea and the navy. Two were Master Mariners and some of his grandchildren were mariners and counted Masters amongst them. James and his family lived at Quay Street where brothers Denis and Daniel also lived. All three of them worked at Larne Harbour.

Children of JAMES MCFAUL and CECILIA GRIBBEN.

FRANCIS[4] MCFAUL, b. 1900, Larne; d. 1901, Larne.

ELLEN MCFAUL, b. 1901, Larne; d. 1914, Larne.

JOSEPHINE MCFAUL, b. 1901, Larne; d. 1959.

ALICE MCFAUL, b. 10 May 1904, Larne; d. 10 Oct 1975,

CECELIA MCFAUL, b. 1910, Larne; d. 20 Aug 1980,

BRIDGET MCFAUL, b. 1912, Larne; d. 06 May 1972,

DENIS MCFAUL, b. 1912, Larne; d. 1915, Larne.

ELLEN MCFAUL, b. 1918, Larne.

JOSEPH D. MCFAUL, b. 21 Jul 1920; d. 02 Mar 1994

JAMES DENNIS MCFAUL, b. 18 Oct 1923, Larne.

The Gribbens

1812

1. JOHN[1] GRIBBIN

John was born in 1812.

He married CECELIA MC CALLION 1934.

Cecelia was born in 1815.

Children of JOHN GRIBBIN and CECELIA MC CALLION;

THOMAS[2] GRIBBIN, b. Aug 1837.

JOHN GRIBBIN, b. 1840.

HENRY GRIBBIN, b. Jul 1844.

WILLIAM GRIBBIN, b. Jul 1845;

ROBERT GRIBBIN, b. Dec 1851.

FRANCIS GRIBBIN, b. Jan 1855.

1855

FRANCIS² GRIBBIN *(JOHN¹)* was born Jan 1855.

He married ELLEN MCKAY Sep 1876 in Larne.

Children of FRANCIS GRIBBIN and ELLEN MCKAY ;

CECILIA³ GRIBBEN, b. 14 June 1879

JOHN.GRIBBEN, b. 17 June 1877.

SUSAN GRIBBEN, b. 1882.

FRANCIS GRIBBEN, b. 1884.

MARY ELIZABETH GRIBBEN, b. 1888.

ELLEN GRIBBEN, b. 1891.

1879

CECILIA³ GRIBBEN *(FRANCIS² GRIBBIN, JOHN¹)*

Was born 14 June 1879 in Larne, and died 11 May 1944.

She married JAMES MCFAUL 15 Nov 1900 in Larne.

He was a son of DENIS MCFAUL and ELLEN MCADOREY.

James was born 05 Aug 1871 in Larne, and died 06 Jul 1944.

Cecelia was the daughter of Francis Gribben and Ellen McKay.

1881

NELLIE³ GRIBBEN *(FRANCIS² GRIBBIN, JOHN¹)*

Mary Ellen (Nellie) was born in 1881.

She married Edward Mc Cambridge.

Nellie died in 1959.

Auntie Nellie had a large influence in Dennis Linton's early life and his education.

1884

FRANCIS³ GRIBBEN *(FRANCIS² GRIBBIN, JOHN¹)*

Frank Gribbin was born in 1884.

He was the son of Francis Gribbin and Ellen Mc Kay.

According to the 1901 census of Larne Frank was living with his mother and his stepfather Joseph McLean at 19 Quay Lane in Larne.

Frank was at the time working as a 17 year old general labourer, probably at Larne Harbour.

Frank later joined up for the First World War (1914 – 1918) and sadly he lost his life in battle at the Dardinells; on 15 august 1915.

I must apologize for my spelling of the name Gribbin. The truth is that I have no idea how it is spelt. I have had it spelt to me as Gribben, Gribbon, and Gribben from different sources. For what it is worth, the family that I knew in Larne all those years ago spelt their name as Gribben. This I got from the church records. I of course have no way of telling that this was not the interpretation by the church official as his way to spell the name.

1873

ELLEN³ MCFAUL *(DENIS², DAN¹)*

Daughter of

Denis McFaul & Ellen Mc Adorey

Was born 30 Aug 1873 in Larne, and died 05 Feb 1943 in Larne. In this case the naming tradition seems to exist as Ellen being the second female child is called after her mother Ellen.

Children of ELLEN MCFAUL are:

LISA⁴ MCFAUL, b. 1894; d. 18 Dec 1971.

BRIDGET MCFAUL, b. 1898; d. 23 Sep 1957.

ALICE MCFAUL, b. 1899;

An extract from Larne Workhouse census of 1901.

Mc F. E 27 Female - R C. Co Antrim Factory Worker

Mc F E J. 7 Female - R C. Co Antrim Scholar Read and write.

Mc F B   3 Female - R C. Co Antrim

Mc F A   2 Female - R C. Co Antrim

1878

BRIDGET³ MCFAUL *(DENIS², DAN¹)*

Daughter of

Denis McFaul & Ellen Mc Adorey

Was born 12 Dec 1878 in Larne, and died 12 Apr 1951 in Larne. She married SAM BAXTER 02 Jan 1900 in Larne, son of SAMUEL BAXTER. He was born 1880 in Larne, and died 17 Feb 1918 in Plymouth Hospital England.

Children of BRIDGET MCFAUL and SAM BAXTER are:

BRIDGET⁴ BAXTER, b. 1899;

MARY ANN BAXTER, b. 1901, Larne; d. 22 Nov 1982, Larne.

NELLIE BAXTER, b. 31 Mar 1903;

m. GEORGE MURDOCK, 20 Dec 1963, Belfast St. Patrick's.

SAM BAXTER, b. 1905, Larne; d. 06 Oct 1976, Larne.

ALICE BAXTER, b. 15 Jan 1908, Larne; d. Larne.

ISABELLE BAXTER, b. 19 Mar 1910, Larne; d. 03 Nov 1977

Dan Mc Faul The Weaver

The Baxter's lived at number 18 Portland Street Larne. Samuel was a fisherman so it was no surprise that he joined the Royal Naval Reserves during the Great War. Samuel was attached to HMS "Wellington". Very sadly Samuel was one of the 147 Larne men who lost their lives during The Great War.

HMS Wellington

Samuel Baxter died in Plymouth Hospital aged 38 on 17 February 1918. Samuel was a seaman by rank and his service number is 1319C. Samuel Baxter is buried in FORD PARK CEMETERY PLYMOUTH.

Dan Mc Faul The Weaver

1881

DANIEL 3 Mc FAUL (DENIS3 DENIS 2 DAN1)

Son of

Denis McFaul & Ellen Mc Adorey

DANIEL³ MCFAUL *(DENIS², DAN¹)* was born 10 Jun 1881 in Larne, and died 06 Feb 1957 in Larne. He married (1) ANNIE HOGG 20 Nov 1898 in the Chapel Larne County Antrim Northern Ireland, daughter of WILLIAM HOGG and SARAH MARTIN. She was born 12 Jul 1880 in Ahogill, and died in Larne. He married (2) MARGARET CLAXTON.

Daniel lived for a long time at Quay Lane where he was born. My father was also born at Quay Lane which was redeveloped in 1929 and renamed Quay Street. He would not have attended McKenna Memorial PES where all the McFaul male children went to in Larne. The school was opened in 1896 when he was 15 years old. The forerunner of McKenna Memorial School

Dan Mc Faul The Weaver

was called North End National School; and that is the school that he attended. He worked in one of the Factories in the town and he married Annie Hogg who also worked at the same factory, The Larne Weaving Company.

They were both 18 years of age at the time when they married in 1898. She was the daughter of William John Hogg and Sarah Martin, who lived at the time in Ahogill near Ballymena.

My Grandparents were married on 20 November 1898.

They had seven children between the years of 1900 and 1918.

Daniel was the youngest of Denis and Ellen Mc Adorey's children and he lived through the Boer War and both World Wars One and Two; and part of the Cold War. Daniel was born on 10, June 1881and for the greater part of his life he worked as a labourer at the boats in Larne Harbour.

Dan Mc Faul The Weaver

This photograph was taken many years after my Grandparents worked there but the working attire would not have changed greatly as the aprons were easy to put on and get off again and offered good protection from stains and dyes and they still do in some industries today.

I worked in Brown's Factory for a brief time. I had my right arm trapped in the "softening" machine rollers at that factory and it left a bad "Burn" mark that is very plain to see today. I was very lucky that another worker dashed very quickly to switch the machine off. There was no safety guard around the machine as health and safety regulations in the workplaces were not as stringent as they are today. My accident happened in the early 1950s

Children of DANIEL MCFAUL and ANNIE HOGG .

WILLIAM JOHN[4] MCFAUL, b. 1900, Larne; d. 26 Jan 1984,

ANNIE MCFAUL b. 20 Jun 1902 Larne; d. Larne.

DENIS MCFAUL, b. 07 Aug 1904, Larne; d. 28 Mar 1943,

SARAH MCFAUL, b. 10 Jun 1907, Larne; d. 08 Jan 1974.

NELLIE MCFAUL, b. 11 Mar 1909, Larne; d. 11 May 1970,

CHARLOTTE MCFAUL, b. 1915, Larne; d. 29 Jan 1986,

DANIEL MCFAUL, b. 31 Jan 1918, Larne; d. 30 Aug 2006;

m. LILY ENGLISH, 20 Jun 1944;

My Grandfather married a lady called Margaret Claxton in 1941.

1906

Margaret Claxton

Wife of

Daniel Mc Faul

Margaret Claxton was born in Larne in 1906.

She died in Larne on 6 August 1992 at the age of 86.

Margaret was the daughter of Charles Claxton and Annie McConnell.

Children of DANIEL MCFAUL and MARGARET CLAXTON ;

CHARLES[4] MCFAUL, b. 1943.

DENIS MCFAUL, b. 1944.

 d. 22 July 2003

JAMES MCFAUL, b. 1946.

KATHLENE MCFAUL, b. 1948.

1871

Charles Claxton

Margaret's father Charles Claxton was yet another casualty of the Great War, his details are as follows.

CLAXTON CHARLES BORN 1871.

Royal Naval Reserve; H.M. Yacht "Zaida."

Date of Death: 17/08/1916

Age: 40 Rank Leading Seaman

Service Number 2090D

Leading Seaman Charles Claxton RNR was a member of an armed Yacht…ZAIDA of 350 tons that that was owned by former British Prime Minister the Earl of Rosebury prior to the First World War. Some say it was sunk by a German Submarine, whilst others say that it struck a mine in the Gulf of Alexandretta.

The fact is that it sunk with the loss of thirteen lives. At least another four men died as Turkish POW, one on 30 September and one each on 15, 17, 25 November 1916.

It seems that the ZAIDA was engaged in Intelligence work as a Military Intelligent Officer Captain Woolley was on board at Port Said and he was one of the prisoners that were taken by the Turks. The following are the names of those who did not survive.

BURNLEY, Samuel, Assistant Cook, MMR, 696361

CAWTE, William G, Able Seaman, MMR, (none given)

CLAXTON, Charles, Leading Seaman, RNR, D 2090

DIXON, Frederick, Carpenter, MMR, 742459

GRIFFITHS, Edwin, Ty/Sub Lieutenant, RNR

JOHNSTON, Edward C, 3rd Engineer, MMR, (none given)

LAMONT, George, Assistant Steward, MMR, 700964

MYALL, William, Able Seaman, MMR, (none given)

NOBLE, James D, Act/Petty Officer, RNR, D 2269

ROYLE, William, Able Seaman, MMR, (none given)

SPENCE, Samuel G S, Engine Room Artificer, RNR, EC 18

STONE, Frederick W, Ty/Engineer Sub Lieutenant, RNR

THIRLWELL, Robert, Ty/Sub Lieutenant, RNR

Charles and his wife Annie were living at 22 Chapel Lane as boarders in 1901. Charles was a sailor then.

Generation No. 4

1889

ELLEN[4] MCFAUL *(DENIS[3], DENIS[2], DAN[1])*

Daughter of

Denis McFaul & Maggie Mc Mullan

Was born 16 Mar 1889 in Larne, and died 16 May 1945 in Larne. She married JAMES MCKEOWN 25 Jul 1914 in Larne, son of THOMAS MCKEOWN and ROSE QUINN. He was born 10 May 1888 in Larne, and died 29 Jan 1967 in Larne.

Children of ELLEN MCFAUL and JAMES MCKEOWN are:

ROSE[5] MCKEOWN, b. 03 Mar 1922, Larne; d. 10 Feb 1999,

MALACHY MCKEOWN, b. Larne; d. 03 Sep 1984, Larne.

MARGARET MC KEOWN, b. Larne; d. 27 Feb 1997;

ROBERT JOSEPH MCKEOWN.

GERARD MAJELA MCKEOWN.

1891

JANE 4 Mc FAUL (DENIS3 DENIS 2 DAN1)

Daughter of

Denis McFaul & Maggie Mc Mullan

Jane was born on 19 April 1891.

She married James Agnew on 4 August 1930.

Jane died 17 November 1959

James died 9 June 1967.

1893

WM JOHN[4] MCFAUL *(DENIS[3], DENIS[2], DAN[1])*

Son of

Denis McFaul & Maggie Mc Mullan

Was born 23 Jul 1893 in Larne. He married ELLEN HOEY 13 Feb 1916 in Larne, daughter of SAM HOEY and SARAH DUFFIN.

Children of WM MCFAUL and ELLEN HOEY are:

NELLIE[5] MCFAUL.

RUBY MCFAUL.

BETTY MCFAUL.

1896

JOSEPH 4 Mc FAUL (DENIS3 DENIS 2 DAN1)

Son of

Denis McFaul & Maggie Mc Mullan

Joseph was born in July 1896

He married Jeannie Ramsey on 27 November 1930

Joseph died 12 November 1944

Joseph worked as a message boy as his first job, after leaving school.

Joseph is buried in the same grave as his sister Jane and her husband James Agnew.

1903

DENIS[4] MCFAUL *(DENIS[3], DENIS[2], DAN[1])*

Son of

Denis McFaul & Maggie Mc Mullan

Was born 1903 in Larne, and died 23 Nov 1950 in Larne. He married JANE PURDY 05 Aug 1926 in Larne, daughter of JOHN PURDY and MARY MCNEILL. She was born 1905 in Larne, and died 16 Jan 1948

Children of DENIS MCFAUL and JANE PURDY are:

CLARE[5] MCFAUL, b. 07 Dec 1926, Larne; d. 20 Jul 1987,

JOHN MCFAUL, b. 20 Jan 1928, Larne; d. 06 Jan 2008,

DENIS MCFAUL, b. 27 Dec 1929, Larne.

MARGARET MCFAUL, b. 25 Mar 1931, Larne.

NELLIE MCFAUL, b. 26 Jun 1933, Larne

VERONICA MARY MCFAUL, b. 11 Sep 1935, Larne.

JAMES LEO MCFAUL, b. 1937, Larne; d. 17 Jun 1981,

Dan Mc Faul The Weaver

1892

JAMES HAYES 4 (ALICE 3 DENIS 2 DAN1)

Son of

Alice McFaul & Alexander Hayes

James Hayes was born 1892

James died on 29 May 1933.

1897

REBECCA HAYES 4 (ALICE3 DENIS 2 DAN1)

Daughter of

Alice McFaul & Alexander Hayes

Rebecca Hayes was born 1897.

1900

FRANCIS Mc FAUL 4 (JAMES3 DENIS 2 DAN1)

Son of

James McFaul & Cecelia Gribbin

Francis was born in 1900.

He died of a Children's disease.

1901

ELLEN Mc FAUL 4 (JAMES3 DENIS 2 DAN1)

Daughter of

James McFaul & Cecelia Gribbin

Ellen was born in 1901.

She was a twin to Frances Josephine.

Ellen died in her early teenage years in 1914.

1901

JOSEPHINE[4] MCFAUL *(JAMES[3], DENIS[2], DAN[1])*

Daughter of

James McFaul & Cecelia Gribbin

Was born 1901 in Larne, and died 1959.

She married PETER MEEKIN.

Peter Meekin was a Soldier and then a Coal miner.

Child of JOSEPHINE MCFAUL and PETER MEEKIN is:

EILEEN[5] MCFAUL, b. 1928, Larne; d. 01 Sep 1987, Larne;

m. DAVID ROSENTHAL, 1948.

Dan Mc Faul The Weaver

1904

ALICE Mc FAUL 4 (JAMES3 DENIS 2 DAN1)

Daughter of

James McFaul & Cecelia Gribbin

ALICE was born 10 May 1904 in Larne, and died 10 Oct 1975 in Larne. She married JACK MC CULLOUGH 29 Jun 1931 in Larne. He was born 23 Nov 1903 in Larne, and died 09 Aug 1987 in Larne.

Children of ALICE MCFAUL and JACK MC CULLOUGH;

JACKIE[5] MC CULLOUGH, b. 08 Jan 1932, Larne;

DONALD MC CULLOUGH, b. 06 Feb 1933, Larne.

JAMES MC CULLOUGH, b. 06 Feb 1934, Larne.

KATHLEEN MC CULLOUGH, b. 28 Jun 1935, Larne.

CECELIA MC CULLOUGH, b. 24 Oct 1948, Larne.

1910

CECELIA Mc FAUL 4 (JAMES3 DENIS 2 DAN1)

Daughter of

James McFaul & Cecelia Gribbin

Was born September 20, 1910 in Larne Co Antrim, and died August 20, 1980 in Liverpool, Merseyside. She married (1) THOMAS LINTON, son of JAMES LINTON and ELLEN LINTON. He was born March 12, 1915 in Larne, Northern Ireland, and died October 24, 1942 in El Alemein, Lybia North Africa. She then married (2) JAMES COLLINS NURSE. He was born on 27 January 1900.

Children of CECILIA LINTON and THOMAS LINTON

THOMAS[5] LINTON, b. May 5, 1934; d. May 7, 1934,

DENNIS ANTHONY LINTON, b. February 21, 1938,

Dan Mc Faul The Weaver

Cecelia and her new husband left Larne and went to live and work in Elland, a small town in Yorkshire. After the birth of her second child she returned to weaving as a job and helped her sister Ellen and her husband's brothers to move there from Ireland; jobs being more plentiful in England.

At the outbreak of war in 1939 Thomas volunteered for the Army and joined the Seaforth Highlanders. One of his brothers returned to Larne and the other stayed to work in the mills. Cecilia sent her son Dennis to live in Larne with her mother for safety instead of sending him away as an evacuee to live with strangers. She joined the Queen Alexandra Nursing Unit and saw service in the blitz in London. After her husband was killed in North Africa in 1942 she joined the Royal Navy and served until 1947.

1915

Thomas Linton Husband of

Celia Linton (Nee McFaul)

Thomas is the son of James Linton and Ellen Jane Linton (Nee Weir). He was born in the town of Larne on 12 March 1915. Thomas was a Dyer in the spinning/weaving industry in N. Ireland and also in Elland Yorkshire before joining the British Army as a volunteer. He was in signals within the Seaforth Highlanders, a famous Scottish Regiment. Thomas Linton died on 24 October 1942 at El Alimein in North Africa. He was killed on the first night of the battle for El Alamein and is buried at the Tobruck Cemetery. His comrades-in-arms on the battlefield cut off his uniform buttons and insignia and privately returned them, along with his bible, to his wife in his tobacco pouch which still contained grains of desert sand. The battle at El Alamein lasted until November 4th. In all, 35,476 British and Commonwealth soldiers lost their lives in the three years of the North African campaigns of WW 2. The British Cemetery at

Dan Mc Faul The Weaver

El Alamein has thousands upon thousands of rock inscribed tombstones arranged in straight rows within a fenced garden. Most of the soldiers were British 8th Army led by General Montgomery. The Battle began on October 23, 1942. Private Thomas Linton was killed the following day.

This collection is Thomas Linton's Cap Badge, the buttons and badges from his Tunic, his War Medals and a broach that he gave to his wife Cecelia.

1947

BERNADINE[5] NURSE *(CECELIA[4] MCFAUL, JAMES[3], DENIS[2], DAN[1])*

Daughter of

Cecelia McFaul & James Nurse

Was born 27 Sep 1947

She married JOHN BROADFOOT.

He was born October 28, 1947 in Bootle, Liverpool

Children of BERNADINE NURSE and JOHN BROADFOOT

TRACEY[6] BROADFOOT, b. 24 Jul 1970,

CHERYL BROADFOOT, b. 24 Jul 1970,

DAVID BROADFOOT, b. 14 Apr 197.

1949

CORINNE[5] NURSE *(CECELIA[4] MCFAUL, JAMES[3], DENIS[2], DAN[1])*

Daughter of

Cecelia McFaul & James Nurse

Was born 23 Jul 1949.

She married FRANCIS SUMNER.

Child of CORINNE NURSE and FRANCIS SUMNER i

STACEY[6] SUMNER.

1912

BRIDGET Mc FAUL 4 (JAMES3 DENIS 2 DAN1)

Daughter of

James McFaul & Cecelia Gribbin

Bridget was born in 1912.

She was a twin to Dennis.

Bridget had no off springs.

She died 6 May 1972.

Bridget is buried in the RC cemetery in Larne with her father James and her mother Cecelia.

1912

DENNIS 4, MCFAUL (JAMES 3.DENIS 2, DAN1)

Son of

James McFaul & Cecelia Gribbin

Dennis was born in 1912.

He was a twin to Bridget.

Dennis died of a child disease at the age of three years.

1918

ELLEN[4] MCFAUL *(JAMES[3], DENIS[2], DAN[1])*

Daughter of

James McFaul & Cecelia Gribbin

Was born 1918 in Larne

She married FRANK SUNDERLAND 1940.

Children of ELLEN and FRANK SUNDERLAND

MARIE[5] SUNDERLAND, b. 13 Oct 1943;

m. KEITH HOLROYD.

JACQUELINE SUNDERLAND, b. 28 Nov 1945.

1920

JOSEPH DANIEL[4] MCFAUL *(JAMES[3], DENIS[2], DAN[1])*

Son of

James McFaul & Cecelia Gribbin

Was born 21 Jul 1920 in Larne, and died 02 Mar 1994 in Larne. He married (1) AGNES MCQUADE in Larne. She was born 1915 in Larne, and died 18 Dec 1965 in Larne.

Children of JOSEPH DANIEL MCFAUL are:

MICHAEL[5] MCFAUL.

KEVIN MCFAUL.

DANNY MCFAUL.

SEAN MCFAUL

Dan Mc Faul The Weaver

Though he was baptised Joseph Daniel, he was always referred to as Dan. Captain Dan I was told when I first discovered that we were related to each other. Due to circumstances beyond our control I have not had the privilege of meeting or knowing Dan. This is because I left Larne many years ago and only returned to visit. But one of my brothers knew him and he told me that Captain Dan had told him that "Our relations came from down the Shore" and he pointed my brother in the direction of Waterfoot in Glenariff.

I went to Waterfoot in the late 1970s and I found a Daniel McFaul buried in the Layde cemetery; he had died on 6 September 1881 aged 62. This Daniel would therefore have been born in 1819. But when I visited the records office and later the church at Cushendall I found that the records there start from 1885. I was therefore unable to connect this Daniel to any generation of our family. Yet he may have been Denis's Father and I live in hope that someday I will find the "Real Dan the Weaver". Joseph Daniel was a Master Mariner and during the 1940s and 1950s he owned a small shipping company with a fellow Sea Captain. They traded round the British Isles with three ships dealing in everything from Tea to Tobacco. Dan was a popular family member who was ever ready to help out at weddings and other family events. Dan helped to sort out my Grandfather's funeral arrangements when he died in 1957.

Dan Mc Faul The Weaver

1923

JAMES DENNIS Mc FAUL 4 (JAMES3 DENIS 2 DAN1)

Son of

James McFaul & Cecelia Gribbin

Was born 18 Oct 1923 in Larne

He married MARY BERNADETTE MCMULLAN.

Children of JAMES MCFAUL and MARY MCMULLAN;

JAMES[5] MCFAUL

BERNADETTE MCFAUL.

LIAM MCFAUL.

DEIDRIE MCFAUL, d. 31 Dec 2002.

ANGELA MCFAUL.

ANTHONY MCFAUL.

Descendants of John Gribben

1. JOHN[1] GRIBBIN

He married CECELIA MC CALLION 1834.

Children of JOHN GRIBBIN and CECELIA MC CALLION;

JOHN[2] GRIBBIN, b. Aug 1840

HENRY GRIBBIN, b. Jul 1844

WILLIAM GRIBBIN, b. Jul 1846;

m. ELIZABETH MC DOWELL.

ROBERT GRIBBIN, b. Dec 1851.

FRANCIS GRIBBIN, b. Jan 1855, Larne.

Generation No. 2

2. FRANCIS[2] GRIBBIN *(JOHN[1])* was born Jan 1855 in Larne. He married ELLEN MCKAY Sep 1876 in Larne.

Children of FRANCIS GRIBBIN and ELLEN MCKAY are:

CECILIA[3] GRIBBEN, b.14 June 1879,

JOHN GRIBBEN, b. 17 June 1877.

SUSAN GRIBBEN, b. 1882.

FRANCIS GRIBBEN, b. 1884.

MARY ELIZABETH GRIBBEN, b. 1888.

ELLEN GRIBBEN, b. 1891.

Generation No. 3

3. CECILIA³ GRIBBEN *(FRANCIS² GRIBBIN, JOHN¹)* was born 1879 in Larne, and died 11 May 1944 in Larne. She married JAMES MCFAUL 15 Nov 1900 in Larne, son of DENIS MCFAUL and ELLEN MCADOREY. He was born 05 Aug 1871 in Larne, and died 06 Jul 1944 in Larne.

Children of CECILIA GRIBBEN and JAMES MCFAUL are:

FRANCIS⁴ MCFAUL, b. 1900, Larne; d. 1901, Larne.

ELLEN MCFAUL, b. 1901, Larne; d. 1914, Larne.

JOSEPHINE MCFAUL, b. 1901, Larne; d. 1959.

ALICE MCFAUL, b. 10 May 1904, Larne; d. 10 Oct 1975,

CECELIA MCFAUL, b. 20 Sep 1910, Larne; d. 20 Aug 1980,

BRIDGET MCFAUL, b. 1912, Larne; d. 06 May 1972, Larne.

DENIS MCFAUL, b. 1912, Larne; d. 1915, Larne.

ELLEN MCFAUL, b. 1918, Larne.

JOSEPH DANIEL MCFAUL, b. 21 Jul 1920, d. 02 Mar 1994,

JAMES DENNIS MCFAUL, b. 18 Oct 1923, Larne.

Generation No. 4

4. JOSEPHINE[4] MCFAUL *(CECILIA[3] GRIBBEN, FRANCIS[2] GRIBBIN, JOHN[1])* was born 1901 in Larne, and died 1959.

She married PETER MEEKIN.

Child of JOSEPHINE MCFAUL and PETER MEEKIN ;

EILEEN[5] MCFAUL, b. 1928, Larne

d. 01 Sep 1987, Larne;

m. DAVID ROSENTHAL, 1948.

5. ALICE[4] MCFAUL *(CECILIA[3] GRIBBEN, FRANCIS[2] GRIBBIN, JOHN[1])* was born 10 May 1904 in Larne, and died 10 Oct 1975 in Larne. She married JACK MC CULLOUGH 29 Jun 1931 in Larne. He was born 23 Nov 1903 in Larne, and died 09 Aug 1987.

Children of ALICE MCFAUL and JACK MC CULLOUGH are:

JACKIE[5] MC CULLOUGH, b. 08 Jan 1932, d. 26 Apr 2000

DONALD MC CULLOUGH, b. 06 Feb 1933, Larne.

JAMES MC CULLOUGH, b. 06 Feb 1934, Larne.

KATHLEEN MC CULLOUGH, b. 28 Jun 1935, Larne.

CECELIA MC CULLOUGH, b. 24 Oct 1948, Larne.

6. CECELIA[4] MCFAUL *(CECILIA[3] GRIBBEN, FRANCIS[2] GRIBBIN, JOHN[1])* was born 20 Sep 1910 in Larne, and died 20 Aug 1980 in Liverpool. She married (1) THOMAS LINTON 12 Mar 1934 in Raloo Larne. He was born 12 Mar 1915 in Larne, and died 24 Oct 1942 in Egypt.

She married (2) JAMES COLLINS NURSE.

He was born 27 Jan 1900 in Trinadad

Children of CECELIA MCFAUL and JAMES NURSE are:

BERNADETTE[5] NURSE, b. 27 Sep 1947.

CORINNE NURSE, b. 23 Jul 1949.

Children of CECELIA MCFAUL and THOMAS LINTON;

THOMAS[5] LINTON, b. 07 May 1934, Larne; d. 09 May 1934

DENNIS LINTON, b. 21 Feb 1938, Halifax England.

7. ELLEN[4] MCFAUL *(CECILIA[3] GRIBBEN, FRANCIS[2] GRIBBIN, JOHN[1])* was born 1918 in Larne.

She married FRANK SUNDERLAND 1940.

Children of ELLEN MCFAUL and FRANK SUNDERLAND;

MARIE[5] SUNDERLAND, b. 13 Oct 1943.

JACQUELINE SUNDERLAND, b. 28 Nov 1945.

8. JOSEPH DANIEL[4] MCFAUL *(CECILIA[3] GRIBBEN, FRANCIS[2] GRIBBIN, JOHN[1])* was born 21 Jul 1920 in Larne, and died 02 Mar 1994 in Larne. He married (1) AGNES MCQUADE in Larne. She was born 1915 in Larne, and died 18 Dec 1965 in Larne. He married (2) MARGARET GLOVER 04 Nov 1966 in Larne.

Children of JOSEPH MCFAUL and AGNES MCQUADE;

MICHAEL[5] MCFAUL.

KEVIN MCFAUL.

DANNY MCFAUL.

SEAN MCFAUL.

9. JAMES DENNIS[4] MCFAUL *(CECILIA[3] GRIBBEN, FRANCIS[2] GRIBBIN, JOHN[1])* was born 18 Oct 1923 in Larne. He married MARY BERNADETTE MCMULLAN.

Children of JAMES MCFAUL and MARY MCMULLAN ;

JAMES[5] MC FAUL.

BERNADETTE MC FAUL.

LIAM MC FAUL.

DEIDRIE MC FAUL, d. 31 Dec 2002.

ANGELA MC FAUL.

ANTHONY MC FAUL.

Generation No. 5

10.   JACKIE[5] MC CULLOUGH *(ALICE[4] MCFAUL, CECILIA[3] GRIBBEN, FRANCIS[2] GRIBBIN, JOHN[1])* was born 08 Jan 1932 in Larne, and died 26 Apr 2000 in Larne.

He married TERESA LYNCH.

Children of JACKIE MC CULLOUGH and TERESA LYNCH;

TERESA[6] MC CULLOUGH, b. 26 Jun 1968.

SEAN MC CULLOUGH, b. 22 Nov 1958.

GERALDINE MC CULLOUGH, b. 26 Nov 1959.

MICHAEL MC CULLOUGH, b. 26 Oct 1963.

11.   JAMES[5] MC CULLOUGH *(ALICE[4] MCFAUL, CECILIA[3] GRIBBEN, FRANCIS[2] GRIBBIN, JOHN[1])*

Was born 06 Feb 1934.

He married MARIE CAMPBELL.

Children of JAMES and MARIE CAMPBELL are:

CAMPBELL[6] MC CULLOUGH, b. 08 Jan 1959.

PAUL MC CULLOUGH, b. 18 Feb 1960.

CHARMAINE MC CULLOUGH, b. 05 Oct 1962.

MARRIANNE MC CULLOUGH, b. 08 Apr 1965.

12. KATHLEEN[5] MC CULLOUGH *(ALICE[4] MCFAUL, CECILIA[3] GRIBBEN, FRANCIS[2] GRIBBIN, JOHN[1])* was born 28 Jun 1935 in Larne. She married JOHN BROWN.

Children of KATHlEEN and JOHN BROWN are:

MARLENE[6] BROWN, b. 22 Oct 1955.

RONALD BROWN, b. 21 Sep 1957.

ROBERT BROWN, b. 10 Jan 1960.

DAVID BROWN, b. 28 Nov 1963.

MONA BROWN, b. 22 Jun 1964.

CAROL BROWN, b. 31 Oct 1965.

BRIAN BROWN, b. 15 Oct 1970.

JAMES BROWN, b. 01 Nov 1975.

13. CECELIA[5] MC CULLOUGH *(ALICE[4] MCFAUL, CECILIA[3] GRIBBEN, FRANCIS[2] GRIBBIN, JOHN[1])* was born 24 Oct 1948 in Larne. She married DANNY MCCORMICK 21 Sep 1968 in Larne. He was born 04 Apr 1948 in Larne.

Children of Cecelia and DANNY MCCORMICK.;

MARC[6] MC CORMICK, b. 13 Jan 1969, Larne.

PETER MC CORMICK, b. 22 Sep 1974, Larne.

14. BERNADETTE^5 NURSE *(CECELIA^4 MCFAUL, CECILIA^3 GRIBBEN, FRANCIS^2 GRIBBIN, JOHN^1)* was born 27 Sep 1947. She married JOHN BROADFOOT.

Children of BERNADETTE and JOHN BROADFOOT are:

TRACEY^6 BROADFOOT, b. 24 Jul 1970, Liverpool.

CHERYL BROADFOOT, b. 24 Jul 1970, Liverpool.

DAVID BROADFOOT, b. 14 Apr 1972, Liverpool.

15. CORINNE^5 NURSE *(CECELIA^4 MCFAUL, CECILIA^3 GRIBBEN, FRANCIS^2 GRIBBIN, JOHN^1)* was born 23 Jul 1949. She married FRANCIS SUMNER.

Child of CORINNE NURSE and FRANCIS SUMNER is:

STACEY^6 SUMNER.

16. DENNIS^5 LINTON *(CECELIA^4 MCFAUL, CECILIA^3 GRIBBEN, FRANCIS^2 GRIBBIN, JOHN^1)* was born 21 Feb 1938 in Halifax England. He married ADRIENNE WATSON 1959 in Liverpool.

Children of DENNIS LINTON and ADRIENNE WATSON;

SHARON^6 LINTON, b. 07 Oct 1962.

ANDREW LINTON, b. 18 Jul 1966.

JAMES LINTON, b. 01 Sep 1967.

JOHN DOMINIC LINTON, b. 28 May 1970.

KATE LINTON, b. 30 Nov 1972;

17.   MARIE[5] SUNDERLAND *(ELLEN[4] MCFAUL, CECILIA[3] GRIBBEN, FRANCIS[2] GRIBBIN, JOHN[1])* was born 13 Oct 1943. She married KEITH HOLROYD.

Children of MARIE SUNDERLAND and KEITH HOLROYD:

CHRISTOPHER[6] HOLROYD, b. 09 Nov 1969.

SUZANNE HOLROYD b. 22 Mar 1972.

18.   JACQUELINE[5] SUNDERLAND *(ELLEN[4] MCFAUL, CECILIA[3] GRIBBEN, FRANCIS[2] GRIBBIN, JOHN[1])* was born 28 Nov 1945. She married IAN WALKER.

Children of JACQUELINE and IAN WALKER

MARK[6] WALKER, b. 20 Mar 1970.

NICHOLAS WALKER, b. 03 May 1972.

PAUL WALKER, b. 25 Jun 1973.

19.   JAMES[5] MCFAUL *(JAMES DENNIS[4], CECILIA[3] GRIBBEN, FRANCIS[2] GRIBBIN, JOHN[1])* He married GILLIAN WILSON.

Child of JAMES MCFAUL and GILLIAN WILSON is:

CHRISTOPHER[6] MCFAUL

20.   BERNADETTE[5] MCFAUL *(JAMES DENNIS[4], CECILIA[3] GRIBBEN, FRANCIS[2] GRIBBIN, JOHN[1])* She married DANNY ROWAN.

Children of BERNADETTE MCFAUL and DANNY ROWAN;

DANNY[6] ROWAN.

BARRY ROWAN.

JAMES ROWAN.

21.   LIAM[5] MCFAUL *(JAMES DENNIS[4], CECILIA[3] GRIBBEN, FRANCIS[2] GRIBBIN, JOHN[1])*

He married CHRIS DECKERS.

Children of LIAM MCFAUL and CHRIS DECKERS are:

LIAM DENIS[6] MCFAUL.

LISA MARIE MCFAUL.

BOBBY EDWARD MCFAUL.

22.   ANTHONY[5] MCFAUL *(JAMES DENNIS[4], CECILIA[3] GRIBBEN, FRANCIS[2] GRIBBIN, JOHN[1])* He married JOANNE DONNELLY.

Children of ANTHONY and JOANNE DONNELLY are:

MICHAEL[6] MCFAUL.

JOANNE MCFAUL, b. 1984

Generation No. 6

23. MARC[6] MCCORMICK *(CECELIA[5] MC CULLOUGH, ALICE[4] MCFAUL, CECILIA[3] GRIBBEN, FRANCIS[2] GRIBBIN, JOHN[1])* was born 13 Jan 1969 in Larne. He married ANNE CONNOR.

Children of MARC MCCORMICK and ANNE CONNOR are:

LAUREN[7] MCCORMICK, b. 25 Sep 1995, Larne.

ERIN MCCORMICK, b. 10 Jul 2001, Larne.

24. TRACEY[6] BROADFOOT *(BERNADETTE[5] NURSE, CECELIA[4] MCFAUL, CECILIA[3] GRIBBEN, FRANCIS[2] GRIBBIN, JOHN[1])* was born 24 Jul 1970 in Liverpool.

Child of TRACEY BROADFOOT is:

SHKIESHA[7] BROADFOOT, b. Jan 1989.

25. CHERYL[6] BROADFOOT *(BERNADETTE[5] NURSE, CECELIA[4] MCFAUL, CECILIA[3] GRIBBEN, FRANCIS[2] GRIBBIN, JOHN[1])* was born 24 Jul 1970 in Liverpool.

Children of CHERYL BROADFOOT are:

MATTHIAS[7] BROADFOOT, b. Apr 1995.

KYNA BROADFOOT, b. Oct 2002.

BOBBIE BROADFOOT, b. Jun 2006.

26. DAVID[6] BROADFOOT *(BERNADETTE[5] NURSE, CECELIA[4] MCFAUL, CECILIA[3] GRIBBEN, FRANCIS[2] GRIBBIN, JOHN[1])* was born 14 Apr 1972 in Liverpool.

Children of DAVID BROADFOOT are:

LUCCA[7] BROADFOOT, b. 1991.

GALI BROADFOOT, b. 2001.

1894

LISA Mc FAUL 4 (ELLEN3 DENIS 2 DAN1)

Daughter of Ellen McFaul

Was born 1894 in Larne, and died 18 Dec 1971 in Larne. She married JAMES CRAIGEN 11 Sep 1916 in Larne. He died 20 Feb 1971 in Larne.

Children of LISA MCFAUL and JAMES CRAIGEN are:

ISABELE[5] CRAIGEN, b. 28 Jan 1917, Larne.

ELLEN CRAIGEN, b. 26 May 1919, Larne.

1898

BRIDGET Mc FAUL 4 (ELLEN3 DENIS 2 DAN1)

Daughter of Ellen McFaul

Bridget Mc Faul was born 1898

She died 23 September 1957

Bridget is buried in the Larne RC cemetery with her mother Ellen and her sister Lisa.

The 1911 census shows a Bridget McFall was working as a domestic servant in a residence at Kilwaughter near Larne. She was the same age as Bridget.

1899

ALICE Mc FAUL 4 (ELLEN3 DENIS 2 DAN1)

Daughter of Ellen McFaul

Was born 1899. She married ROBERT DEEHAN 18 Oct 1918 in Larne, son of WILLIAM DEEHAN and MARGARET FARRELL. He was born 1897.

Children of ALICE MCFAUL and ROBERT DEEHAN;

WM. JOHN[5] DEEHAN, b. 07 Nov 1919, Larne.

ROBERT DEEHAN, b. 21 Aug 1921, Larne.

ELLEN DEEHAN, b. Sep 1923, Larne.

BRIDGET DEEHAN, b. Dec 1929, Larne.

ALICE DEEHAN, b. Mar 1932, Larne.

1900

WILLIAM JOHN[4] MCFAUL *(DANIEL[3], DENIS[2], DAN[1])*

Son of Daniel McFaul & Annie Hogg

was born 1900 in Larne, and died 26 Jan 1984 in Larne. Willie John married Sara Gillon, from Lanark in Scotland. She was the daughter of Patrick Gillon and Mary O'Donnell. The marriage took place in the Chapel at Larne on 31 December 1925. I don't know as yet what happened to Sara Gillon but Willie John married again on 20 October 1931 to Lily McBride the daughter of Denis McBride and Mary Peoples. Lily was born in Larne and died 27 Feb 1994 in Larne.

Children of WILLIAM MCFAUL and LILY MCBRIDE;

DANIEL[5] MCFAUL, d. 30 Apr 1953, Larne.

DENIS MCFAUL, b. 11 Jun 1933, d. 01 Mar 1985,

KATHLEEN MCFAUL.

LILY MCFAUL.

MAUREEN MCFAUL,

PATRICK MCFAUL,

DANIEL MCFAUL, b. 28 Aug 1932; d. 1932,

1902

ANNIE Mc FAUL 4 (DANIEL 3 DENIS 2 DAN1)

Daughter of

Daniel McFaul & Annie Hogg

Was born 20 June 1902 in Larne, and died in Larne. She married TOM REID

Children of ANNIE MCFAUL and TOM REID are:

MARGARET[5] REID, m. ROBERT EVANS, 24 Oct 1947.

DANNY REID.

MARIE REID.

Dan Mc Faul The Weaver

1907

SARAH[4] MCFAUL *(DANIEL[3], DENIS[2], DAN[1])*

Daughter of

Daniel McFaul & Annie Hogg

Was born 10 Jun 1907 in Larne, and died 08 Jan 1974. She married JOHN MC CLUSKEY 08 Jul 1941, son of JOHN MC CLUSKEY and ROSETTA MC CARRY.

Children of SARAH ALICE MCFAUL are;

ANNIE[5] MC FAUL, b. 18 Nov 1929, Larne; d. 07 Jan 1999,

MARY MC FAUL, b. 03 Mar 1933, d. 14 August 2009

  m. ALEX ELLIOT, 22 Jul 1954, Larne;

Children of SARAH and JOHN MC CLUSKEY

  DANNY MC CLUSKEY, b. 1934, Larne;

  ROSE MC CLUSKEY, b. 1935, Larne; d. 30 Jan 1990.

Sarah then married Hugh McAuley on 8 July 1948.

He was the son of John McAuley and Mary Magill.

Sarah died 8 January 1974

Hugh died 1 November 1995

But for my dear old Aunt Sarah, I have often wondered what would have happened to us all and I shudder to think about it. She got no real recognition for her efforts during the War years, trying to bring us all up so that her dead brother would be proud of us. Well I can tell you that she succeeded. She was the sort of person who didn't want any praise or reward. My brothers and I drifted away from Larne and sadly in time Aunt Sarah was gone, but certainly not forgotten, as we started to rear families of our own.

1909

NELLIE[4] MCFAUL *(DANIEL[3], DENIS[2], DAN[1])*

Daughter of

Daniel and Annie Hogg

was born 11 Mar 1909 in Larne, and died 11 May 1970 in Larne. She married JOHNNY MAGUIRE 30 Nov 1928 in Larne, son of JAMES MAGUIRE and REBECCA CRANEY. He died 30 Mar 1978 in Larne.

Children of NELLIE and JOHNNY MAGUIRE are:

PATRICK[5] MCAGUIRE,

DANIEL MAGUIRE,

NELLIE MAGUIRE, b. 01 Nov 1937.

JOAN MAGUIRE.

1915

CHARLOTTE 4, (DANIEL 3, DENIS 2, DAN1)

Daughter of

Daniel and Annie Hogg

Was born 1915 in Larne, and died 29 Jan 1986 in Larne. She married MICHAEL O'TOOLE 28 Jun 1934 in Larne, son of JOSEPH O'TOOLE and ELLEN CLARKE. He died 27 Jan 1981 in Larne. Michael was a Gent's Barber in the town of Larne.

Children of CHARLOTTE and MICHAEL O'TOOLE;

EILEEN[5] O'TOOLE,

MICHAEL O'TOOLE.

NAN O'TOOLE, b. 27 Oct 1934;

RAYMOND O'TOOLE.

TERRY O'TOOLE.

DANIEL PATRICK O'TOOLE, b. 23 Dec 1937.

JOSEPH O'TOOLE, d. 19 Nov 1943.

1918

DANIEL 4, (DANIEL 3, DENIS 2, Dan1)

Son of

Daniel McFaul and Annie Hogg

Was born 31 Jan 1918 in Larne, and died 30 Oct 2006. He married ELIZABETH ENGLISH 20 Jun 1944 in.

Elizabeth was born 04 May 1921, and died 04 May 1993.

Children of DANIEL and ELIZABETH ENGLISH;

ANNE[5] MCFAUL, b. 05 Oct 1945.

JAMES MCFAUL, b. 06 Nov 1949.

Dan Mc Faul The Weaver

Danny as young Daniel was known to friends and family was a very good footballer, he played for Larne FC in the late 1930 – 40s. He is the first player seated on the left and Johnny McAuley is next to him. Johnny was the elder brother of Gerald and Jimmy McAuley who married two of my sisters Anna and Eileen McFaul daughters of Denis and Mary Ellen Sullivan during the Second World War.

When I was a boy I looked forward to playing football for the School team each week at Inver Park which is still the home ground of Larne FC. This was Larne FC team in the early 1940s.

This generation of our McFaul Family History who lived through the Great War would have seen some of them as both children and parents; having to contend with many problems and changes that were taking place not only in Larne but worldwide as the new century brought lots of new creations inventions and a certain amount of prosperity, mixed with sectarian strife in Ulster. In 1912 the Home Rule Bill was considered. This caused much concern among Protestants leading to the formation of the Ulster Volunteer Force and Home Rule was delayed due to the Great War in 1914. These factors influenced the lifestyle of the population in country life Ulster. Ireland was part of the United Kingdom but they were not the only paupers. Victorians didn't understand poverty. The ruling classes had the opinion that if you were not employed it was because you are lazy.

Benjamin Disraeli's novel Sybil published in 1845 sums it up. He said that we were a country of two nations. "Two nations between whom there is no intercourse and no sympathy; who are ignorant of each other's habits, thoughts and feelings. As if they were dwellers in different zones or inhabitants of different planets. He was of course referring to;

THE RICH AND THE POOR.

Dan Mc Faul The Weaver

1904

DENIS 4, (DANIEL 3, DENIS 2, Dan1

Son of

Daniel Mc Faul & Annie Hogg

Was born 07 Aug 1904 in Larne, County Antrim Northern Ireland, and died 28 Mar 1943 in North Africa in World War Two. He married MARY ELLEN SULLIVAN on 31 Jan 1924 in Larne. Mary Ellen is the daughter of BERNARD SULLIVAN and MARY ELLEN CRILLY. She was born 05 Apr 1901 in Larne, and died on her birthday 05 Apr 1942 in the Bann Hospital Coleraine.

Dan Mc Faul The Weaver

I guess that my parents had known each other for some time as my father's family and the Sullivan family both lived in Quay Lane in Larne in the early part of the 1900s. My father's years at school were during the First World War when Larne Harbour was regarded as a vitally important anti-submarine base as two hundred trawlers dispatched from Hull, Aberdeen, Lowestoft and other fishing ports operated from there.

The Larne - Stranraer steamer was full of soldiers moving to and from the front line. These channel crossings ran during the war without a break. Many wrongly thought that this war would be over quickly and with hindsight I think that my father may have been one of them. Nevertheless some left their families never realizing that the war would last for over four years and around 5 million would fall in battle. Sadly 147 of them came from our home town of Larne.

1914 was a historical time in the town of Larne for on the night of Friday 24th April events took place that was to be etched in the annals of Ulster and in the minds of every Ulster Loyalist. On that night the ship Clyde Valley slipped into Larne Harbour to unload arms and ammunition for the Ulster Volunteer Force. 500 vehicles moved a vast arsenal of rifles and ammunition from the Quayside whilst movement out of and into the town were restricted. The Ulster Volunteer Force was intent on showing the British Government that Loyalists of Ulster would resist Home Rule to the death. The events of the night thankfully passed into folklore. It all took place a few hundred yards from where my Parent's families were asleep; or maybe not, at Quay Lane in Larne.

Several of our family tree members lost their lives in both World Wars as can be seen on the Roll of Honour names on the War memorial at Larne. For the most part, during World War One the British troops were pinned down in their trenches by the effectiveness of the Germany machine gun power.

Many troops were killed or wounded the moment that they stepped out of the trenches into No Man's Land, laden with supplies and expecting little or no opposition. They were very easy targets for the German machine gunners. 58, 000 British troops alone were included in the losses on the first day. The country as a whole had endured a horrific loss of life.

Trench warfare involved bombardment of enemy lines followed by infantry attacks. Soldiers leapt out of the trenches into machine-gun fire, gaining only a few yards of territory or dying where they stood.

Nevertheless when the war ended there was jubilation and dancing in the streets of Britain despite the fact that almost all essential goods were in short supply.

Food shortages and limited coal supplies for heating lowered the resistance to an influenza epidemic which caused the death of 150,000 people nationwide.

Many soldiers returned home to find little support or little chance of finding work like these First World War veterans who were reduced to selling matches to earn a living. Some stayed in the Army and were sent to Ireland to "Keep the Peace".

Prime Minister Lloyd George had promised a country, "Fit for heroes to live in". But the four million servicemen who returned to civilian life found little glory.

Dan Mc Faul The Weaver

In 1940 my father was a member of the North Irish Horse Regiment that went to Tunisia in January 1943 During World War Two. The Regimental War Diaries state that a three ton Bedford truck, which my father was driving along the BEJA-DJEBEL ABOID road on Sunday 21st March 1943, was mortared and my father was badly wounded. He subsequently died of his wounds seven days later on Sunday 28th March 1943. His travelling companion on that fateful day was a Regimental Quartermaster Sergeant, whose body was sadly never recovered.

When I took this picture my father's grave stone was badly pitted having been there for some 65 years. I did meet the person in charge of the War graves in that area and as he promised the headstone has now been replaced.

Tabarka where my father is buried is so unlike the rest of Tunisia. It is situated on the border with Algeria where the Torch Landings took place in 1942 as the Battles for North Africa continued. I say Battles, as there were many of them in little villages and many that were unrecorded. It is a lovely part of Tunisia with pine forests rain and greenery that I never expected to see so near to the Sahara Desert. Incidentally, in one of the many books that I have read about the War in Tunisia stated that the reason that many of the Battles were not reported was that the village names and locations could not be pronounced,nor could they be spelt correctly. My father's grave is, through the gates, turn left the reference is 3 B 10.

British War Cemetery at Tabarka in Tunisia

Dan Mc Faul The Weaver

This photograph I know was taken at Portrush in 1941 as the date is on the back. Unfortunately there were no names but my father is the soldier nearest to the Nissan Hut. I would guess that it was taken early morning as the soldier in the middle looks as if he was woken up to have his picture taken and the one sat down seems to be cooking breakfast.

With respect to those brave men the photo is a bit "Dads Armyish". I could swear that the soldier on the left is Frazer. I can just hear him saying. "We are all doo..oomed" in his Scottish accent.

This photograph was taken in 1940 at Ballykinler Camp. The date is on the back of the photograph.

Back Row; Stevenson (Ballymena), Kennedy (Larne), My father Denis McFaul (Larne), Sempey (Larne, Reid (Larne), Mooney , Moore, and Duff, all (Ballymena),

Middle Row; Agnew (Kells), Lorimar (Ballymena), Lindsay and Montgomery (Larne).

Front Row; Blackadder and Houston (Larne).

Dan Mc Faul The Weaver

The Fallen of Larne World War Two.

TO THE MEMORY OF THE MEN OF LARNE
WHO FELL IN THE 1939-1945 WAR.

BAXTER, JAMES	MAXWELL, ARTHUR
BLAIR, JAMES	MILLS, D. NELSON
CLARKE, JAMES	MILLS, JAMES
COCHRANE, QUINTON	MOORHEAD, ALFRED
CRAIG, DAVID	McALLISTER, RANDAL
CRAIG, JOSEPH	McALLISTER, WILLIAM
CRAWFORD, DANIEL	McCLELLAND, ROBERT
DAVID, GEORGE	McCLUGGAGE, EDWARD
DURRELL, ERNEST R.	McCORMICK, GEORGE
EVANS, JOSEPH	McCORMICK, TERENCE
FRASER, S. LOVAT	McCULLOUGH, DONALD
GAMBLE, FRANK	McFAUL, DENIS
GARDINER, ANGUS T.	McILHINNEY, DAVID
GOWDY, Wm JOHN	McILHINNEY, JOHN
GREER, ALEXANDER	McKAY, Wm JOHN
GREER, THOMAS C.	McKINSTRY, JOHN
HANNA, JAMES	McNEILL, JAMES M.
HAVERON, FRANCIS G.	McSEVENEY, HUGH C.
HAVERON, HENRY	PERRY, SAMUEL J.
HAVERON, JAMES	REID, HUGH
HEYBURN, WILLIAM	RICHMOND, RICHARD M.
HIGGINS, DANIEL	ROBINSON, Wm JOHN
HILLIS, JOHN	ROSS, SAMUEL
HOLDEN, JAMES	SEMPLE, JOHN
HOOD, JOHN	SHIELDS, Wm HUGH
HOUSTON, FRANK	SLOAN, JOHN
HOUSTON, JAMES	SMYTH, JOHN T.
KINGWOOD, EDWARD J.	SNODDON, HUGH McW.
LAW, Wm ALFRED	SPENCE, Wm JOHN
LEWIS, CECIL T.	SWANN, JAMES
LILLY, Wm JAMES	SWANN, ROBERT M.
LILLY, WILSON	SWANN, JOHN W.
LINTON, THOMAS	TEARE, JOHN McI.
MAGEE, WILLIAM	THOMPSON, WILLIAM
MARTIN, WILLIAM	WATT SMYTH, BRIAN
MARTIN, THOMAS	WRIGHT, JOHN N.

"WE WILL REMEMBER THEM."

MALAYA 1948
SGT. HEYBURN, DAVID — ROYAL ARTILLERY
1950 — KOREAN WAR — 1953
R.F.N. WRIGHT, THOMAS — 1ST BATT. R.U.R.
R.F.N. ROBINSON, SAMUEL — 1ST BATT. R.U.R.
ADEN 1988

Dan Mc Faul The Weaver

Larne War Memorial

During the 1960s I spent some time in the Libyan Desert. It was then that I began to wonder what my father had died for in that god forsaken land. I tried to imagine how it must have felt twenty five years earlier fighting a War in the Desert. As I have read many books on the North African campaign I can visualize a truck journey by my father, (he was killed driving a three ton Bedford truck which was mortared). Driving where there were mine-fields surrounded by masses of barbed wire, it was essential to know that to leave your position in the Desert one had to follow a definite path or compass bearing.

When I was there we lived and slept in the open, just as those soldiers did in the 1940s. The weather conditions would have been the same. During the day, it was really hot and during the night it was very, very cold. The soldiers in the War would each have had one blanket. Their main meal of the day was eaten at camp, if they happened to be there at the time, or depending upon their location a main meal might have been sent to them "At the front line". Otherwise it was dry rations that consisted of mainly biscuits, tinned fish and bully beef, which would be anything but solid, with the intense heat, it would have been quite liquefied I should imagine. They would have two pints of water in their water bottle, this they would have to treat like gold water being a premium in the desert. They would not have had sufficient water for personal hygiene, or washing clothes. I had landed at RAF El Adam and it was not long before I was passing burnt out vehicles and tanks as I headed into the desert in the direction of Tunisia; this was a battle area some 20 years before where my father had lost his life. To my left was sand, to my right was sand; sand, sand and more sand, miles of it. I thought about Lawrence of Arabia and I half expected to see him appeared on the horizon. (Incidentally, about twenty years later I bought a house a few hundred yards away from Laurence's grave near Dorchester).

One minute we were going along at 30 miles per hour in that desert then the vehicle stopped, bogged down in soft sand axle deep. Fortunately we had more up to date help to rescue us and there were thankfully no bombs or shells dropping around me. The heat was really intense 120 degrees during the day and in the haze I began to understand the meaning of the word Mirage. I could also understand why the war time vehicles often could not be moved during the hours of daylight, the dust clouds would obviously give away their position and no doubt have brought down more shells around the convoys. To make life more difficult in that god forsaken place, a plague of flies always seemed to be around, millions of them, they covered everything, even the food and oneself. Nothing would have been different in this respect during the war. The mosquitoes would also make sure that there was no respite in the cooler evening. I tried to imagine the conditions fighting in a War there for months on end. These pests were swarming everywhere, the shells may have missed their target on some occasions but these swarming pests didn't miss theirs. I have struggled to find an answer as to the reason why my father joined the Army. There was no conscription in Northern Ireland so he didn't have to go to war. Perhaps he thought it was his duty, or that the more men who joined the sooner the conflict would end. The most likely reason I came up with is the fact that he could not find a reasonable job to support his family in the manner that he would have liked to. He like all the other Irish people from the South as well as the North of Ireland were Volunteers, which is a word that I also find hard to understand especially when it is used by the Government.

Many of our young men and women during the two World Wars were volunteering for work that we were told was beneficial to the Country (just like those in Afghanistan are fighting to keep terrorists off the streets of Britain) and if all this is true then it's a good thing. Perhaps if you don't let them into the country in the first place, they would not get on to the streets. But "Volunteerism" is not so wonderful that every young person should have to do it. The problem with these grand schemes like universal voluntary Military Service is that they cannot be both universal and voluntary. The way I see it if everybody has to do it then it's not voluntary is it? On the other hand if it truly is up to the individual, then it is certainly not universal. What the politicians (who know that they are not going to fight in a War) have in mind, is to use the pressures of conformity, as well as the powers of Government to remove as much freedom of choice as possible when it comes to making decisions about things like National Service compulsory; at the same time making it appear that everyone who joins up is a volunteer. Their plans include Military Service advertising campaigns, with words like Combat, Travel, Defence, Your country needs you and exciting reports and revues from rubber stamped commissions. Speeches from politicians and goody-goody council types who would infect every school with pop Stars, footballers, religious freaks, and the like.

The British Parliament is very good at marshalling all the forces of bullshit in our society toward what they want us to believe is a good and noble cause; like banning Fox hunting or hounding those who are in receipt of invalidity benefit. Putting pressure on people to serve for a year or two is a perfect subject for such campaigns as these. But you never hear Politicians mention OIL very much these days, only to justify the rise in petrol costs. We can all think up "Good Ideas"; what about making student loans depending on the years of service signed up for. That would cover all but the richest young students. The hope would then be that some element of these "volunteers" would be inspired to dedicate their lives or at least a part of their lives, to the service of the country. I regard these exercises as a bit cynical. For a start, the very concept of volunteering under this kind of pressure would turn the very word itself into a joke. The exclusion of young people whose parents were wealthy enough to buy them out of the Army, (as during The Cold War days), would do nothing to reduce my cynicism.

I can sit here and ask the question; "Why for example were farmers not required to "volunteer" for a year or two in exchange for the massive subsidies they have enjoyed from the taxpayers for years; not to mention having been paid **not** to till their land in the days of the European "Butter Mountains"?

There were also those hiding behind so called "reserved occupations". If they had jobs such as Doctors, Miners, Farmers, Scientists, Merchant Seamen, School teachers, Railway and dock workers or Utility Workers - Water, Gas, Electricity that was fine. I have read many stories from various forums regarding reserved occupations and surprisingly enough most people wanted to join the services. In my father's case he told a couple of little white lies. His attestation form states that he was born on 7/8/1906 when he joined the North Irish Horse Regiment in March 1940, aged 33 years. His birth certificate states that he was born on 7/8/1904. He also declared that he had 4 dependent children instead of 5. The only logical reason that I can think of for this is that he was fearful that he would be considered to be too old to join. I base my assumption on the fact that as I said before; he didn't have to join it was not compulsory for people born in Northern Ireland. Interestingly enough during World War II the Stormont government called on Westminster to introduce conscription several times, as this was already the case in Britain. The British government consistently refused, no doubt remembering how a similar attempt in 1918 had backfired as nationalist opposition made it unworkable. Much of the population of serving age were either in essential jobs or had already joined voluntarily making the potential recruitment from conscription very low.

A National Service draft would raise certain issues such as when "voluntary", requires the said Volunteer to pay the ultimate price. It is tempting to argue that this really is something you should not be able to buy your way out of. I admit that the armed services are more socially diverse today while in National Service days, "dying on the job" was no greater in the Military than in any other career like the Fire Service or down the Coal Mines.

One of the comforts of old age is that I can sit here and start making demands on young people, safe in the knowledge that they won't apply to me; having safely escaped National Service in the days of the Cold War. But I have a feeling that future generations may not be so lucky.

Dan Mc Faul The Weaver

Having been there this poem of mine sums up my thoughts about the place where my father died.

This place is just a barren **land**

With mile after mile of nothing but **sand**

The heat of the sun, and the Flies that **torment**

There were signs of the battles, wherever I **went**.

Other nasty creatures, live in this **land**

Most you wouldn't want, to hold in your **hand**

I saw some Chameleons, funny creatures were **they**

Their eyes sort of swivelled, in a very odd **way**

It's said they change colours I know that they **Do**

I put them on various things, and found it is **true**

The flies were a menace, and buzzed round all **day**

Hundreds of the pests, giving a flying **display**

I had to covered up, to keep the "mosies" at **bay**

My shorts I wore in the daytime, not the end of the **day**.

There was always a risk of Malaria, it was common **enough**

So I took a dose of Perri something, yellow hideous **stuff**

Mans fascination with the desert, I find hard to **understand**

I'll never know why Dad had to go, to that God forsaken **land**

The odd Oasis here and the odd well there, hardly a tree to **see**

The Arabs they can have their land I know where I prefer to **be**

Dan Mc Faul The Weaver

This is a photograph taken before ships were equipped with opening bow doors and ramps. In fact they were first developed during the Second World War to land vast amounts of men, equipment and supplies on invasion beaches without the use of piers and port equipment. The first dedicated Roll on Roll off ramps in the British Isles were built at Larne and Stranraer in 1938 to serve the first purpose built Roll on Roll off car ferry in Britain the Princess Victoria which entered service in the summer of 1939.

Easy does it!

A car drives onto the Princess Margaret back in 1932. James Boyd took the train which includes John McLarnon (crane driver), Dan McFaul, John Houston, Denis McAuley, Peter McCorkle (cargo man), Denis McFaul, William Clements and John Blair (foreman). 2760/9.

The Dan Mc Faul mentioned is my Grandfather and the Denis McFaul mentioned is most probably my grandfather's brother's son, born in 1903, when he worked at Larne harbour as a labourer.

Mc Kenna Memorial Boys School 1913

Provided that they were at school that day, my father and his brother Willie John should be in this photograph. Willie John would be about thirteen years old and my father about nine. Unfortunately I have not got the names of any of the pupils so I cannot identify anyone, not even my father if he is there. There are also possibilities that my mother's brothers Barney, Michael and George are also in this photograph.

Dan Mc Faul The Weaver

St. Mary's Convent School for girls 1913

The same situation arises here in this photograph of the girls of St. Mary's taken in 1913. I cannot identify which of the girls is my mother Mary Ellen Sullivan. Perhaps some reader may know the answer and be kind enough to let me know. Because of her long jet black hair I would guess that the girl 5th in from the right in the front row is my mother.

The Old Town

Mill Street and Mill Lane which ran from Pound Street to High Street are named after the mills which dated as far back as the Inver Priory. It seems that the manufacturing industry in Larne was centred in this area and it included trades ranging from Barrel and Keg making to Flour Mills.

Trow Lane as I knew it ran from Mill Street to Mill Lane. It was originally known as Trough Lane because the water that was used in the local flour mill flowed down from the Inver River in a trough to the water wheel which powered the machinery for the mill. In those days there was an easy logic when naming places unlike the fancy names that are thought up by people who are paid by the tax payer's money. One that comes to mind is Boulevard, and as far as I am concerned the Midsummer Boulevard in Milton Keynes is just like all the other roads and Boulevards in the town.

Pound Street during the eighteenth century was the business part of Larne. The name again is quite self explanatory as it was the place (a walled enclosure) where "impounded" stray animals were kept. It was common practice for towns to have a Pound in those times. It was also the place where contraband or the proceeds of illegal trafficking in goods were taken.

Coopers Lane This is where Barrels and Kegs were made, just off High Street. In those days Larne was a busy port and when ships went to sea it was eight or ten weeks to America. But the provisions for a journey at sea, especially the raw meat were stored in Coopers Lane salted Kegs. Salt was used for curing and preserving then and Larne had a salt works at the Bank near the town. Larne had a good trade with other countries in the import of Salt Rock.

The Open was what it was, an open space. It was where Mill Street began and straight over was Dunluce Street. The other two corners of the Open were High Street and Bridge Street.

The Open was the place where the Town Stocks were once situated. This is where wrongdoers were securely fastened to repent for their misdeeds. I believe that the Stocks were in need of repair on several occasions in the 1760s which suggests that they were widely used, hopefully not by many by the name of McFaul. The Stocks in Larne were the Leg Type only.

The Naggy Burn was the Pound Water that flowed through the Pound Green. The water just ran through the street uncovered and like many other places that I have visited, pedestrians and vehicles had to just splash their way through. To - day most of these places that I come across have a bridge or stile for crossing purposes. It was essential that our Naggy Burn passed through the Pound, because at the time the Law demanded that water is available for the livestock that had been impounded there.

The Pound was situated between Pound Street and St. Johns Place. When my Great Grandfather Denis McFaul married Ellen Mc Adorey in 1864 he was living in Pound Street, and since then there has been quite a few Mc Fauls who have resided in Pound Street. In those days the Inver River wound its way down to the town jail that was situated at Henning's Chemist shop on the corner of Main Street and Cross Street, it carried on to meet the sea near the Larne Paper Mill in Circular Road.

Blacks Lane lay between Mill Street and Mission Lane. Blacks Lane was I presume named after someone called Black. But Mission Lane which ran on to Pound Street was where there was a Mission Hall. It was originally called Methodist Lane as the founder of Methodism, John Wesley (an Englishman) used to preach in the open at Blacks Lane and Mission Lane.

Bridge Street was the main approach to Station Road, the Market Place and the village of Glynn, Magheramorne and Carrickfergus, over the Inver River bridge hence the name Bridge Street. If someone mentions Bridge Street I think of The Thatch Pub just after turning right at the bottom of Mill Street on my way to the Railway station to catch the train to Belfast when I attended the Christian Brothers School in Harding Street. The Thatch was a large building on the other side of Bridge Street on the corner of Point Street.

Meetinghouse Street ran from the bottom of Mill Brae across Pound Street into Church Lane. The names were derived from what was the Old Presbyterian Church.

Dan Mc Faul The Weaver

LARNE'S SQUINT; In one of the local churches (St. Cedmas, Inver) there is a small window known as a "Squint". This goes back to the days of leprosy when lepers were kept away from the rest of the congregation and had to watch the ceremony through a small peep-hole known as a Squint. The current church was part of the Augustinian monastery at Invermore, signs of which remained until the 19th century. Following the dissolution of the monasteries by Henry VIII, the church has been in continuous use as the parish church of Inver. This makes St Cedma's the second-oldest church in continuous use in Co Antrim. A great concern is that St Cedma's could potentially cease to be viable as a church if retail giant Tesco were to be given permission to build a supermarket at Inver Park.

In time the buildings in the old part of the town began to develop problems. Some of the wealthier people moved to the new part of the town. By the 1940s some of the properties were in a poor condition and towards the end of the War some people were moved to the Antiville Estate or Ferris Park and to a new idea of Pre-fabricated accommodation. Pre-Fabs as we used to call them.

During my researching in Larne I have had to hunt through the Larne Times archives on several occasions in the town Library. Some of the articles that I have stumbled upon in the process have been quite amusing, but one in particular sticks in my mind. It refers to a fire in Mill Street that took place in March 1898. It is believed to have originated from sparks falling on the thatch from an adjoining chimney. I cannot imagine thatched houses in Mill Street, as they seemed so tall to me in my schooldays; but I suppose all the houses had thatched roofs at one time just as most houses today are tiled roofs.

Generation No. 5

1922

ROSE[5] MCKEOWN *(ELLEN[4] MCFAUL, DENIS[3],)*
DENIS[2], DAN[1]

Daughter of

Ellen & James Mc Keown

Was born 03 Mar 1922 in Larne, and died 10 Feb 1999 in Larne. She married JOSEPH WILLIAM LONGMORE 04 Aug 1941 in Larne. He was born in Larne, and died 16 Apr 1993 in Larne.

Children of ROSE MCKEOWN and JOSEPH LONGMORE;

MARGARET[6] LONGMORE.

BILL LONGMORE.

ELLEN LONGMORE.

JOSEPH LONGMORE,

MALACHY LONGMORE, d. 03 Sep 1984.

NELLIE[5] MCFAUL *(WM JOHN[4], DENIS[3], DENIS[2], DAN[1])*

Daughter of

Wm. John & Ellen Hoey

She married JAMES MC ILROY.

Child of NELLIE MCFAUL and JAMES MC ILROY is:

JAMES [6] MC ILROY.

RUBY[5] MCFAUL *(WM JOHN[4], DENIS[3], DENIS[2], DAN[1])*

Daughter of

Wm. John & Ellen Hoey

She married PATRICK BONNAR 25 Aug 1944 in Larne.

Child of RUBY MCFAUL and PATRICK BONNAR is

PATRICK[6] BONNAR.

BETTY[5] MCFAUL *(WM JOHN[4], DENIS[3], DENIS[2], DAN[1])*

Daughter of

Wm. John & Ellen Hoey

She married PATRICK MCCLURE.

Children of BETTY MCFAUL and PATRICK MCCLURE are:

LORAINE[6] MCCLURE.

ELEANOR MCCLURE.

JEAN MCCLURE.

1926

CLARE[5] MCFAUL *(DENIS[4], DENIS[3], DENIS[2], DAN[1])*

Daughter of

Denis & Jane Purdy

Clare was born 07 Dec 1926 in Larne.

She died 20 Jul 1987 in Larne.

Child of CLARE MCFAUL is:

DEREK[6] MCFAUL, b. 1949.

1928

EILEEN Mc FAUL 5 (FRANCES 4, JAMES 3 DENIS 2 DAN1)

Daughter of

Frances Josephine Mc Faul

Eileen Mc Faul was born in 1928 and Died 1981

She married David Rosenthal in 1948.

Eileen died on 1 September 1987

She is buried with her grandparents James and Cecelia in Larne RC cemetery.

Dan Mc Faul The Weaver

1932

JACKIE[5] MC CULLOUGH *(ALICE[4] MCFAUL, JAMES[3], DENIS[2], DAN[1])*

Son of

Alice & Jack Mc Cullough

Was born 08 Jan 1932 in Larne, and died 26 Apr 2000 in Larne. He married TERESA LYNCH in 1954.

Children of JACKIE MC CULLOUGH and TERESA LYNCH

TERESA[6] MC CULLOUGH, b. 26 Jun 1968.

SEAN MC CULLOUGH, b. 22 Nov 1958.

GERALDINE MC CULLOUGH, b. 26 Nov 1959.

MICHAEL MC CULLOUGH, b. 26 Oct 1963.

1933

DONALD Mc CULLOUGH 5 (ALICE 4, JAMES 3 DENIS 2 DAN1)

Son of

Alice & Jack Mc Cullough

Donald Mc Cullough was born 6 February 1933

He married Collette in February 1963

Collette died in 1995.

1934

JAMES[5] MC CULLOUGH *(ALICE[4] MCFAUL, JAMES[3], DENIS[2], DAN[1])*

Son of

Alice & Jack Mc Cullough

Was born 06 Feb 1934 in Larne.

He married MARIE CAMPBELL.

Children of JAMES and MARIE CAMPBELL ;

CAMPBELL[6] MC CULLOUGH, b. 08 Jan 1959.

PAUL MC CULLOUGH, b. 18 Feb 1960.

CHARMAINE MC CULLOUGH, b. 05 Oct 1962.

MARRIANNE MC CULLOUGH, b. 08 Apr 1965.

1935

KATHLEEN[5] MC CULLOUGH *(ALICE[4] MCFAUL, JAMES[3], DENIS[2], DAN[1])*

Daughter of

Alice & Jack Mc Cullough

Was born 28 Jun 1935 in Larne.

She married JOHN BROWN.

Children of KATHLEEN and JOHN BROWN;

MARLENE[6] BROWN, b. 22 Oct 1955.

RONALD BROWN, b. 21 Sep 1957.

ROBERT BROWN, b. 10 Jan 1960.

DAVID BROWN, b. 28 Nov 1963.

MONA BROWN, b. 22 Jun 1964.

CAROL BROWN, b. 31 Oct 1965.

BRIAN BROWN, b. 15 Oct 1970.

JAMES BROWN, b. 01 Nov 1975.

1948

CECELIA[5] MC CULLOUGH *(ALICE[4] MCFAUL, JAMES[3], DENIS[2], DAN[1])*

Daughter of

Alice & Jack Mc Cullough

Was born 24 Oct 1948 in Larne.

She married DANNY MCCORMICK 21 Sep 1968.

He was born 04 Apr 1948 in Larne.

Children of CECELIA and DAN MC CORMICK ;

MARC[6] MCCORMICK, b. 13 Jan 1969, Larne.

PETER MCCORMICK, b. 22 Sep 1974, Larne.

1934

THOMAS LINTON 5 (CECELIA 4, JAMES 3 DENIS 2 DAN1)

Son of

Cecelia Mc Faul & Thomas Linton

Thomas Linton was born on 7 May 1934.

Sadly Thomas only lived for two days.

1938

DENNIS[5] LINTON (CECELIA[4] MCFAUL, JAMES[3], DENIS[2], DAN[1])

Son of

Thomas Linton & Cecelia Mc Faul

Was born on 21 Feb 1938 in Halifax England. He married ADRIENNE WATSON 1959 in Liverpool.

Dennis was brought up in Larne Co Antrim Northern Ireland from the age of 18 months old. He was educated at St McNissi College Garron Tower. At age 17 traditionally, within this family, he became a sailor like his grandfather before him there being little other work available.

In 1957 Dennis left Ireland, like so many others, and settled in Liverpool. Dennis has had jobs and occupations from a Police Officer to College Lecturer.

Children of DENNIS LINTON are:

ANDREW[6] LINTON, b. 18 Jul 1966.

JAMES LINTON, b. 01 Sep 1967.

JOHN DOMINIC LINTON, b. 28 May 1970.

SHARON LINTON, b. 07 Oct 1962.

KATE LINTON, b. 30 Nov 1972.

Dennis retired in 1996 and gave back some of his time and energy to the community in a number of high profile positions finally retiring completely in 2000. He was married and divorced and re-married and had five children. None of his children went to sea. Mostly they are in the medical or caring professions.

1942

MARIE SUNDERLAND 5 (ELLEN 4, JAMES 3 DENIS 2 DAN1)

Daughter of

Ellen & Frank Sunderland

Marie Sunderland was born 13 October 1943

Marie married Keith Holroyd.

Children of Marie Sunderland and Christopher Holroyd;

CHRISTOPHER[6] HOLROYD, b. November 9, 1969;

SUZANNE HOLROYD, b. March 22, 1972.

1945

JACQUILINE SUNDERLAND 5 (ELLEN 4, JAMES 3 DENIS 2 DAN1)

Daughter of

Ellen & Frank Sunderland

Jacqueline was born 28 November 1945

She married Ian Walker.

Children of JACQUELINE and IAN WALKER are:

MARK[6] WALKER, b. March 20, 1970.

NICHOLAS WALKER, b. May 3, 1972.

PAUL WALKER, b. June 25, 1973.

JAMES[5] MCFAUL *(JAMES DENNIS[4], JAMES[3], DENIS[2], DAN[1])*

He married GILLIAN WILSON.

Child of JAMES MCFAUL and GILLIAN WILSON is:

CHRISTOPHER[6] MCFAUL.

BERNADETTE[5] MCFAUL *(JAMES DENNIS[4], JAMES[3], DENIS[2], DAN[1])*

She married DANNY ROWAN.

Children of BERNADETTE MCFAUL and DANNY ROWAN

DANNY[6] ROWAN.

BARRY ROWAN

JAMES ROWAN.

LIAM[5] MCFAUL *(JAMES DENNIS[4], JAMES[3], DENIS[2], DAN[1])*

He married CHRIS DECKERS.

Children of LIAM MCFAUL and CHRIS DECKERS are:

LIAM DENIS[6] MCFAUL.

LISA MARIE MCFAUL.

BOBBY EDWARD MCFAUL.

ANTHONY[5] MCFAUL *(JAMES DENNIS[4], JAMES[3], DENIS[2], DAN[1])*

He married JOANNE DONNELLY.

Children of ANTHONY and JOANNE DONNELLY are:

MICHAEL[6] MCFAUL.

JOANNE MCFAUL, b. 1984.

Dan Mc Faul The Weaver

1926

ANNA[5] MCFAUL *(DENIS[4], DANIEL[3], DENIS[2], DAN[1])*

Daughter of

Denis & Mary Ellen Sullivan

Was born 16 Aug 1926 in Larne, and died 11 Sep 1987 in Larne. She married (1) GERALD MCAULEY 08 Oct 1943 son of JOHN MCAULEY and MARY MAGILL. He was born 23 Aug 1919 in Larne, and died 23 Nov 1963 in Larne. She married (2) ALEXANDER MC ATACKNEY 05 Nov 1966.

Children of ANNA MCFAUL and GERALD MCAULEY are:

ANNMARIE[6] MCAULEY, b. 17 Oct 1944, Larne.

m. William Purvis.

GERALDINE MCAULEY, b. 1948, Larne; d. 17 Mar 1972.

Gerald Mc Auley worked at Howden Brothers the Coal Merchants at Bank Quay in the Bank Road, where a familiar sight was seeing the steam and smoke belching out of the funnels, which were painted black with a large red band, as Howden ships sailed into Larne Lough and up to the Quay at the Bank Road where Gerald worked. Gerald was born in Larne and sadly he was killed in a road accident on his way home from work.

Gerald was a good man and he was the one who paid for me to go to College in Belfast for a year (including paying my rail fares from Larne to Belfast each day). I am grateful for what he and my sister Anna tried to do for me in those difficult years for me just after the War.

1928

EILEEN⁵ MCFAUL *(DENIS⁴, DANIEL³, DENIS², DAN¹)*

Daughter of Denis & Mary Ellen Sullivan

was born 10 Dec 1928 in Larne, and died 23 Aug 1978 in Larne. She married JAMES MCAULEY 27 Jun 1945 in the Chapel at Larne County Antrim Northern Ireland. He was born 25 May 1927 in Larne, and died 16 Oct 1975 in Larne.

Children of EILEEN MCFAUL and JAMES MCAULEY are:

MARY⁶ MCAULEY. b. 12 April 1946.

JOHN MCAULEY.

DENIS MCAULEY.

GERALD MCAULEY. b. 9 December 1957.

Dan Mc Faul The Weaver

Eileen's husband Jimmy McAuley is a brother to Gerald who married my sister Anna. With hind sight I don't think that my two sisters Anna and Eileen could have married nicer people. Their husbands both accepted me and my wife into their homes at varying times when I was at that awful age when I thought that I knew everything and didn't have two half pennies two rub together. An interesting thing is that Jimmy was born on the same date as me 25 May and he died on the date that my wife and I were married, 16 October.

This was Eileen and Jimmy McAuley on their wedding day 27 June 1945 three weeks to the day after D-day, the official ending of hostilities in Europe.

In my difficult teenage years Eileen was not just my sister, she was my father and my mother and my sister, all rolled into one and I loved her dearly.

When I needed money for the pictures or the snooker hall Eileen was the one who would go out and borrow the money for me until I got paid on Friday.

Dan Mc Faul The Weaver

1930

DENIS[5] MCFAUL *(DENIS[4], DANIEL[3], DENIS[2], DAN[1])*

Son of

Denis & Mary Ellen Sullivan

Was born 09 Feb 1930 in Larne, and died 29 Oct 1998 in Larne. He married MARY LOUGHRANE in Larne.

Children of DENIS MCFAUL and MARY LOUGHRANE are:

ROBERT[6] MCFAUL.

SHAMUS MCFAUL.

ELIZABETH MCFAUL

My brother Denis spent some time in the Army including a year or so in the Malayan Jungle during the 1950s. He was quite a handsome looking man my brother and he was always very smart in his appearance. Circumstances were such that we really didn't get the time or the opportunity to get to know each other as we would have liked to. Denis had a good sense of humour and he was good fun to be with, most of the time. When he was in the Army, I went to see him when he was in the Military Hospital at Catterick Camp in Yorkshire. He had some sort of thyroid trouble. Denis had been admitted to Mill Hill Hospital in London and was then sent to Catterick Military Hospital to recuperate.

We walked around the gardens of the Hospital, talking over old times and then we went and sat down on a bench by the Fish Pond. In those days some of the more permanent inmates of the Military Hospitals wore those horrible Blue coloured "Hospital Suits" that they had to wear if they were going out of the Hospital Grounds.

As Denis and I sat there talking, a person appeared from the hospital entrance, he spied us sitting there and turned to walk in our direction.

"Oh no" said Denis, "This ginger haired guy is a nut case".

Denis then quickly told me that he was forever saying that he had done this and he had done that and usually bored everyone to tears with his exploits. Denis then said that he would show me what he meant. When the chap came up to us Denis said to him, "This is my brother Dan Ginger". I said; "Pleased to meet you Ginger" or something such as that. The fellow sat down beside us and Denis said to him; "My brother Dan and I were just talking about when I was the long jump and the standing jump Champion at the Army Championships a few years ago".

Immediately the ginger haired soldier said, "I won a jumping competition once", to which Denis replied "Of course I was much younger then, I am not sure how good I am now, I don't know if I could even clear this pond".

Denis's words were like a red rag to a bull. "I could clear that pond easily" said Ginger. "I don't know it looks a long way across to me" said Denis before adding; "But of course I haven't got the technique any more". Within seconds ginger took off his blue coat and hung it on the edge of the bench. He stepped up on to the wee wall that surrounded the Fish Pond and took his stance. "You're a brave man ginger" said Denis, "It's too far for me".

No sooner had Denis said that when there was an almighty splash, the fish must have thought that there was an earthquake. There was this poor chap lying in the middle of the Fish Pond, the only dry thing of his was his coat, still hanging on the bench.

I never did find out why the fellow was in the Hospital but I do know that during the time of National Service some people tried some very strange ways to get themselves discharged. Was Ginger one of them, we will never know. But I did notice that Denis had that Impish smile of his on his face once again.

Dan Mc Faul The Weaver

Denis spent some time in the British army. He was a wireless operator in the Royal Corps of Signals. He was in Singapore and Malaya before he was posted back to the United Kingdom to Pendine in South Wales in the early 1950s where he found me a job near the barracks on a building site.

Dan Mc Faul The Weaver

This photograph was taken in the Laharna Hotel in Larne and as you may guess, it was not fancy dress it was taken some time in the "Swinging Sixties". I do not know what the occasion was but the following are the members of our McFaul family.

From the left is my sister Anna McFaul. The next lady I do not know. Next is my dear sister Eileen McFaul. Then there is Eileen's son Gerald and his girlfriend (later his wife), Deborah Campbell. Then on the end right is my Brother Denis' son Shamus who used to work on the oil rigs off the coast of Aberdeen. It may have been one of his frequent visits to see his Aunties families in Larne. Shamus looks tired from his trip from Aberdeen.

Dan Mc Faul The Weaver

1931

CHARLOTTE[5] MCFAUL *(DENIS[4], DANIEL[3], DENIS[2], DAN[1])*

Daughter of

Denis & Mary Ellen Sullivan

Was born 12 Feb 1931 in Larne

She married WILLIAM EDGAR 10 Sep 1962 in Larne.

Children of CHARLOTTE MCFAUL and WILLIAM EDGAR;

GERALDINE[6] EDGAR, b. 15 Jun 1962, Larne.

BRIAN EDGAR, b. 11 Feb 1963, Larne.

William Edgar died and several years later Charlotte married a Larne chap called Gerry Brady whom I did know when I was a schoolboy. I had left Ireland at an early age and never returned to live there. I unfortunately lost touch with some of the family and Charlotte and her family members were amongst them. I did spend some time with her when I visited Larne in 2004 – 2009 years we also spent some time at our mother's grave in Portstewart. We also had a very pleasant day with her daughter and one of her Granddaughters, driving through the Glens of Antrim and taking in the famous sights such as the Waterfalls in Glenariffe.

Charlotte's Granddaughter Martine with one of the two famous cats, resident at the excellent restaurant at the Forest Trail.

Dan Mc Faul The Weaver

In this picture Charlotte looks on as my daughter Bernadette nearest the camera and Charlotte's daughter Geraldine prepare to place some fresh flowers on our mother's grave in the cemetery at Portstewart in Northern Ireland.

Dan Mc Faul The Weaver

1940

BERNARD⁵ MCFAUL *(DENIS⁴, DANIEL³, DENIS², DAN¹)*

Son of

Denis & Mary Ellen Sullivan

Was born 25 May 1940 in Larne

He married MARGARET KEENAN on 12 January 1963.

Children of BERNARD and MARGARET KEENAN

BRIAN⁶ MCFAUL, b. 01 Mar 1964, Larne.

RICHARD MCFAUL, b. 01 Oct 1965, Larne.

GEMMA MCFAUL, b. 04 Aug 1968, Larne.

DESMOND MCFAUL, b. 12 Aug 1970, Larne.

SUSANE MCFAUL, b. 24 Nov 1973, Larne.

DARREN MCFAUL, b. 09 Aug 1977, Larne.

1935

ROSE[5] MC CLUSKEY *(SARAH[4] MCFAUL, DANIEL[3], DENIS[2], DAN[1])*

Daughter of

Sarah Alice McFaul & John McCluskey

Was born 1935 in Larne, and died 30 Jan 1990 in Larne.

She married JOSEPH LONGMORE.

Child of ROSE MC CLUSKEY and JOSEPH LONGMORE is:

ANTHONY[6] LONGMORE.

1945

ANNE[5] MCFAUL *(DANIEL JOSEPH[4], DANIEL[3], DENIS[2], DAN[1])*

Daughter of

Daniel McFaul & Elizabeth English

Was born 05 Oct 1945

She married DON HOMER.

Children of ANNE MCFAUL and DON HOMER are:

MICHELLE[6] HOMER, b. 11 May 1967.

DONNA HOMER, b. 20 Feb 1970.

PAULA HOMER, b. 25 Jul 1973.

1949

JAMES[5] MCFAUL *(DANIEL JOSEPH[4], DANIEL[3], DENIS[2], DAN[1])*

Son of

Daniel McFaul & Elizabeth English

Was born 06 Nov 1949

He married LINDA WILLIAMS.

She was born 06 Nov 1949.

Children of JAMES MCFAUL and LINDA WILLIAMS are:

CHRISTOPHER[6] MCFAUL, b. 14 Oct 1972.

DAMIEN MCFAUL, b. 06 Apr 1975.

1934

DANIEL Mc FAUL 5 (DENIS 4, DANIEL 3, DENIS 2, DAN1)

Son of

Denis McFaul and Mary Ellen Sullivan

I was born on 25th May 1934 at number 19 Ronald Street Larne. The only event in the town of any note in the year of my birth was that a new Post Office was opened in Main Street Larne. I was educated at McKenna Memorial Public Elementary School in Chapel Lane Larne and the Christian Brother College in Harding Street Belfast.

Unfortunately my education at the Christian Brothers College only lasted for one year as circumstances were such that I had to find a job to help with the income to the household. My sister Anna's husband was paying for my schooling and my train fares to Belfast from Larne each day.

By and large, women didn't go to work then, not in Larne anyway, and Gerald was just an ordinary worker who had a family of his own to keep as well as me.

The town of Larne was a much better place to live at in those days. In the network of Lanes in the Mill Street area where I grew up Catholics and Protestants lived side by side and no one seemed bothered about that. There was no graffiti, no boarded up houses and no windows with bullet holes in them, as I seen when I visited the street where I was born in 2004.

I am sure that my parents never thought that as a family we would have to live through another World War, just like they did as children less than two decades before. Political and industrial unrest maybe, as this has always been part of the history of Ireland, but not another World War.

My time growing up then, was during World War Two and by 1942 some of my early recollections are of American Servicemen in the town. Some were billeted at Kilwaughter Castle. Soon after their arrival, children like me learned that if we were friendly to them we would always get the odd bar of chocolate or a packet of chewing gum. And with hindsight, judging by the number of local girls that were now wearing Nylon Stockings, we children were not the only ones who were being friendly.

Dan Mc Faul The Weaver

This is a picture taken in 1949 it shows the members of the 2nd Antrim Catholic Boys Scouts (Larne).

A few of my first cousins are pictured including me. I am the Patrol Leader with the Staff on the right next to the priest father Hugh O'Donnell. My cousins are Denis McFaul (3rd in from the left second row). Denis's Brother Patrick (5th in on that row) and Danny O'Toole (sitting second in from the left Front row).

This is me and Dennis Linton as boy scouts. Dennis is not in the above picture as there is a slight age gap between us.

Dan Mc Faul The Weaver

This was the McKenna Memorial School football team that won the Irish schools Cup in the 1940s. I was very proud to be a member of that team.

Back Row; Sean Fulton, Francis Shaw (Ferris Lane) , Barry,   (Bryan Street), Pat Heggarty,

Jimmy Ramsey (Mill Lane), Gerry Campbell (Mill Street).

Sitting; David O'Neill , Danny McFaul (Mill Street), Steve Mc Auley (Mill Lane), Jim Mc Kinstry, Sean Kearney (Mill Brae), Bertie Fulton.

In Front; Charlie Brown and John Hamill.

Dan Mc Faul The Weaver

The Old Town area was a network of Mill Street, Mill Lane, Black's Lane, Ferris Lane, Church Lane, Mission Lane, Trowe Lane, Cooper's Lane and The Knowe. The house where I and my brothers and sisters lived at with our Aunt Sarah and her four children during World War Two was 22 Mill Street.

Number 22 is the house past the large building on the right (The Mourne Clothing Company) which produced uniforms for the armed forces when I was living there during the 1940s. There is a gap between the Mourne building and number 22, just where you see the Chimney Breast. That gap led into Mill Lane and a Water Pump where the residents of Mill Lane got their Water supply from.

Dan Mc Faul The Weaver

In 1940 when I was six years old my father had joined the Army. I of course don't remember this happening. But it seems that at the time the common belief was that the War would be over quite quickly. They could not have been more wrong. My father joined the North Irish Horse, which I later thought very dashing, charging into battle on a great white horse. The North Irish Horse was a Tank Regiment and they done their dashing in their Tanks in the Desert of North Africa and other War torn places and their Roll of Honour tells us the price that was paid. My father was one such casualty of that War as he was killed in action less than a year after my mother's death. I with my brothers and sisters were then sent to live with my father's sister Sarah. It seems that aunt Sarah was the only one who wanted to know about the plight of we six orphans when we were sent to Larne from Portrush after our father was sent with his regiment to North Africa. Sarah was the one who spared us the trauma of being brought up in an establishment similar to the dreaded Workhouse where my mother had been born more than forty years earlier. That could well be the reason why Aunt Sarah agreed to take all six of us, for if she hadn't, there is no doubt that we would have been taken into the care of the local authorities. All eleven of us lived in number 22 Mill Street but we could not be regarded as a "Typical Family" of the 1940s and the only places that housed more people than 22 Mill Street, were Hotels and Lodging Houses.

Dan Mc Faul The Weaver

This was the kind of Morrison type Air Raid Shelter that was my sleeping quarters for a year during the War. It also doubled as a dining table which was handy with so many people living in the same house.

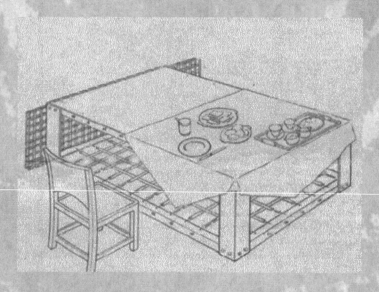

I remember it as a very cold place to sleep in the back room of the house at number 22 Mill Street. I was always the first one up each morning and first to use the cold water tap just outside the door for washing before going to school, (winter and summer). We had no running water inside the house and it took too long a time to heat water from the chain that hung over the open fire in the "sitting room" which would not be lit at that time of the morning anyway otherwise I would probably have slept in there.

1901

Mary Ellen Sullivan

Wife of Denis McFaul

Mary Ellen Sullivan was born in the Workhouse at Larne in 1901. At the 1901 census the population of the Union was 33,029 with 11 officials and there were 195 inmates in the workhouse. At the time the dreaded workhouse was the last resort for poor families if the bread winner happened to get sick, or lost their job for some reason, or more to the point, couldn't find a job. The Victorian authorities didn't understand Poverty. They simply believed that if you had no job it was because you were a lazy sod and that it was up to you to provide for your family. I would agree in principle that we should provide for our family in the same way that the authorities should encourage and create jobs for those who are unskilled and less fortunate.

Dan Mc Faul The Weaver

Most local Larne people may recognise this workhouse building as once being the Moyle Hospital in the Old Glenarm Road.

In 1929, the workhouse became Larne District Hospital, later Moyle. The former fever hospital was extended in 1936 and became the nurses' home. The front building has now been demolished. When these huge shared Workhouses were built under the new Poor Law of 1834 they were meant to be frightening places. The authorities didn't mind terrible stories about them being told to people outside, because the main purpose was to save money and to encourage people to look after themselves and their families. Which is not a bad thing in itself it's the way that the authorities went about it that horrifies us to read about it today.

The inconsistency of good harvests, the scarcity of jobs and the disruption by trouble making Religious factions, meant that the fine line between a decent existence and extreme poverty in the Province of Ulster was a line that was not so easy to change. For many years the usual way to provide help for the very poorest people in the community including those who were old and sick, was to pay for them to stay in their homes, it was much cheaper than finding them a home and paying someone to look after them. The money for this came from the Poor Rate, collected from the people of the parish and this system of caring for the poor was called Outdoor Relief. But there were many complaints from parishioners about the cost of the poor rate, and wealthy landowners were among those demanding an even cheaper way of dealing with the poor people in the community. The government's answer was a new Act of Parliament in 1834 which forced parishes to combine together into Unions and build large workhouses for the whole area. These were almost like prisons, with bare walls, hard beds, and little food and people in British prisons today are better treated than paupers were in the early 19th century Britain. They have the same hours of Free Phone Calls to their families as the Soldiers who are risking their lives daily, in Iraq and Afghanistan have. By comparison, the only crime that most people who entered the Workhouse committed was being poor. Once in the workhouses family members were split up and could never meet as long as they were in the workhouse.

People were terrified of having to commit to the workhouse and who could blame them. One of these awful places was built in 1841 at Larne, in the County of Antrim in Northern Ireland. Like everything else that goes wrong in this world, the problem is about the cost to put it right. Workhouses were no exception and the Poorhouse Act put at the centre of provision the guideline that; Workhouse conditions should be worse than the lowest living standards of the labourer. This was obviously to keep people from rushing into the Workhouses and it was evident that only the poorest and the destitute were tempted to do so. The everyday lives of the poor people in a Workhouse were bad enough. The surroundings were very grim, there was very little to eat, and what they were given was of poor quality and tasteless. The sleeping quarters were bare, with iron beds laid out in rows and almost no other furniture. But things became even worse for anyone who did not do as they were told as they were quickly punished.

The workhouse rules were very strict, particularly in the early years. If for instance someone was ordered to be confined for 24 hours and to be fed on Bread and Water, he or she, would have been locked up in the punishment block, probably with no windows, for at least a day and a night. It was also quite common for people in the workhouse to be ordered to be whipped in front of the other inmates, so that they would know what to expect if they didn't comply with the rules. During the famine years in the mid-1840s a 40-bed fever hospital was erected at the north east of the workhouse in Larne. Sleeping galleries were erected for an additional 130 inmates.

The Poor Law Union in Larne was formed in 1840 and the new workhouse was built in 1841. Harsh new rules for dealing with paupers were brought in under the hated New Poor Laws of 1834. All the new workhouses were meant to look like prisons and many were sited on high ground to serve as a warning to the community that this could be where they might end up unless they worked hard and avoided the evils of Drink; that was the doctrine at the time. But of course it wasn't all beggars and drunks who sought refuse in the workhouse Most among the ruling classes believed that the poor were just lazy, work shy drunkards who chose to live off the parish instead of supporting their families. They accepted that some of the poorest people of the local parishes were unable to help themselves because they were old or sick or injured. These were called the deserving poor, but all other homeless people who were fit to work, were harshly treated. They were looked upon as rogues and vagabonds, or simply idle beggars. The reality was that the cost of outdoor relief had been increasing and again the government's answer was to put all the people supported by the ratepayers into Workhouses and spend as little as possible on them by putting them to work. That is why they were called Workhouses; and they made sure that the inmates did work.

I can only imagine what my Grandparent's life must have been like at that time, when no working class person could afford to own his or her own home. Accommodation was usually rented from the local Council, or in lodging houses.

At the time just before my mother was born in 1901, my Grandparents were living in one of the Lodging houses at 14 Mill Lane Larne, two doors below where my wife Margaret and I got our first little house together; (this was over fifty years later in 1953).

The intensive cold in the February of 1901 only added to my Grandfather Sullivan's bad luck. He worked as a Chimney Sweep, but due to the weather conditions he couldn't find other employment as all Outdoor work had come to a halt since the start of the New Year and the onset of the bad weather. Those who were unemployed were in a desperate state. None who could afford it, stayed outside for very long. The poor huddled beside their inadequate stoves or open fires, if they could find something to burn in them, while the rich built fires in every room. My Grandfather his wife Mary Ellen and their young 4 year old son John were living at number 14 Mill Lane along with 11 other people and I can testify that they only comprised of an Attic upstairs, not proper stairs like today, just like step ladders and two rooms downstairs which were not much larger than my bathroom is today. That is where my Grandparents were lodging, and any day my mother was due to be born. My Grandfather and my Grandmother had a tough decision to make. Bring their child into the world in that heavily overcrowded house among strangers, (who had to sleep and eat, in "Shifts" to ensure that everyone got some food and rest), or agree to my Grandmother entering the dreaded Workhouse until my mother was born and well enough to move elsewhere. My Grandfather would have known that a birth was difficult in those days, even at the best of times and that a labouring mother needed to be sustained by food and warmth. As a result of the weather my Grandmother became very poorly and reluctantly, they decided that my Grandmother should volunteer to be admitted to the Workhouse with their son John until after the new baby was born. This was not a satisfying solution to their problems but at least it was a last resort to make sure that my Grandmother and their children would be looked after at this very trying time.

And so; it was in that horrid place on the 5th day of April 1901 that my mother Mary Ellen Sullivan spent her first day on this earth.

We should be mindful that in 1901 there was no old age pension. No disability allowance. No invalidity pension, nor was there the vast array of benefits and credits that there are today. It was a time when you worked or you starved and so did your family. It was also a time when people were very afraid of taking sick or growing old as any expense with regards to their health was their own responsibility or that of the family. And while we are on the subject of Pensions we must not forget that in rural Irish communities of the early 1800s, weather forecasting was anything but a precise science. There were tales of people who could accurately predict turns in the weather and without the science that we take for granted today. Weather events were often viewed with superstition. One particular storm in 1839 was so peculiar that rural folk in the west of Ireland, stunned by its ferocity, feared it could be the end of the world. Some blamed it on the "fairies," and elaborate folk tales sprang from the event. Those who lived through the "Big Wind" never forgot it. And for that reason the horrendous storm became, seven decades later, a famous question formulated by the British bureaucrats who ruled Ireland.

The Great Storm Struck Ireland and Snow fell across the country on Saturday January 5, 1839. Sunday morning dawned with cloud cover that amounted to a typical Irish sky in winter. The day was warmer than usual, and the snow from the night before began to melt. By midday it began to rain heavily, and the precipitation coming in off the North Atlantic slowly spread eastward. By early evening heavy winds began to howl. Then on Sunday night an unforgettable fury was unleashed. Hurricane force winds began to batter the west and north of Ireland, as the freak storm roared out of the Atlantic. For most of the night, until just before dawn, the winds mauled the countryside, uprooting large trees, tearing the thatched roofs off houses, and toppling barns and church spires. There were even reports that grass was torn off hillsides. As the worst part of the storm occurred after midnight, and the relentless winds extinguished any candles or lanterns, people were particularly terrified as they couldn't see what was happening. And in many cases homes were burned because the bizarre winds blasting down chimneys threw hot embers from hearths across the floors of houses, igniting entire structures.

Casualties and Damage from the Big Wind in Newspaper reports claimed that more than 300 people were killed in the wind storm, but accurate figures are difficult to pin down.

There were reports of houses collapsing on people as well as houses burning to the ground, so there's no doubt there was considerable loss of life as well as many injuries. Many thousands were made homeless, and the economic devastation inflicted on a population that was already impoverished must have been massive. Stores of food meant to last through the winter were destroyed and scattered. Livestock and sheep were killed in vast numbers. Wild animals and birds were likewise killed and crows and jackdaws were nearly made extinct in parts of the country.

But it must be kept in mind that the storm struck in a time before government disaster response programs were implemented, so the people affected essentially had to fend for themselves.

The storm or The Big Wind as it was commonly known in Folklore by the Traditional Rural Irish. They believed in the "wee people," (what we think of today as leprechauns or fairies) and by tradition held that the feast day of a particular saint, Saint Ceara, which was held on January 5, was when these supernatural beings would hold a great meeting. As the mighty wind storm struck Ireland on the day after the feast of Saint Ceara, a storytelling tradition developed that the "wee people" held their grand meeting on the night of January 5, and decided to leave Ireland. As they left the following night they created the "Big Wind."

The Big wind then became a Milestone and the night of January 6, 1839 was so profoundly memorable that it was always known in Ireland as the "Big Wind" or "The Night of the Big Wind." Things date from it: and people would recall that such and such a thing happened before or after the Big Wind, when they were such and such an age, so much so that the

British Bureaucrats Relied on the "Big Wind". But a quirk in Irish tradition was that birthdays were never celebrated in the 19th century and no special heed was given to precisely how old someone was. This creates problems for we genealogists today, and it created problems for bureaucrats as well 100 years ago. You see in 1909 the British government, which was still ruling Ireland, instituted a system of old age pensions. When dealing with the rural population of Ireland where the written records might be scanty, the ferocious storm that blew in from the North Atlantic 70 years earlier proved to be useful as one of the questions asked of elderly people was if they could remember the "Big Wind." If they could, they qualified for a pension. Many of the claimants were watched by spectators, such was the novelty and the excitement as many of them seemed a lot younger than 70 and there was concern also about the massive queues in some places. In Ennis the rush was such that a police presence was required to keep order.

The pension, which had a maximum rate of five shillings per week, was payable to those whose incomes did not exceed £31.10 shillings per annum. Those whose income did not exceed £21 yearly were entitled to the full five shillings. For the first time the state assumed financial responsibility for family members through direct payment of cash. Prior to that the only assistance provided for the elderly was the Poor Law and the dreaded workhouse.

At the time of the introduction of the pension, many Irish who were not so old rushed to collect payments. In fact, so many people claimed the pension that the British Government was flabbergasted. The legislation that governed the pension came into force in January 1909 and by the following month, 177,000 pensions had been granted in Ireland, representing 4.1% of the population, compared with 370,000 people in England, representing 1.1% of the population. Granted, the proportion of older people in Ireland was higher than England and there was more poverty in Ireland, but luckily for those wishing to chance their arm and brazen it out compulsory registration of births only began in 1864, so determining age was open to debate, a debate the Irish won handsomely. Bogus claims abounded and, as a result, the pension cost much more than planned. This ensured pension officials began to pay much closer attention to Irish claims. O'Gráda has highlighted the response of one Irish MP to this. He described the officials as being in the particularly foolish and not very admirable position of men who have done some good by accident; and now blush to find how expensive it is and are now trying to diminish the cost of the good they have done". However it is a fact that when the fist pensions were paid, all the old-timers, male and female, who were able to walk, collected the first payment; but for many it was the last. Some celebrated the event by having a few drinks and were injured after falling over, while others contracted colds or pneumonia. This was all true and one might say that it was a double-edged sword for some. In Roscommon their neighbours ferried cartloads of aged female pensioners to the post office and in Birr, Co Offaly where a 93-year-old woman fell ill on the way home from the post office, the reason being that she had not been out of doors for many years before". But there seemed to be few as advanced in age as she was.

Five shillings was not an insignificant sum of money in Ireland a century ago when labourers were not earning much more than 10 shillings per week. But of course, the party had to be spoiled because in 1910, 38,495 pensions were revoked in Ireland in comparison to 29,217 in the rest of the UK. Nevertheless Ireland's share was still 22.2% of those claiming by 1911, when there were 243,000 recipients of the pension in the 32 counties. In 1919 the pension was doubled to a maximum of 10 shillings a week.

We might also be mindful that some of the so called "pillars of the community", or Masters as they were referred to, who were in charge of the Workhouses were not all that they appeared to be as can be seen from this extract of Hansard on 17th July 1894 in the House of Commons shows.

Mr. Mains (Donegal North)

I beg to ask the Chief Secretary to the Lord Lieutenant of Ireland (1) whether it has been reported to him that the Local Government Inspector (Mr. Agnew) on recent visits to the following unions—namely, Carrickmacross, Castleblaney, Larne, and Ballymena, found that the masters of these unions had more paupers entered on the books and charged for than were in the establishments; and, if so, in what other unions has he found a similar state of things; (2) whether the Local Government Board will in future instruct all their Inspectors, when they visit the unions in their districts, to see that the number of paupers in the house corresponds with the number in the books; and (3) what steps the Local Government Board will take in face of this loss to the ratepayers?

Mr. J. Morley

The fact is as stated in the first paragraph; and a similar state of things was also found to exist in the case of the Newtownards Workhouse. The Local Government Board will consider whether it is possible to adopt steps to prevent the occurrence of similar abuses in these and other unions in Ireland. The masters of the workhouses named have been called upon for written explanations as to the discrepancies in question, and upon the receipt of these explanations the Board will decide what further action should be taken in the matter.

The master at the time of my mother's birth in the Larne Workhouse was a Malcolm Fleming. As you can see he signed the birth certificate to say that her name was Ellen Jane Sullivan and that her mother's maiden name was O'Hara. This is completely wrong. My mother's name is Mary Ellen Sullivan and her mother's name is Mary Ellen Crilly. The obvious answer to the BLUNDER is that he signed the certificate on 4th June 1901; 76 days after my mother's birth and at the time of her birth there were 195 inmates in the Workhouse. This clown was so efficient that he described my mother as Male and Doctor Killen didn't fare too well either as he also signed the document.

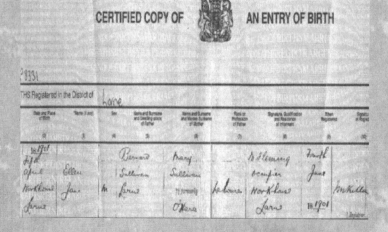

HC Dec 10 May 1894.

MR. M'CARTAN

I beg to ask the Chief Secretary to the Lord Lieutenant of Ireland whether his attention has been called to a letter from the Secretary to the Local Government Board to the Larne (County Antrim) Board of Guardians, subsequently published in The Irish News of the 3rd instant, in which it is stated that there are, in the infirmary of the workhouse, 62 patients, of whom 27 are lunatics in charge of one nurse who is unable to go about the wards without the aid of a stick; whether he is aware the letter alleges that this infirm nurse is assisted by three female inmates of an inferior class, two of whom are of immoral character; that on the male side three old and infirm men are the only assistants; and that the Inspector found in a ward with five female imbeciles an infant, one and a-half years old, in charge of a pauper attendant who belongs to the same class she is supposed to mind; and whether immediate steps will be taken to make such nursing and other arrangements as the necessity of the case demands?

Hansard 29 May 1894

MR. M'CARTAN (Down, S.)

I beg to ask the Chief Secretary to the Lord Lieutenant of Ireland whether his attention has been called to the report in The Irish News of the 17th instant of the proceedings at the special meeting of the Larne (County Antrim) Board of Guardians, held on the 16th instant, to consider the letter sent to the Guardians by the Secretary of the Local Government Board of Ireland; whether he is aware that, out of 61 inmates in the infirmary of the workhouse, 27 are lunatics; that the medical officer of the workhouse stated at the meeting that, of the three assistants who were helping the infirm nurse in charge at the time when the Inspector visited the house, the two who were then doing the work were regular prostitutes; and whether, considering the disclosures made at this meeting, some inquiry will be held into the working of the institution, or some steps taken to have a sufficient number of proper nurses engaged to attend to the wants of the patients? It is perfectly plain to me that the "master" at Larne Workhouse never took a blind bit of notice of the authorities as can be seen by this further copy of Hansard plainly shows.

WORKHOUSE IRREGULARITIES IN IRELAND;

Hansard 09 August 1894

MR. J. MORLEY

The masters of the workhouses named in this question have submitted their explanations to the Local Government Board. They allege that the discrepancies were entirely the result of an oversight. The Board have reprimanded these officers, and have called their auditor's attention to the matter in order that the cost of maintenance entered in the workhouse books in respect of the paupers who have left the house may be surcharged to the workhouse masters. (2) The Board believe that it is the practice on the part of some of the Inspectors to count the paupers in the workhouses, and they have intimated to all of them, in view of what has transpired in the district in question, that it is desirable that this should periodically be done.

So these people who were fiddling the Books and employing prostitutes and very disturbed people instead of nurses; got a slap on the wrist and now I cannot get anyone to supply me with my mother's proper birth certificate. Am I am supposed to put this down to another "oversight" on their part. So much for the freedom of information act, I seem to have got the freedom of **miss** information; and I had to pay for the privilege as it cost me £10 for what was supposed to be my mother's birth certificate. It has also cost me a hell of a lot more since then, to find out the truth about these evil, corrupt officials who were responsible for my grandmother and my mother's health whilst in their care and the correct administration of my mother's birth.

The Kirkbrides

1732

1. **John[1] Kirkbride** was born 1732.

Children of John Kirkbride are:

Martha[2] Kirkbride, born 21 Dec 1752.

James Kirkbride, born 01 Dec 1757; died 22 Jul 1825.

John Kirkbride, born 19 Jun 1759.

Mary Kirkbride, born 01 Sep 1761.

Sarah Kirkbride, born 25 Apr 1769; died Mar 1775.

1757

James[2] Kirkbride (John[1])

Was born 01 Dec 1757, and died 22 Jul 1825.

He married **Elizabeth Sunderland** 27 Jan 1785.

She was born 1761, and died 21 Jan 1838.

Children of James Kirkbride and Elizabeth Sunderland are:

John[3] Kirkbride, born 30 Dec 1786 in St. Andrews Penrith.

Margaret Kirkbride, born 06 Jul 1785.

Martha Kirkbride, born 07 Sep 1789.

James Kirkbride, born 24 Dec 1790; died 1852.

Elizabeth Kirkbride, born 06 Apr 1793; died 01 Nov 1816.

Johnathon Kirkbride, born 24 Dec 1796; died Oct 1874.

Thomas Kirkbride, born 27 Oct 1798; died 21 Feb 1837

Isaac Kirkbride, born 28 May 1803; died 16 Feb 1811.

1786

John[3] Kirkbride (James[2], John[1])

Was born 30 Dec 1786 in St. Andrews Penrith.

He married **Elizabeth Black** 13 Jun 1808 in St. Mary's Carlisle.

She was born 1786 in Carlisle, and died in Carlisle Cumberland.

Children of John Kirkbride and Elizabeth Black are:

Isaac[4] Kirkbride, born 23 Jan 1816 in Carlisle;

died 07 Feb 1873.

Margaret Kirkbride, born 02 Jan 1826 in Carlisle;

died 27 Jan 1906.

1816

Isaac⁴ Kirkbride (John³, James², John¹)

Was born 23 Jan 1816 in Carlisle, and died 07 Feb 1873 in Carlisle. He married **Sarah Rome** 13 Jun 1835 in Carlisle. She was born 1812 in Isle of Skye, and died 20 Mar 1883 in Carlisle

Children of Isaac Kirkbride and Sarah Rome are:

John⁵ Kirkbride, born 12 Dec 1835; died 18 Nov 1867.

Marie Charlotte Kirkbride, born 17 Jun 1840; died 18 Apr 1897.

Elizabeth Kirkbride, born 25 Dec 1842; died Jul 1905.

Margaret Ann Kirkbride, born 24 Apr 1845; died 1883.

William Kirkbride, born 04 Jul 1847; died 03 Sep 1904.

Isaac James Kirkbride, born 16 Jan 1849 in Carlisle; died 1901.

James Kirkbride, born 28 Jun 1851; died 19 Mar 1904.

Sarah Hannah Kirkbride, born 17 Jun 1853; died 08 Oct 1892.

John Kirkbride, born 12 Dec 1835.

1849

Isaac James[5] Kirkbride (Isaac[4], John[3], James[2], John[1])

Was born 16 Jan 1849 in Carlisle, and died 1901.

He married **Mary Howarth**, daughter of John Howarth and Hannah Stretch. She was born 04 Jun 1857 in Badcock Row Pendleton / Salford.

Children of Isaac Kirkbride and Mary Howarth are:

Charles[6] Kirkbride, born 1881.

James Kirkbride, born 1882.

Mary Lily Kirkbride, born 31 Jul 1891.

John Kirkbride, born 1892.

Clara Kirkbride, born Jul 1895 in Salford Lancashire.

She married Bertie Pollitt 13 Mar 1914 in Salford.

1891

Mary Lily[6] **Kirkbride** (Isaac James[5], Isaac[4], John[3], James[2], John[1])

Was born 31 Jul 1891.

She married **William Cody** 18 Jun 1910 in Salford.

He was born 1880 in Hulme Manchester.

Children of Mary Kirkbride and William Cody are:

Mary Lilian[7] Cody, born 24 Apr 1911 in Pendleton / Salford;

She died June 1970 in Manchester.

Patricia Cody, born 21 Dec 1929 in 33 Richmond St. Pembleton.

1911

Mary Lilian⁷ Cody (Mary Lily⁶ Kirkbride, Isaac James⁵, Isaac⁴, John³, James², John¹)

Mary Lilian Cody was born 24 Apr 1911 in Pendleton / Salford, and died Jun 1970 in Manchester.

She married **Alexander McKay Thompson** 24 Nov 1934 in Salford Manchester. He was born 20 Jun 1912, and died 24 Mar 1985 in Manchester.

Children of Mary Cody and Alexander Thompson are;

Alex Thompson, born 12 May 1935 in 240 Ellor St. Pendleton.

Margaret Thompson, born 13 Sep 1936 at 13 Woodbine St.

Salford; died 28 Oct 1996 in Northampton England.

Mary Lilian Cody married Alexander Thomson and during the Second World War he served for a time in the Black Watch Regiment. They had a son called Alex born in 1935 and a daughter called Margaret Nancy. But sometime between Margaret's birth in 1936 and the end of the War her parent's marriage had broken up. Mary was left with the two children and a mortgage to pay. Mary worked for a Brewery Company during the war years. She drove a horse and cart delivering barrels of beer to pubs in the Manchester area. She died in 1970, but not before she told me that the horse that she drove around the streets of Manchester was called Sonny. She said that the horse knew every delivery on her round without her having to remind the wise old horse when to stop. But in a strange way Sonny was the cause of her eventual death. It seems that one day during a brewery delivery Mary had occasion to "Back Sonny and his cart into a Brewery yard". The cellar to be supplied that day was close to a wall. Mary was at the rear of the Cart and as Sonny backed up towards the wall in the cobbled yard, Mary was pinned to it by the cart. As a result of this mishap (and that is all that she thought it was at the time) a black mark appeared above one of Mary's breasts. She was a very determined lady my mother in law and she refused to consult anyone about the mark as she said that she couldn't afford to have any time off work with the children to feed and a mortgage to pay, not to mention rationing and all the other hardships of coping on her own with working and looking after two school age children. It was some years later (after I first met her in 1952) that the "Black Mark" was diagnosed as Cancer which undoubtedly contributed to her premature death.

1936

Margaret Nancy[8] Thompson (Mary Lilian[7] Cody, Mary Lily[6] Kirkbride, Isaac James[5], Isaac[4], John[3], James[2], John[1]) was born 13 Sep 1936 in 13 Woodbine St. Salford, and died 28 Oct 1996 in Northampton England. She married **Daniel McFaul** 16 Oct 1954 in Chapel Larne County Antrim Northern Ireland, son of Denis McFaul and Mary Sullivan. He was born 25 May 1934 in Larne.

Children of Margaret Thompson and Daniel McFaul are:

Denis[9] McFaul, born 18 Mar 1955 in Larne County Antrim

AnnaMarie McFaul, born 10 Oct 1957 in Manchester.

Lilian Bernadette McFaul, born 01 Apr 1959 in Catterick Camp.

Denise Alexis McFaul, born 14 Apr 1961 in Taunton Somerset.

Margaret Nancy Thomson was born at number 13 Woodbine Street Salford on 13 September 1936. She was baptised in Salford Cathedral on 28 September 1936. She was educated at St. Wilfred's School Salford. She later lived at number 48 Upper Moss Lane in the Hulme area of Manchester when I first met her in 1952. She was working in a factory called Dannimac as a machinist. Some may remember the name Dannimac it became famous when it made the Macs that were worn by Prime Minister Harold Wilson in the 1960s. Margaret was one of many children who were evacuated from Manchester to Blackpool during World War Two. She once told me that they were sent by train and all the children had labels tied round their neck with their names and other basic details on them, just like parcels have when going through the postal system. Even before the war started the Government was worried that a new war might begin when Hitler came to power in 1933. They figured that British cities and large towns would be targets for bombing raids by aircraft. So at the start of the Second World War many children from cities and large towns were moved temporarily from their homes to places that were considered to be much safer; usually to a seaside town or out in the countryside. Those who were evacuated were schoolchildren and teachers, mothers with children under five years of age, pregnant women and certain disabled people.

During the war about 3.5 million people, mainly children had experienced evacuation. No one was forced to go but the Government encouraged parents with the aid of posters that their children would be safer from German bombs in they moved to the seaside and country towns. Parents and children alike were nervous at the thought of being separated and not knowing when or if they will see each other again.

Generation No. 6

1949

DEREK Mc FAUL 6 (CLARE 5, DENIS 4, DENIS 3, DENIS 2, DAN1)

Son of Clare McFaul

Derek was born in 1949

He married Marie Sayers.

Marie was born in 1953

Children of DEREK MCFAUL and MARIE SAYERS are:

CIARA[7] MCFAUL, b. 1982.

JOANNE MCFAUL, b. 1984.

CLARE MCFAUL, b. 1987.

1969

MARC⁶ MCCORMICK *(CECELIA⁵, ALICE⁴, JAMES³, DENIS², DAN¹)*

Was born 13 Jan 1969 in Larne.

He married ANNE CONNOR.

Children of MARC MCCORMICK and ANNE CONNOR are:

LAUREN⁷ MCCORMICK, b. 25 Sep 1995, Larne.

ERIN MCCORMICK, b. 10 Jul 2001, Larne.

1970

TRACEY⁶ BROADFOOT *(BERNADINE⁵ NURSE, CECELIA⁴ MCFAUL, JAMES³, DENIS², DAN¹)*

Was born 24 Jul 1970.

Child of TRACEY BROADFOOT is;

SHKIESHA⁷ BROADFOOT, b. Jan 1989.

1970

CHERYL⁶ BROADFOOT *(BERNADINE⁵ NURSE, CECELIA⁴ MCFAUL, JAMES³, DENIS², DAN¹)*

Was born 24 Jul 1970

Children of CHERYL BROADFOOT are:

MATTHIAS⁷ BROADFOOT, b. Apr 1995.

KYNA BROADFOOT, b. Oct 2002.

BOBBIE BROADFOOT, b. Jun 2006.

1972

DAVID⁶ BROADFOOT *(BERNADETTE⁵ NURSE, CECELIA⁴ MCFAUL, JAMES³, DENIS², DAN¹)*

Was born 14 Apr 1972 in Liverpool.

Children of DAVID BROADFOOT are:

LUCCA⁷ BROADFOOT, b. 1991.

GALI BROADFOOT, b. 2001.

BEAU BROADFOOT, b. Dec 2004.

1944

MARIE McAULEY 6 (ANNA 5, DENIS 4, DENIS 3, DENIS 2, DAN1)

Daughter of

Anna McFaul and Gerald McAuley

Was born 17 Oct 1944 in Larne.

She married WILLIAM PURVIS 15 Apr 1963, son of ANDREW PURVIS and LAVINIA TAGGART.

He was born 13 Dec 1943.

Children of ANNMARIE MCAULEY and WILLIAM PURVIS;

ERIC GEORGE[7] PURVIS, b. 12 Sep 1963, Larne.

JACQUELINE PURVIS, b. 20 Dec 1964, Larne.

GERALDINE PURVIS, b. 29 Aug 1966, Larne.

AMANDA PURVIS, b. 12 Sep 1967, Larne;

m. ANTONY STANTON, 27 Jun 2009;

ANDREA PURVIS, b. 01 Jun 1972, Larne.

WILLIAM PURVIS, b. 27 Sep 1973, Larne.

1948

GERALDINE McAULEY 6 (ANNA 5, DENIS 4, DENIS 3, DENIS 2, DAN1)

Daughter of Anna McFaul and Gerald McAuley

GERALDINE^6 MCAULEY *(ANNA^5 MCFAUL, DENIS^4, DANIEL^3, DENIS^2, DAN^1)* was born 1948 in Larne, and died 17 Mar 1972 in Larne. She married GIRVAN MORRIS 1965 in Larne.

Children of GERALDINE MCAULEY and GIRVAN MORRIS;

PAUL^7 MORRIS, b. 1966.

GIRVIN MORRIS, b. 1969.

GERALDINE LORRAINE MORRIS, b. 1972

In 1972 tragedy struck at my sister Anna's family when her daughter Geraldine was murdered as she was visiting a block of flats in the town. The story is that a man who lived in the town thought that his wife was cheating on him, so he followed her to the tower blocks at the top of Main Street. Geraldine used to sell fabric products and she was delivering some goods to customers in the flats. Geraldine came out of one of the flats and while she was walking to her next customer, she was stabbed to death. The man thought that Geraldine was his wife in the dimly lit surroundings, as she was wearing a similar type of coat to that of his wife. The incident was reported in the local press something like this;

Man Charged With Murder

A 21 year old man appeared at a special court in Larne on Saturday afternoon charged with the murder of Mrs Geraldine Morris (24) on Saint Patrick's night. He was remanded to appear at Armagh Magistrate's court on March 30th. When charged on Saturday morning at Larne police station, the man is alleged to have told the Police that he had nothing to say. Mrs. Morris's body was found on the ninth floor of Shane House a multi-storey block of flats at 8.30 pm on Friday evening. She was lying on the communal stairway and had been stabbed to death. She was a part time agent for a clothing and supply firm and had called at Shane House to collect for her firm. A spokesman for the firm said she had been working for them for two years but she never had large sums of money to collect. She lived at 50 Millbrae with her husband Girvan, a coal man, and her three children Paul six, Girvan three and Geraldine Lorraine who is seven weeks. She has been married eight years.

1972

KATE LINTON 6 (DENNIS⁵ *CECELIA*⁴, *JAMES*³, *DENIS*², *DAN*¹)

Daughter of Dennis and Adrienne Watson

Kate

Sophie

Kate was born on 30 November 1972

She married Roger Hutchinson in 2000

Child of Kate Linton and Roger Hutchinson is:

Sophie[7] Hutchinson, b. 2001

1962

SHARON⁶ LINTON *(DENNIS⁵, CECELIA⁴ MCFAUL, JAMES³, DENIS², DAN¹)*

Daughter of

Dennis and Adrienne Watson

Sharon was born 07 Oct 1962.

Child of SHARON LINTON is:

ROWEN JADE⁷ b. 22 Dec 1995.

1966

ANDREW6 LINTON (DENNIS5, CECELIA4 MCFAUL, JAMES3, DENIS2, DAN1)

Son of

Dennis and Adrienne Watson

Andrew was born on 18 Jul 1966.

Children of ANDREW LINTON ;

EMILY JANE7 LINTON, b. 22 Oct 1988.

ELOISE LINTON b. 4 Sept. 1995

EVE LINTON b. 29 Jan. 2004

CECELIA ROSE LINTON b. 24 Jan. 2007

1947

MARY McAULEY 6 (EILEEN 5, DENIS 4, DENIS 3, DENIS 2, DAN1)

Daughter of

Eileen McFaul and James McAuley

MARY[6] MCAULEY *(EILEEN[5] MCFAUL, DENIS[4], DANIEL[3], DENIS[2], DAN[1])* was born on 12 April 1946. She married ROB VANDE LANGKRUIS 28 Nov 1964. Rob was born on 8 May 1944.

Children of MARY and ROB VANDE LANGKRUIS;

SHAUN[7] VANDE LANGKRUIS. b. 21 Mar 1965

JANETTE VANDE LANGKRUIS. b. 14 April 1966

ALLISON VANDE LANGKRUIS. b. 15 June 1968

1957

GERALD[6] MCAULEY *(EILEEN[5] MCFAUL, DENIS[4], DANIEL[3], DENIS[2], DAN[1])*

Son of

Eileen McFaul and James McAuley

Was born on 9 December 1957.

He married DEBRAH CAMPBELL;

Debrah was born on 10 October 1955.

Children of GERALD MCAULEY and DEBRAH CAMPBELL;

MARK[7] MCAULEY.

MICHAEL MCAULEY.

NAOMI MCAULEY.

1962

GERALDINE⁶ EDGAR *(CHARLOTTE⁵ MCFAUL, DENIS⁴, DANIEL³, DENIS², DAN¹)*

Daughter of

Charlotte McFaul and William Edgar

Was born 15 Jun 1962 in Larne

She married JIM RICE.

Children of GERALDINE EDGAR and JIM RICE are:

MARTINE⁷ RICE, b. 21 Jan 1994, Larne

STEVEN RICE, b. 12 Mar 1992, Larne.

Dan Mc Faul The Weaver

1963

BRIAN[6] EDGAR *(CHARLOTTE[5] MCFAUL, DENIS[4], DANIEL[3], DENIS[2], DAN[1])*

Son of

Charlotte McFaul and William Edgar

Was born 11 Feb 1963 in Larne

He married KAREN Mc RANDAL. on 29 October 1992.

Children of BRIAN EDGAR and KAREN Mc RANDAL are:

CHRISTOPHER[7] EDGAR, b. 1993, Larne.

DAVID EDGAR, b. 23 Apr 1994, Larne.

KATIE EDGAR, b. 03 Jan 2003, Larne.

Dan Mc Faul The Weaver

1955

DENIS[6] MCFAUL *(DANIEL[5], DENIS[4], DANIEL[3], DENIS[2], DAN[1])*

Son of Daniel McFaul and Margaret Thompson.

Was born 18 Mar 1955 in Larne

He married JACQULINE BEAK in Upminster Essex

Children of DENIS MCFAUL and JACQULINE BEAK are:

CHRISTOPHER DANIEL[7] MCFAUL, b. 10 May 1980.

JENNIFER LOUISE MCFAUL, b. 05 Oct 1985.

Denis was born at 16 Mill Lane in Larne on 18 March 1955. His education started in 1960 when he was five years of age at Taunton in Somerset. It continued for three years until the family moved to Bunde in West Germany. Two years later he had moved to Northern Ireland for a further four years and finally King Richard's School at Dekalia in Cyprus. Then it was back to Germany again in 1973.by which time he was a young man and ready to make his mark on the workforce.

Like some Army units, NAAFI was a place where a person in a job with a rank such as Warehouse Manager would have to retire, or even die, before a vacancy would be created for someone to be promoted. But it was a steady reliable job and Denis had become a fluent speaker of the German language. He was transferred to the United Kingdom in 1976 as assistant manager at a warehouse in Darlington, where the manager was soon to be retired.

Denis married Jacquline Beak whom he met as a working colleague when Jackie, as she was affectionately known, was working as a Secretary at the same establishment. Their marriage took place at Upminster in Essex in 1978. In June 1985 Denis was seconded from NAAFI into the Army as a 2nd Lieutenant in the Royal Army Ordnance Corps to serve in the Falkland Islands where he gained valuable experience in the logistics of the movement of personnel and equipment. This experience was very useful to him in his later life. He served in the Falkland Islands as a Logistics Officer and attained the rank of Captain.

Dan Mc Faul The Weaver

Whilst in the Falkland Islands Denis developed stomach ulcers and he had eventually to return to England to have an operation. After his recovery from his operation Denis was demobbed from the Army and he resumed his employment with NAAFI at a depot in Darlington, near Catterick Camp in Yorkshire. Denis, I am pleased to say was born in Larne like myself and many of his Ancestors and other relations. He was naturally called Denis because his Grandfather was called Denis. Unfortunately he was not to get to know his paternal Grandfather although he did know his Grandfather and his Grandmother on his mother's side. Denis, though born in Larne didn't start his school days at McKenna Memorial where so many of the McFaul males have done throughout the generations.

This photograph was taken in the Falkland Islands in 1985. Denis is the Officer in the middle of the back row.

1957

ANNAMARIE[6] MCFAUL *(DANIEL[5], DENIS[4], DANIEL[3], DENIS[2], DAN[1])*

Daughter of

Daniel McFaul and Margaret Thompson

Was born 10 Oct 1957 in Manchester.

She married RICHARD THOROGOOD in Dekelia. Cyprus on 24 March 1973.

Children of ANNAMARIE and RICHARD THOROGOOD

RICHARD[7] THOROGOOD, b. 15 Aug 1975 Cyprus.

HAYLEY THOROGOOD, b. 29 Jun 1978.

Anna Marie's education started in an Army School and continued in the same vane until she left school at King Richard's School, Cyprus in 1973. Anna Marie later continued her education and obtained a Degree in Northampton and until early retirement in 2009 held a senior position with the local Borough as a Welfare Officer for the County. She has been the Lady Captain of one of the Local Golf Clubs in the area. Anna Marie is also a Justice of the Peace.

This is my daughter Anna Marie and I with the Golf Ryder Cup.

1959

LILIAN BERNADETTE[6] MCFAUL *(DANIEL[5], DENIS[4], DANIEL[3], DENIS[2], DAN[1])*

Daughter of

Daniel McFaul and Margaret Thompson

was born 01 Apr 1959 in Catterick Camp Yorkshire.

She married JOHN GEORGE FISHER in Krefeld Germany.

Children of LILIAN MCFAUL and JOHN FISHER are:

ANGELA[7] FISHER, b. 15 Sep 1977;

CLARE FISHER, b. 21 Dec 1979.

Bernadette was born in Catterick Camp Yorkshire on April Fool's day 1959. She is the daughter of Daniel and Margaret McFaul. Her stay in England was short lived as her father was posted to Germany shortly afterwards. Returning again to Germany with her parents some years later, Bernie had spent most of her childhood there. She became quite fluent in the German language and finished her schooling at Kent school near Rheindarlen in West Germany. In 1976 she married John Fisher, in Krefeld Germany. Her husband was a serving soldier and they were posted to Belgium.

On 15 September 1977 she gave birth to a baby daughter which they named Angela. Eleven days after the birth they were off to Holland as her husband had been posted once again in the line of duty. Three years later on 21 December 1979 Bernadette gave birth to another daughter, Clare Elizabeth, at RAF Wegberg hospital. Eleven weeks later they were off again to Northern Ireland.

After this tour of duty was up they all moved to Belgium. Unfortunately the marriage broke up, but Bernadette and Clare remained in Belgium. They later moved to Blackpool where Bernadette went to College and obtained two teaching qualifications and an Honours degree in modern languages. She taught English and French at local colleges in Lancashire to mainly foreign students.

1961

DENISE⁶ MCFAUL (DANIEL⁵, DENIS⁴, DANIEL³,

DENIS², DAN¹)

Daughter of

Daniel McFaul and Margaret Thompson

Denise was born on 14th April 1961. She is the youngest and the fourth child of Margaret and Daniel Mc Faul. Denise worked for many years as an employee of one of the large well known Supermarket chains. She settled down to a family life with partner Paul and his daughter Tammy.

1967

MICHELLE⁶ HOMER *(ANNE⁵ MCFAUL, DANIEL JOSEPH⁴, DANIEL³, DENIS², DAN¹)*

Daughter of

Daniel McFaul & Elizabeth English

Was born 11 May 1967.

She married RYAN TWEEDIE.

Child of MICHELLE HOMER and TWEEDIE is:

RYAN⁷ TWEEDIE, b. 07 Apr 1993.

1970

DONNA[6] HOMER *(ANNE[5] MCFAUL, DANIEL JOSEPH[4], DANIEL[3], DENIS[2], DAN[1])*

Daughter of

Anne McFaul & Don Homer

Was born 20 Feb 1970.

She married Michael IRVINE.

Children of DONNA HOMER and Michael IRVINE are:

RACHEL[7] IRVINE, b. 08 Dec 1996.

MICHAEL IRVINE, b. 21 Feb 2002.

1970

CHRISTOPHER[6] MCFAUL *(JAMES[5], DANIEL JOSEPH[4], DANIEL[3], DENIS[2], DAN[1])*

Son of

James McFaul & Linda Williams

Was born 14 Oct 1972

He married EMMA WINKLES 02 Sep 2000.

Children of CHRISTOPHER MCFAUL and EMMA WINKLES

DANIEL[7] MCFAUL, b. 07 Mar 1997.

JACK MCFAUL, b. 31 Dec 2002.

1975

DAMIEN[6] MCFAUL *(JAMES[5], DANIEL JOSEPH[4], DANIEL[3], DENIS[2], DAN[1])*

Son of

James McFaul & Linda Williams

Was born 06 Apr 1975

He married ZOE SOUTHGATE 10 Sep 2006.

Children of DAMIEN MCFAUL and ZOE SOUTHGATE are:

PHOEBE[7] MCFAUL, b. 15 Dec 2005.

VIOLET MCFAUL, b. 01 Jan 2008.

Generation No. 7

1963

ERIC GEORGE⁷ PURVIS *(ANNMARIE⁶ MCAULEY, ANNA⁵ MCFAUL, DENIS⁴, DANIEL³, DENIS², DAN¹)*

Son of

Ann Marie McAuley & William Purvis

Was born 12 Sep 1963 in Larne

He married JANICE MARTIN 23 Aug 1985 in Larne.

She was born 19 Nov 1965.

Children of ERIC PURVIS and JANICE MARTIN are:

RICHARD⁸ PURVIS, b. 12 Feb 1985, Larne.

LINDA PURVIS, b. 28 Aug 1986, Larne.

LAURA PURVIS, b. 19 Apr 1992, Larne.

STEPHEN PURVIS, b. 03 Oct 1996, Larne.

Dan Mc Faul The Weaver

Richard   Linda

Stephen   Laura

Dan Mc Faul The Weaver

1964

JACQUELINE[7] PURVIS *(ANNMARIE[6] MCAULEY, ANNA[5] MCFAUL, DENIS[4], DANIEL[3], DENIS[2], DAN[1])*

Daughter of

Ann Marie McAuley and William Purvis

Was born 20 Dec 1964 in Larne

She married TREVOR TWEED 25 Sep 1992 in Larne.

He was born 18 Jul 1966

Child of JACQUELINE PURVIS and TREVOR TWEED is:

JORDAN[8] TWEED, b. 12 Oct 1995.

1966

GERALDINE[7] PURVIS *(ANNMARIE[6] MCAULEY, ANNA[5] MCFAUL, DENIS[4], DANIEL[3], DENIS[2], DAN[1])*

Daughter of

Ann Marie McAuley and William Purvis

Was born 29 Aug 1966 in Larne.

She married JOHN ROSS 14 Jul 1997.

Children of GERALDINE PURVIS and JOHN ROSS are:

JONATHAN[8] ROSS, b. 22 Apr 1996, Larne.

LEAH ROSS, b. 04 Dec 2003, Larne.

Dan Mc Faul The Weaver

1972

ANDREA[7] PURVIS *(ANNMARIE[6] MCAULEY, ANNA[5] MCFAUL, DENIS[4], DANIEL[3], DENIS[2], DAN[1]*

Daughter of

Ann Marie McAuley and William Purvis

Was born 01 Jun 1972 in Larne.

She married MICHAEL JOHN DAVIDSON 31 Aug 1991.

He was born 31 Dec 1969.

Children of ANDREA PURVIS and MICHAEL DAVIDSON

NICOLE[8] DAVIDSON, b. 30 Mar 1994.

CHLOE DAVIDSON, b. 28 Sep 2002

Dan Mc Faul The Weaver

1973

WILLIAM[7] PURVIS *(ANNMARIE[6] MCAULEY, ANNA[5] MCFAUL, DENIS[4], DANIEL[3], DENIS[2], DAN[1]*

Son of

Ann Marie McAuley and William Purvis

Was born 27 Sep 1973 in Larne.

He married JOANNE PEACOCK 06 Jul 2001.

She was born 10 Oct 1978.

Child of WILLIAM PURVIS and JOANNE PEACOCK is:

COURTNEY NATASHA[8] PURVIS, b. 14 Oct 2002.

1980

CHRISTOPHER Mc Faul 7 (DENIS⁶, *DANIEL⁵*, *DENIS⁴*, *DANIEL³*, *DENIS²*, *DAN¹*)

Son of

Denis McFaul and Jacquiline Beak

Was born on 10 May 1980. Christopher is the first male where the traditional naming has been broken in 140 years. His ancestors are; father Denis, Grandfather Daniel; Great/Grandfather Denis; Great/ Great /Grandfather Daniel; Great /Great /Great/ Grandfather Denis; and Great/ Great/ Great /Great/ Grandfather Dan the weaver.

1985

JENNIFER Mc Faul 7, (DENIS⁶ , *DANIEL⁵, DENIS⁴, DANIEL³, DENIS², DAN¹*)

Daughter of

Denis McFaul and Jacquiline Beak

Jennifer was born on 5 May 1985. Like her brother Christopher she is at university and at present has a Master's degree in creative writing. I would like to think that perhaps in the future she may rewrite and transform this book to what will be her family history.

1975

RICHARD[7] THOROGOOD *(ANNAMARIE[6] MCFAUL, DANIEL[5], DENIS[4], DANIEL[3], DENIS[2], DAN[1])*

Son of

Anna Marie McFaul and Richard Thorogood

Was born 15 Aug 1975 in Dekelia Cyprus.

He married SVETLANA STEFANOVIC 19 Aug 2006.

She was born 21 Nov 1981.

Children of RICHARD and SVETLANA STEFANOVIC.

DANIEL THOROGOOD, b. 05 Jul 2007.

DAVID THOROGOOD, b. 05 Jul 2007.

1978

HAYLEY[7] THOROGOOD *(ANNAMARIE[6] MCFAUL, DANIEL[5], DENIS[4], DANIEL[3], DENIS[2], DAN[1]*

Daughter of

Anna Marie McFaul and Richard Thorogood

Was born 29 Jun 1978. She married ANDREW BRADBURY 15 Jul 2000 in Northampton, son of ROBIN BRADBURY and SUSAN LARDER.

He was born 09 Jan 1967.

Dan Mc Faul The Weaver

Children of HAYLEY and ANDREW BRADBURY

JOSHUA⁸ BRADBURY, b. 21 Oct 2001,

ISABELLE BRADBURY, b. 30 Jan 2008,

Hayley and Andrew were married in the old Church at Geddington in Northampton, made famous by the Eleanor Cross in the middle of the village. History records that Eleanor daughter of Ferdinand 3rd, King of Leon married Edward, who on the death of Henry 3rd was to become Edward 1, the most powerful of all the Plantagenet Kings. He was 15 Eleanor was 9. They both stayed on many occasions at their royal palace at Geddington attending the church (originally Saxon but it was the Norman's who created the Church we see today.

Dan Mc Faul The Weaver

On 28th November 1290, while on her way to join the King in Scotland the Queen was taken gravely ill and died at Harby near Lincoln. Her body was taken to Westminster Abbey.

The King was so grief stricken he gave orders that every place where the escorts had rested, a cross be erected in her memory. In total there were 12 crosses but today only three remain. The one at Geddington is in best condition and represents her love for the area and that the escorts rested here on 7th December 1290.

1977

ANGELA[7] FISHER *(LILIAN BERNADETTE[6] MCFAUL, DANIEL[5], DENIS[4], DANIEL[3], DENIS[2], DAN[1])*

Daughter of

Bernadette McFaul and John Fisher

Was born 15 September 1977

She married LEE AUSTIN 01 July 2000.

Angela commenced her schooling at Smallwood Manor near Stafford in the England. The school caters for pupils between the ages of two and a half and eleven years of age. She then went on to Smallwood's senior school Denstone College before going to Swansea University where she obtained a degree in Marine Biology. Angela likes to travel and has been to Africa, India, Ecuador, Peru, and Tibet. She plays the piano and reads as much as she can. She is also a fluent speaker of the French language.

1979

CLARE[7] FISHER *(LILIAN BERNADETTE[6] MCFAUL, DANIEL[5], DENIS[4], DANIEL[3], DENIS[2], DAN[1])*

Daughter of

Bernadette McFaul and John Fisher

Was born 21 Dec 1979

She married (1) COLIN OAKES 07 Dec 2000.

She married (2) ANTHONY DRAPER 18 Aug 2007.

He was born 19 Mar 1975.

Clare was born on 21 December 1979 she is the daughter of Bernadette McFaul and John Fisher. Most of her young life was spent in Belgium and at an American School and also High School. She joined the American Air Force Cadets and played American Football and Basketball and she was quite athletic. The family moved back to the United Kingdom in the summer of 1998. In 1999 Clare joined the Royal Air Force and attained the rank of Corporal. She married Colin Oakes who was also in the Royal Air Force on 7th December 2000. Clare left the RAF in 2004. Clare speaks French and Russian, enjoys music. Plays the Piano, she is also very artistic and trendy.

Child of CLARE FISHER and COLIN OAKES is:

HANNAH^8 OAKES, b. 22 Feb 2001,

Child of CLARE FISHER and ANTHONY DRAPER is:

LUKE^8 DRAPER, b. 01 Mar 2006,

HANNAH  LUKE

Generation No. 8

Children of ERIC PURVIS and JANICE MARTIN

RICHARD[8] PURVIS, b. 12 Feb 1985, Larne.

LINDA PURVIS, b. 28 Aug 1986, Larne.

LAURA PURVIS, b. 19 Apr 1992, Larne.

STEPHEN PURVIS, b. 03 Oct 1996, Larne.

Child of JACQUELINE PURVIS and TREVOR TWEED

JORDAN[8] TWEED, b. 12 Oct 1995.

Children of GERALDINE PURVIS and JOHN ROSS

JONATHAN[8] ROSS, b. 22 Apr 1996, Larne.

LEAH ROSS, b. 04 Dec 2003, Larne.

Children of ANDREA PURVIS and MICHAEL DAVIDSON

NICOLE[8] DAVIDSON, b. 30 Mar 1994.

CHLOE DAVIDSON, b. 28 Sep 2002.

Child of WILLIAM PURVIS and JOANNE PEACOCK

COURTNEY NATASHA[8] PURVIS, b. 14 Oct 2002.

Children of RICHARD and SVETLANA STEFANOVIC

DANIEL[8] THOROGOOD, b. 05 Jul 2007.

DAVID THOROGOOD, b. 05 Jul 2007.

Children of HAYLEY and ANDREW BRADBURY

JOSHUA[8] BRADBURY, b. 21 Oct 2001, Northampton England.

ISABELLE BRADBURY, b. 30 Jan 2008, Northampton .

Child of CLARE FISHER and COLIN OAKES

HANNAH[8] OAKES, b. 22 Feb 2001, Lincoln England.

Child of CLARE FISHER and ANTHONY DRAPER

LUKE[8] DRAPER, b. 01Mar 2006.

Statistics for descendants of Dan the Weaver.

Total number of individuals	*569*
Total number of marriages	*146*
Average life span	*56. years*
Earliest birth date	*1815*
Latest birth date	*2008 (Isabelle Bradbury).*
Number of text records	*2753*
Number of generations	*11*
Number of different surnames	*134*

The Sullivans

1864

BERNARD1 SULLIVAN was born 1864 in County Antrim, and died in Larne Lough.

He married MARY ELLEN CRILLEY 1895.

She was born 1871 in County Down.

Children of BERNARD SULLIVAN and MARY CRILLEY

JOHN SULLIVAN, b. 1897, Louth; d. 1966, Larne;

MARY SULLIVAN, b. 05 Apr 1901; Larne

MICHAEL SULLIVAN, b. 04 Nov 1902, Antrim.

BARNEY SULLIVAN, b. 04 Dec 1904, Larne;

GEORGE SULLIVAN, b. 01 Aug 1906, Larne.

Both Bernard and Mary Ellen's birth years and counties of their birth were confirmed in the 1901 census of Larne when they were living in a lodging house at 14 Mill Lane. At that time they also had a son John who was 4 years old and according to them John was born in County Louth.

They were documented as being called O'Sullivan which suggests that they themselves did not complete the Census form, in fact I know they didn't as they could not read or write.

1897

JOHN2 SULLIVAN (BERNARD1)

Johnny Sullivan was born in Louth in Republic of Ireland in 1897. He died in 1966 in Larne Northern Ireland. I knew my uncle Johnny very well as I used to go to see him nearly every day when he lived in the second little house at the Knowe just off the top of Mill Lane after World War two. He was a real character and I loved to listen to the tales that he used to tell. He was unfortunately very short sighted but I think that this made his other senses much sharper than normal.

I have read lots of books on Clan history and discovered all manner of difficult to understand information, most of which is far too boring to pass on. However my uncle Johnny told me that a McFaul is reputed to have invented Whiskey. He also told me that there is a Town called McFaul in a remote part of Alaska. Some years later I thought that maybe one day I could go there to Alaska and have a tot of Mc Faul Whiskey; and that's about it for my Clan discoveries. I should have known better. Uncle Johnny having been born in 1897 wouldn't have been able to spell Genealogy let alone know anything about it. Nevertheless I used to enjoy my little chats with him when I was a boy and the stories that he would tell me about his time "On the Road" as a Tinker. My Uncle Johnny told me once that he thought that he got his idea for travelling from his Grandmother. She wasn't really a Sullivan traveller as she was his mother's mother and my Great Grandmother. He said that they called her a country woman. My Great Grandfather apparently went off with her as a young girl when they were both teenagers. He was only a boy then himself. Uncle Johnny said that she was looked upon as an outcast for in those days travellers and Gypsies were treated like dirt, they were nobodies. He had it hard in his time ending up in the dreaded workhouse a few times. But my Grandparents had it just as bad and I know that my Grandfather Sullivan couldn't read or write. Johnny told me that generally he only spent time in school when he was in the Workhouse. His told me that his senses were so acute that when he did go to school in Larne he could smell the chalk as he entered the classroom.

1901

Mary Ellen Sullivan wife of Denis McFaul

MARY ELLEN2 SULLIVAN (BERNARD1) was born 05 Apr 1901 in Larne, and died 05 Apr 1942 in Coleraine N. Ireland. She married DENIS MCFAUL 31 Jan 1924 in Larne. He was born 04 Aug 1904 in Larne, and died 28 Mar 1943 in Tunisia North Africa.

My mother is buried in the Agerton Cemetry in Portstewart where we were living in an Army property. Dad was in the North Irish Horse regiment then.

1902

MICHAEL2 SULLIVAN (BERNARD1)

Michael Sullivan was born on 4 November 1902 in the town of Antrim.

Children of MICHAEL SULLIVAN and M are:

ANNA3 SULLIVAN, m. BRIAN MC EVOY;

MICKEY SULLIVAN.

BOBBY SULLIVAN.

Bernard and Mary Ellen's second son Michael was born in Antrim town on November 4th 1902 when they were living at number 285 Castle Street. They soon returned to Larne as son Bernard was born at Mill Lane Larne in December 1904.

Dan Mc Faul The Weaver

Petty Officer Michael Sullivan was a crew member of the HMS Sardonyx "S" Class Destroyer ordered from Alex Stephen of Cowan with the 12th Order of the 1917-18 Build Programme in June 1918 with 37 other ships. The ship was laid down 25th March 1918 and launched on 27th May 1919 as the first RN ship to carry the name. Building was completed on 12th July 1919 and she served with the Fleet until later was placed in Reserve. Brought forward for service in 1939 this ship was adopted by the civil community of Coulsdon and Pursey, Surrey after a successful "WARSHIP WEEK" National Savings campaign in December.

HMS SARDONYX

The following history of the ship's movements during World war Two will help us to understand where Michael was and what was happening at various times.

Dan Mc Faul The Weaver

Heraldic Data

Badge

On a Field Black a Pendant Gold set with geometrical design of Red and White.

Motto 'Clean cuts clean'

Details of War Service

1939

September to October

Deployed on coastal convoy defence.

November

Transferred to Western Approaches for Atlantic convoy.

December

Atlantic convoy defence in continuation

1940

January to August

Atlantic convoy defence in continuation. Nominated for refit.

September to November

Under refit and modifications to improve capability.

December

Resumed duty in Western Approaches.

1941

January to February

Western Approaches convoy defence

March 17th

Joined HM Destroyers WALKER, VANOC, VOLUNTEER, HM Corvettes BLUEBELL And HYDRANGEA in 5th Escort Group on formation. Deployed as escort for Convoy HX112 16th Convoy sighted by Ul10 which carried out attack on escorted ships and called for further U-Boat support. U99, U100 carried out attacks during which both were sunk for the loss of five escorted mercantiles including three Tankers (Note : U 99 was commanded by Otto Kretschmer and U 100 Joachim Schepke both of whom were successful U-Boat commanders wit many sinkings. These two U-Boat sinkings were credited to HMS VANOC and HMSWALKER.

April to July

Deployment with Group in continuation

August to September

Deployed with HM Destroyers MALCOLM, WATCHMAN, SCIMITAR, H M Covettes to ARABIS, VERBENA, VIOLET, MONKSHOOD, PETUNIA and DAHLIA in 8th Escort.

October

Group for convoy defence in NW Approaches.

November

Atlantic convoy defence in continuation With Group. 22nd. Involved in collision with HM Trawler ST APOLLO which was sunk.

December

NW Approaches deployment with Group in continuation.

1942

January

NW Approaches deployment with Group In continuation For details of U-BOAT to operations in the Atlantic.

April 18th

Detached for escort of ships of 1st Minelaying Squadron. Deployed with H M Destroyers CHARLESTOWN, WELLS of Minelaying Squadron, HM Destroyer SALADIN and H Minesweeper SCOTT as escort for HM Auxiliary Minelayers AGAMEMNON, MENESTHEUS, PORT QUEBEC and SOUTHERN PRINCE for minelay in Northern Barrage.

May 23rd

Deployed with HM Cruiser CAIRO, HM Destroyer BEAGLE, DOUGLAS and KEPPEL for Local escort o rms QUEEN MARY during first 24hours of passage in NW Approaches as Convoy WS19W 24th Detached with escort and returned to Clyde. (Note : QUEEN MARY was on passage to Suez with troops for 8th Army) Carried out anti-submarine operations with HM Destroyers NEWARK and INTREPID In Denmark Strait prior to mine lay by H M Minelayer ADVENTURE and above ships of 1st Mine laying Squadron (Operation SN72)

June

Atlantic convoy escort in continuation. Detached for duty in Denmark Strait during a mine laying operation. June On completion of detached duty resumed convoy defence in NW Approaches.

July 11th

Detached for escort of minelayers in NW Approaches. Deployed with Destroyers BRIGHTON, STMARY'S, SALISBURY OF Squadron And HMS SCOTT to escort of same minelayers as Operation SN72 for mine lay in Faeroes Bank (Operation SN3C) Resumed convoy defence in NW Approaches on completion of SN3C.

August 2nd

Deployed as part of escort for military Convoy WS21Sduring initial stage of passage from Clyde in NW Approaches.

September

Atlantic convoy defence in continuation.

October 31st

Deployed with HM Destroyer SKATE as Escort for ships on passage in Irish Sea from Liverpool to join military Convoy WS24 in Clyde.

November to December

Atlantic convoy defence in continuation.

1943

January

Transferred to Iceland for Atlantic convoy Defence with H M Destroyers SALADIN, SABRE, SCIMITAR and SHIKARI as 21st Escort Group.

February to April

Convoy defence based in Iceland with Group in continuation.

May 19th

Deployed for local escort duties in Clyde. Part of escort for joint Convoy KMF15/WS30 For initial stage of passage in NW Approaches to Gibraltar

June to August

Clyde local escort deployment in continuation.

September

Detached with HMS SCIMITAR for escort of minelayers. Escorted HM Auxiliary Minelayers AGAMEMNON, MENESTHEUS and PORT QUEBEC with HMS SCOTT and HM Destroyers LANCASTER and METEOR for mine lay in Faeroes-Iceland Gap.

September 21st

Deployed with HM Destroyers MAHRATTA, OBEDIENT and SHIKARI for anti-submarine search operation in NW. October Withdrawn from Atlantic convoy escort and deployed for convoy defence in coastal waters of UK. due to changes in defence tactics and development of new weapons.

1944

January to September

Coastal convoy escort duty in continuation. support of allied landings in Normandy.

October

Withdrawn from operational service and deployed for training.

November to December

Training deployment in continuation.

1945   January to May.

Training in continuation. Reduced to Reserve status.

Dan Mc Faul The Weaver

1904

BERNARD2 SULLIVAN (BERNARD1)

Barney was born 04 Dec 1904 in Mill Lane Larne.

He married MARY

My grandparents Sullivan were residing in Larne when their next son Bernard (Barney) was born on 11 December 1904 in Mill Lane. I don't know if it was in a lodging house or not as Barney's birth certificate does not specify what number they lived at in Mill Lane. Barney has much the same build as Uncle Johnny.

1926

ANNA3 SULLIVAN (MICHAEL2, BERNARD1)

Was born 16 Aug 1926

She married BRIAN MC EVOY.

Brian was a Sea Captain.

He was born 08 Apr 1923, and died 15 Jul 2000.

Children of ANNA SULLIVAN and BRIAN MC EVOY are:

BRIAN4 MC EVOY, b. 1947.

MARGARET MC EVOY, b. 1951.

MONA MC EVOY, b. 1952.

JOHANNA MC EVOY, b. 1961.

ARLENE MC EVOY, b. 1963.

This is a photograph of Anna and her brothers Bobby and Mickey.

This is an item from the local Glenarm newspaper when Anna was the winner of a Beauty Contest.

* In Glenarm locals' thoughts were turning to those of beauty as Miss Glenarm was chosen by Miss Glens of Antrim, Miss T Spence from Cushendall.

The beauty contest was organised by St Jospeh's Boys Club and was held in the Town Hall.

The winner was Mrs Brian McEvoy. Runners up were Miss Rosemary Davy and Miss McCambridge.

Descendants of Bernard Sullivan

1. BERNARD1 SULLIVAN was born 1864 in County Antrim, and died in Larne Lough. He married MARY ELLEN CRILLEY 1895. She was born 1871 in County Down.

Children of BERNARD SULLIVAN and MARY CRILLEY are:

JOHN2 SULLIVAN, b. 1897, Louth; d. 1966,

m. KATHLEEN.

MARY ELLEN SULLIVAN, b. 05 Apr 1901,

d. 05 Apr 1942. m. Denis McFaul 1924.

MICHAEL SULLIVAN, b. 04 Nov 1902, Antrim.

BARNEY SULLIVAN, b. 04 Dec 1904, Larne; .

GEORGE SULLIVAN, b. 01 Aug 1906, Larne.

2. MARY ELLEN2 SULLIVAN (BERNARD1) was born 05 Apr 1901 in Larne, and died 05 Apr 1942 in Coleraine N. Ireland. She married DENIS MCFAUL 31 Jan 1924 in Larne. He was born 04 Aug 1904 in Larne, and died 28 Mar 1943 in Tunisia North Africa.

Children of MARY SULLIVAN and DENIS MCFAUL are:

ANNA3 MCFAUL, b. 16 Aug 1926; d. 11 Sep 1987,

EILEEN MCFAUL, b. 10 Dec 1928, ; d. 23 Aug 1978

DENIS MCFAUL, b. 09 Feb 1930; d. 29 Oct 1998,

CHARLOTTE MCFAUL, b. 12 Feb 1931, Larne.

DANIEL MCFAUL, b. 25 May 1934, Larne.

BERNARD MCFAUL, b. 25 May 1940, Larne.

3. MICHAEL2 SULLIVAN (BERNARD1) was born 04 Dec 1902 in Antrim. He married M. She died 1935.

Children of MICHAEL SULLIVAN and M are:

ANNA3 SULLIVAN, b. 16 Aug 1926.

MICKEY SULLIVAN, b. 1928.

BOBBY SULLIVAN, b. 1932

ANNA3 SULLIVAN (MICHAEL2, BERNARD1) was born 16 Aug 1926. She married BRIAN MC EVOY. He was born 08 Apr 1923, and died 15 Jul 2000.

Children of ANNA SULLIVAN and BRIAN MC EVOY are:

BRIAN4 MC EVOY, b. 1947.

MARGARET MC EVOY, b. 1951.

MONA MC EVOY, b. 1952.

JOHANNA MC EVOY, b. 1961.

ARLENE MC EVOY, b. 1963.

Because of the information that my Grandfather Bernard Sullivan has provided on Census forms; ie; He was born in County Antrim; His son John was born in Louth and his wife Mary Ellen was born in County Down; I hired a professional researcher to find his birth certificate and that of his son John, all to no avail. If my grandfather's information was correct the only conclusion that I can come to is that he was not registered at birth. This is not surprising as registration only became compulsory in the year of his birth 1864. It may well be that son John was never registered at birth either.

Statistics for Family Sullivan

Total Number of Individuals   *26*

Total Number of Marriages   *6*

Average Life span   *57 years*

Earliest Birth Date   *1864*

Dan Mc Faul The Weaver

A Glimpse of how Larne has changed.

The Royal Mail Coach first came to Larne in **1811** and operated between Larne and Belfast on Mondays, Wednesdays and Fridays. The Mail Officer sat with the mailbag at his feet and his shotgun on his knee. When mail was delivered the recipient had to pay a charge before he or she received their letter. This practice was discontinued in **1840** when the Penny Post was introduced. For the price of a Penny Stamp a letter could travel to any part of the country. A building in Cross Street was to serve as a Market House, Court House, Police Barracks and Post Office. People may remember this building across from the Town Hall as Henning's Chemists, now a Café.

Larne Workhouse was opened in **1842**. Then there was the Great Potato Famine **1845 - 1847** which struck the entire Country. Fortunately the County of Antrim was less affected than most other places.

In **1858** a town improvement Act was introduced and the first town Commissioners were appointed. A Fire service was established in the town and Public Gas Lighting was introduced in some streets.

By **1861** the first Railway Line between **Larne** and **Carrickfergus** was laid and was officially opened in **1862**. The noticeable thing here is that over 700 men and 90 horses were employed to lay this Railway Line. The old Pier at **Quay Lane** where my Great Grandfather Denis sailed in and out of during his early seafaring days was removed.

1863 a new road called **Circular Road** was built.

1864 a market place opened in the new Station Road. A newspaper **Larne Weekly Reporter** was printed for the first time.

1865 saw plans to construct Curran Road and a Town Hall in addition to streets and lanes being named and houses to be numbered within a short time. Lots of changes were being made providing much needed work for the townspeople. Also regular sea crossings between **Larne** and **Stranraer** in Scotland were introduced. With the advent of the **Postal Telegraph System** of sending messages long distances by electric current over a wire, it increased the efficiency of the Post Office service when it was introduced to the town in **1870**. By **1875** the Town Hall was erected and new modern houses were built in a part of the town called **Clonlee** which would later be in what was known as the New Town. In **1877** the first Narrow Gauge Railway in Ireland to carry passengers is opened between **Larne** and **Ballyclare**.

Larne Lough was still claiming its many victims of ships wrecks at sea. In **1878** the! State of Louisiana! Sunk near the **Maidens Lighthouse** on Christmas Eve on its maiden voyage from Glasgow to New York via Larne and shortly after, in **1879** the Shipbuilding industry was established.

1883 The Thatch public house was demolished and another building erected in its place.

1889 William Brown established his weaving factory in Larne.

1897 This was the year that seen the first motor car in Larne.

1900 was the year that Victoria Street that runs from the Fair Hill to Clonlee was constructed. During these times there was no guarantee of a comfortable old age and it is no different today. We have done a complete circle, if the elderly had neither savings nor family to help them there was only the grudging relief granted by the workhouse system. And today they have got to use their savings or sell their homes to pay for health Care.

Kinship of Dan McFaul

Name	Relationship with Dan McFaul		
Agnew, James	Husband of the great-granddaughter		
Mc Atackney, Alexander	Husband of the 2nd great-granddaughter		
Austin, Lee	Husband of the 4th great-granddaughter		
Baxter, Alice	Great-granddaughter	III	3
Baxter, Bridget	Great-granddaughter	III	3
Baxter, Isabelle	Great-granddaughter	III	3
Baxter, Mary Ann	Great-granddaughter	III	3
Baxter, Nellie	Great-granddaughter	III	3
Baxter, Sam	Husband of the granddaughter		
Baxter, Sam	Great-grandson	III	3
Beak, Jacquline	Wife of the 3rd great-grandson		
Bonnar, Patrick	Husband of the 2nd great-granddaughter		
Bonnar, Patrick	3rd great-grandson	V	5
Bradbury, Andrew	Husband of the 4th great-granddaughter		
Bradbury, Isabelle	5th great-granddaughter	VII	7
Bradbury, Joshua	5th great-grandson	VII	7
Broadfoot, Beau	4th great-granddaughter	VI	6
Broadfoot, Bobbie	4th great-grandson	VI	6
Broadfoot, Cheryl	3rd great-granddaughter	V	5
Broadfoot, David	3rd great-grandson	V	5
Broadfoot, Gali	4th great-granddaughter	VI	6
Broadfoot, John	Husband of the 2nd great-granddaughter		
Broadfoot, Kyna	4th great-granddaughter	VI	6
Broadfoot, Lucca	4th great-granddaughter	VI	6

Dan Mc Faul The Weaver

Name	Relation		
Broadfoot, Matthias	4th great-grandson	VI	6
Broadfoot, Shkiesha	4th great-granddaughter	VI	6
Broadfoot, Tracey	3rd great-granddaughter	V	5
Brown, Brian	3rd great-grandson	V	5
Brown, Carol	3rd great-granddaughter	V	5
Brown, David	3rd great-grandson	V	5
Brown, James	3rd great-grandson	V	5
Brown, John	Husband of the 2nd great-granddaughter		
Brown, Marlene	3rd great-granddaughter	V	5
Brown, Mona	3rd great-granddaughter	V	5
Brown, Robert	3rd great-grandson	V	5
Brown, Ronald	3rd great-grandson	V	5
Campbell, Debrah	Wife of the 3rd great-grandson		
Campbell, Marie	Wife of the 2nd great-grandson		
Claxton, Margaret	Wife of the grandson		
Mc Cluskey, Danny	2nd great-grandson	IV	4
Mc Cluskey, John	Husband of the great-granddaughter		
Mc Cluskey, Rose	2nd great-granddaughter	IV	4
Mc Cluskey, Rosie	Wife of the 3rd great-grandson		
Connor, Anne	Wife of the 3rd great-grandson		
Craigen, Ellen	2nd great-granddaughter	IV	4
Craigen, Isabele	2nd great-granddaughter	IV	4
Craigen, James	Husband of the great-granddaughter		
Mc Cullough, Campbell	3rd great-grandson	V	5
Mc Cullough, Cecelia	2nd great-granddaughter	IV	4
Mc Cullough, Charmaine	3rd great-granddaughter	V	5
Mc Cullough, Donald	2nd great-grandson	IV	4
Mc Cullough, Geraldine	3rd great-granddaughter	V	5
Mc Cullough, Jack	Husband of the great-granddaughter		
Mc Cullough, Jackie	2nd great-grandson	IV	4
Mc Cullough, James	2nd great-grandson	IV	
Mc Cullough, Kathleen	2nd great-granddaughter	IV	4
Mc Cullough, Marrianne	3rd great-granddaughter	V	5
Mc Cullough, Michael	3rd great-grandson	V	5
Mc Cullough, Paul	3rd great-grandson	V	5
Mc Cullough, Sean	3rd great-grandson	V	5
Mc Cullough, Teresa	3rd great-granddaughter	V	5
Davidson, Chloe	5th great-granddaughter	VII	7
Davidson, Michael John	Husband of the 4th great-granddaughter		
Davidson, Nicole	5th great-granddaughter	VII	7
Deckers, Chris	Wife of the 2nd great-grandson		
Deehan, Alice	2nd great-granddaughter	IV	4
Deehan, Bridget	2nd great-granddaughter	IV	4
Deehan, Ellen	2nd great-granddaughter	IV	4
Deehan, Robert	Husband of the great-granddaughter		
Deehan, Robert	2nd great-grandson	IV	4
Deehan, Wm. John	2nd great-grandson	IV	4
Donnelly, Joanne	Wife of the 2nd great-grandson		
Draper, Anthony	Husband of the 4th great-granddaughter		

Name	Relation		
Draper, Luke	5th great-grandson	VII	7
Edgar, Brian	3rd great-grandson	V	5
Edgar, Christopher	4th great-grandson	VI	6
Edgar, David	4th great-grandson	VI	6
Edgar, Geraldine	3rd great-granddaughter	V	5
Edgar, Katie	4th great-granddaughter	VI	6
Edgar, William	Husband of the 2nd great-granddaughter		
Elliot, Alex	Husband of the 2nd great-granddaughter		
English, Elizabeth	Wife of the great-grandson		
Evans, Robert	Husband of the 2nd great-granddaughter		
Mc Faul, Annie	2nd great-granddaughter	IV	4
Mc Faul, Mary	2nd great-granddaughter	IV	4
Fisher, Angela	4th great-granddaughter	VI	6
Fisher, Clare	4th great-granddaughter	VI	6
Fisher, John George	Husband of the 3rd great-granddaughter		
Fleck, Tommy	Husband of the great-granddaughter		
Glover, Margaret	Wife of the great-grandson		
Gribben, Cecilia	Wife of the grandson		
Hardy, Leo	Husband of the 2nd great-granddaughter		
Hayes, Alexander	Husband of the granddaughter		
Hayes, James	Great-grandson	III	3
Hayes, Rebecca	Great-granddaughter	III	3
Hilton, Neil Kenneth	Husband of the 3rd great-granddaughter		
Hilton, Rowen Jade	4th great-granddaughter	VI	6
Hoey, Ellen	Wife of the great-grandson		
Hogg, Annie	Wife of the grandson		
Holroyd, Christopher	3rd great-grandson	V	5
Holroyd, Keith	Husband of the 2nd great-granddaughter		
Homer, Don	Husband of the 2nd great-granddaughter		
Homer, Donna	3rd great-granddaughter	V	5
Homer, Michelle	3rd great-granddaughter	V	5
Homer, Paula	3rd great-granddaughter	V	5
Hutchinson, Roger	Husband of the 3rd great-granddaughter		
Mc Ilroy, James	Husband of the 2nd great-granddaughter		
Mc Ilroy, James	3rd great-grandson	V	5
Irvine	Husband of the 3rd great-granddaughter		
Irvine, Michael	4th great-grandson	VI	6
Irvine, Rachel	4th great-granddaughter	VI	6
Keenan, Margaret	Wife of the 2nd great-grandson		
Keenan, Rosie	Wife of the 2nd great-grandson		
VanDe Langkruis, Allison	4th great-granddaughter	VI	6
VanDe Langkruis, Janette	4th great-granddaughter	VI	6
VanDe Langkruis, Rob	Husband of the 3rd great-granddaughter		
VanDe Langkruis, Shaun	4th great-grandson	VI	6
Linton, Andrew	3rd great-grandson	V	5
Linton, Cecelia Rose	4th great-granddaughter	VI	6
Linton, Dennis	2nd great-grandson	IV	4
Linton, Eloise	4th great-granddaughter	VI	6
Linton, Emily Jane	4th great-granddaughter	VI	6

Name	Relation		
Linton, Eve	4th great-granddaughter	VI	6
Linton, James	3rd great-grandson	V	5
Linton, John Dominic	3rd great-grandson	V	5
Linton, Kate	3rd great-granddaughter	V	5
Linton, Sharon	3rd great-granddaughter	V	5
Linton, Thomas	Husband of the great-granddaughter		
Linton, Thomas	2nd great-grandson	IV	4
Longmore, Anthony	3rd great-grandson	V	5
Longmore, Bill	3rd great-grandson	V	5
Longmore, Ellen	3rd great-granddaughter	V	5
Longmore, Joseph	3rd great-grandson	V	5
Longmore, Joseph	Husband of the 2nd great-granddaughter		
Longmore, Joseph William	Husband of the 2nd great-granddaughter		
Longmore, Malachy	3rd great-grandson	V	5
Longmore, Malachy	Husband of the 2nd great-granddaughter		
Longmore, Margaret	3rd great-granddaughter	V	5
Loughran, Elizabeth Jane	Wife of the 2nd great-grandson		
Loughrane, Mary	Wife of the 2nd great-grandson		
Lynch, Teresa	Wife of the 2nd great-grandson		
Lyttle, Clement	Husband of the 2nd great-granddaughter		
Maguire, Daniel	2nd great-grandson	IV	4
Maguire, Joan	2nd great-granddaughter	IV	4
Maguire, Johnny	Husband of the great-granddaughter		
Maguire, Nellie	2nd great-granddaughter	IV	4
Maguire, Patrick	2nd great-grandson	IV	4
Martin, Janice	Wife of the 4th great-grandson		
McAdorey, Ellen	Daughter-in-law		
McAuley, AnnMarie	3rd great-granddaughter	V	5
McAuley, Denis	3rd great-grandson	V	5
McAuley, Gerald	Husband of the 2nd great-granddaughter		
McAuley, Gerald	3rd great-grandson	V	5
McAuley, Geraldine	3rd great-granddaughter	V	5
McAuley, James	Husband of the 2nd great-granddaughter		
McAuley, John	3rd great-grandson	V	5
McAuley, Mark	4th great-grandson	VI	6
McAuley, Mary	3rd great-granddaughter	V	5
McAuley, Michael	4th great-grandson	VI	6
McAuley, Naomi	4th great-granddaughter	VI	6
McBride, Lily	Wife of the great-grandson		
McClure, Eleanor	3rd great-granddaughter	V	5
McClure, Jean	3rd great-granddaughter	V	5
McClure, Loraine	3rd great-granddaughter	V	5
McClure, Patrick	Husband of the 2nd great-granddaughter		
McCormick, Danny	Husband of the 2nd great-granddaughter		
McCormick, Erin	4th great-granddaughter	VI	6
McCormick, Lauren	4th great-granddaughter	VI	6
McCormick, Marc	3rd great-grandson	V	5
McCormick, Peter	3rd great-grandson	V	5
McFaul, Alice	Granddaughter	II	2

Name	Relationship	Generation	
McFaul, Alice	Great-granddaughter	III	3
McFaul, Alice	Great-granddaughter	III	3
McFaul, Angela	2nd great-granddaughter	IV	4
McFaul, Anna	2nd great-granddaughter	IV	4
McFaul, AnnaMarie	3rd great-granddaughter	V	5
McFaul, Anne	2nd great-granddaughter	IV	4
McFaul, Annie	Great-granddaughter	III	3
McFaul, Anthony	2nd great-grandson	IV	4
McFaul, Bernadette	2nd great-granddaughter	IV	4
McFaul, Bernard	2nd great-grandson	IV	4
McFaul, Betty	2nd great-granddaughter	IV	4
McFaul, Bobby Edward	3rd great-grandson	V	5
McFaul, Brian	3rd great-grandson	V	5
McFaul, Bridget	Granddaughter	II	2
McFaul, Bridget	Great-granddaughter	III	3
McFaul, Bridget	Great-granddaughter	III	3
McFaul, Cecelia	Great-granddaughter	III	3
McFaul, Charles	Great-grandson	III	3
McFaul, Charlotte	Great-granddaughter	III	3
McFaul, Charlotte	2nd great-granddaughter	IV	4
McFaul, Christopher	3rd great-grandson	V	5
McFaul, Christopher	3rd great-grandson	V	5
McFaul, Christopher Daniel	4th great-grandson	VI	6
McFaul, Ciara	4th great-granddaughter	VI	6
McFaul, Clare	2nd great-granddaughter	IV	4
McFaul, Clare	4th great-granddaughter	VI	6
McFaul, Damien	3rd great-grandson	V	5
McFaul, Dan	Self		0
McFaul, Daniel	2nd great-grandson	IV	4
McFaul, Daniel	Grandson	II	2
McFaul, Daniel	Grandson	II	2
McFaul, Daniel	2nd great-grandson	IV	4
McFaul, Daniel	2nd great-grandson	IV	4
McFaul, Daniel	4th great-grandson	VI	6
McFaul, Daniel James	2nd great-grandson	IV	4
McFaul, Daniel Joseph	Great-grandson	III	3
McFaul, Danny	2nd great-grandson	IV	4
McFaul, Darren	3rd great-grandson	V	5
McFaul, Deidrie	2nd great-granddaughter	IV	4
McFaul, Denis	Son	I	1
McFaul, Denis	Grandson	II	2
McFaul, Denis	Great-grandson	III	3
McFaul, Denis	Great-grandson	III	3
McFaul, Denis	Great-grandson	III	3
McFaul, Denis	2nd great-grandson	IV	4
McFaul, Denis	2nd great-grandson	IV	4
McFaul, Denis	2nd great-grandson	IV	4
McFaul, Denis	Great-grandson	III	3
McFaul, Denis	3rd great-grandson	V	5

McFaul, Denise Alexis	3rd great-granddaughter	V	5
McFaul, Derek	3rd great-grandson	V	5
McFaul, Desmond	3rd great-grandson	V	5
McFaul, Eileen	2nd great-granddaughter	IV	4
McFaul, Eileen	2nd great-granddaughter	IV	4
McFaul, Elizabeth	3rd great-granddaughter	V	5
McFaul, Ellen	Granddaughter	II	2
McFaul, Ellen	Great-granddaughter	III	3
McFaul, Ellen	Great-granddaughter	III	3
McFaul, Ellen	Great-granddaughter	III	3
McFaul, Francis	Great-grandson	III	3
McFaul, Gemma	3rd great-granddaughter	V	5
McFaul, Jack	4th great-grandson	VI	6
McFaul, James	2nd great-grandson	IV	4
McFaul, James	2nd great-grandson	IV	4
McFaul, James	Grandson	II	2
McFaul, James	Great-grandson	III	3
McFaul, James	2nd great-grandson	IV	4
McFaul, James Dennis	Great-grandson	III	3
McFaul, James Leo	2nd great-grandson	IV	4
McFaul, Jane	Great-granddaughter	III	3
McFaul, Jennifer Louise	4th great-granddaughter	VI	6
McFaul, Joanne	3rd great-granddaughter	V	5
McFaul, Joanne	4th great-granddaughter	VI	6
McFaul, John	2nd great-grandson	IV	4
McFaul, Joseph	Great-grandson	III	3
McFaul, Joseph Daniel	Great-grandson	III	3
McFaul, Josephine	Great-granddaughter	III	3
McFaul, Kathleen	2nd great-granddaughter	IV	4
McFaul, Kathlene	Great-granddaughter	III	3
McFaul, Kevin	2nd great-grandson	IV	4
McFaul, Liam	2nd great-grandson	IV	4
McFaul, Liam Denis	3rd great-grandson	V	5
McFaul, Lilian Bernadette	3rd great-granddaughter	V	5
McFaul, Lily	2nd great-granddaughter	IV	4
McFaul, Lisa	Great-granddaughter	III	3
McFaul, Lisa Marie	3rd great-granddaughter	V	5
McFaul, Margaret	2nd great-granddaughter	IV	4
McFaul, Maureen	2nd great-granddaughter	IV	4
McFaul, Michael	3rd great-grandson	V	5
McFaul, Michael	2nd great-grandson	IV	4
McFaul, Nellie	2nd great-granddaughter	IV	4
McFaul, Nellie	Great-granddaughter	III	3
McFaul, Nellie	2nd great-granddaughter	IV	4
McFaul, Patrick	2nd great-grandson	IV	4
McFaul, Phoebe	4th great-grandson	VI	6
McFaul, Rebecca	Great-granddaughter	III	3
McFaul, Richard	3rd great-grandson	V	5
McFaul, Robert	3rd great-grandson	V	5

Name	Relation		
McFaul, Ruby	2nd great-granddaughter	IV	4
McFaul, Sarah	Great-granddaughter	III	3
McFaul, Sean	2nd great-grandson	IV	4
McFaul, Shamus	3rd great-granddaughter	V	5
McFaul, Susane	3rd great-granddaughter	V	5
McFaul, Threasa	2nd great-granddaughter	IV	4
McFaul, Veronica Mary	2nd great-granddaughter	IV	4
McFaul, Violet	4th great-granddaughter	VI	6
McFaul, William John	Great-grandson	III	3
McFaul, Wm John	Great-grandson	III	3
McFaul, Wm.John	2nd great-grandson	IV	4
McKeown, Gerard Majela	2nd great-grandson	IV	4
McKeown, James	Husband of the great-granddaughter		
McKeown, Malachy	2nd great-grandson	IV	4
McKeown, Margaret	2nd great-granddaughter	IV	4
McKeown, Robert Joseph	2nd great-grandson	IV	4
McKeown, Rose	2nd great-granddaughter	IV	4
McMullan, Margaret	Wife of the grandson		
McMullan, Mary Bernadette	Wife of the great-grandson		
McQuade, Agnes	Wife of the great-grandson		
Meekin, Peter	Husband of the great-granddaughter		
Morris, Geraldine Lorraine	4th great-granddaughter	VI	6
Morris, Girvan	Husband of the 3rd great-granddaughter		
Morris, Girvin	4th great-grandson	VI	6
Morris, Paul	4th great-grandson	VI	6
Murdock, George	Husband of the great-granddaughter		
Nurse, Bernadette	2nd great-granddaughter	IV	4
Nurse, Corinne	2nd great-granddaughter	IV	4
Nurse, James Collins	Husband of the great-granddaughter		
Oakes, Colin	Husband of the 4th great-granddaughter		
Oakes, Hannah	5th great-granddaughter	VII	7
O'Toole, Daniel Patrick	2nd great-grandson	IV	4
O'Toole, Eileen	Wife of the 3rd great-grandson		
O'Toole, Eileen	2nd great-granddaughter	IV	4
O'Toole, Joseph	2nd great-grandson	IV	4
O'Toole, Michael	Husband of the great-granddaughter		
O'Toole, Michael	2nd great-grandson	IV	4
O'Toole, Nan	2nd great-granddaughter	IV	4
O'Toole, Raymond	2nd great-grandson	IV	4
O'Toole, Terry	2nd great-grandson	IV	4
Peacock, Joanne	Wife of the 4th great-grandson		
Purdy, Jane	Wife of the great-grandson		
Purvis, Amanda	4th great-granddaughter	VI	6
Purvis, Andrea	4th great-granddaughter	VI	6
Purvis, Courtney Natasha	5th great-granddaughter	VII	7
Purvis, Eric George	4th great-grandson	VI	6
Purvis, Geraldine	4th great-granddaughter	VI	6
Purvis, Jacqueline	4th great-granddaughter	VI	6
Purvis, Laura	5th great-granddaughter	VII	7

Purvis, Linda	5th great-granddaughter	VII	7
Purvis, Richard	5th great-grandson	VII	7
Purvis, Stephen	5th great-grandson	VII	7
Purvis, William	Husband of the 3rd great-granddaughter		
Purvis, William	4th great-grandson	VI	6
Ramsey, Jeanie	Wife of the great-grandson		
Ramsey, Joseph	Husband of the 2nd great-granddaughter		
Mc Randal, Karen	Wife of the 3rd great-grandson		
Reid, Danny	2nd great-grandson	IV	4
Reid, Margaret	2nd great-granddaughter	IV	4
Reid, Marie	2nd great-granddaughter	IV	4
Reid, Tom	Husband of the great-granddaughter		
Rice, Jim	Husband of the 3rd great-granddaughter		
Rice, Martine	4th great-granddaughter	VI	6
Rice, Steven	4th great-grandson	VI	6
Rosenthal, David	Husband of the 2nd great-granddaughter		
Ross, John	Husband of the 4th great-granddaughter		
Ross, Jonathan	5th great-grandson	VII	7
Ross, Leah	5th great-granddaughter	VII	7
Rowan, Barry	3rd great-grandson	V	5
Rowan, Danny	Husband of the 2nd great-granddaughter		
Rowan, Danny	3rd great-grandson	V	5
Rowan, James	3rd great-grandson	V	5
Sayers, Marie	Wife of the 3rd great-grandson		
Smyth, Jeanie	Wife of the 2nd great-grandson		
Southgate, Zoe	Wife of the 3rd great-grandson		
Stanton, Antony	Husband of the 4th great-granddaughter		
Stefanovic, Svetlana	Wife of the 4th great-grandson		
Sullivan, Mary Ellen	Wife of the great-grandson		
Sumner, Francis	Husband of the 2nd great-granddaughter		
Sumner, Stacey	3rd great-granddaughter	V	5
Sunderland, Frank	Husband of the great-granddaughter		
Sunderland, Jacqueline	2nd great-granddaughter	IV	4
Sunderland, Marie	2nd great-granddaughter	IV	4
Taylor, Sharon	Wife of the 3rd great-grandson		
Thompson, Margaret Nancy	Wife of the 2nd great-grandson		
Thorogood, Daniel	5th great-grandson	VII	7
Thorogood, David	5th great-grandson	VII	7
Thorogood, Hayley	4th great-granddaughter	VI	6
Thorogood, Richard	Husband of the 3rd great-granddaughter		
Thorogood, Richard	4th great-grandson	VI	6
Tweed, Jordan	5th great-grandson	VII	7
Tweed, Trevor	Husband of the 4th great-granddaughter		
Tweedie, Ryan	Husband of the 3rd great-granddaughter		
Tweedie, Ryan	4th great-grandson	VI	6
Walker, Ian	Husband of the 2nd great-granddaughter		
Walker, Mark	3rd great-grandson	V	5
Walker, Nicholas	3rd great-grandson	V	5
Walker, Paul	3rd great-grandson	V	5

Watson, Adrienne   Wife of the 2nd great-grandson
Williams, Linda   Wife of the 2nd great-grandson
Wilson, Gillian   Wife of the 2nd great-grandson
Winkles, Emma   Wife of the 3rd great-grandson

Marriage Report

Husband	Wife	Marriage date
James Agnew	Jane McFaul	04 Aug 1930
Alexander Mc Atackney	Anna McFaul	05 Nov 1966
Lee Austin	Angela Fisher	01 Jul 2000
Sam Baxter	Bridget McFaul	02 Jan 1900
Patrick Bonnar	Ruby McFaul	25 Aug 1944
Andrew Bradbury	Hayley Thorogood	15 Jul 2000
John Mc Cluskey	Sarah McFaul	08 Jul 1941
William Cody	Mary Lily Kirkbride	18 Jun 1910
James Craigen	Lisa McFaul	11 Sep 1916
Jack Mc Cullough	Alice McFaul	29 Jun 1931
Michael John Davidson	Andrea Purvis	31 Aug 1991
Robert Deehan	Alice McFaul	18 Oct 1918
William Deehan	Margaret Farrell	28 Dec 1895
Anthony Draper	Clare Fisher	18 Aug 2007
Brian Edgar	Karen Mc \Randal\	29 Oct 1992
William Edgar	Charlotte McFaul	10 Sep 1962
Alex Elliot	Mary Mc \Faul\	22 Jul 1954
Robert Evans	Margaret Reid	24 Oct 1947
John George Fisher	Lilian Bernadette McFaul	24 Jul 1976
Tommy Fleck	Bridget Baxter	22 Aug 1941
Francis Gribbin	Ellen McKay	Sep 1876
Alexander Hayes	Alice McFaul	07 Jan 1891
Roger Hutchinson	Kate Linton	2000
Hughie Johnston	Margaret Jane McAuley	21 Apr 1949
Isaac Kirkbride	Sarah Rome	13 Jun 1835
James Kirkbride	Elizabeth Sunderland	27 Jan 1785
John Kirkbride	Elizabeth Black	13 Jun 1808
Rob VanDe Langkruis	Mary McAuley	28 Nov 1964
Dennis Linton	Adrienne Watson	1959
Thomas Linton	Cecelia McFaul	12 Mar 1934
Joseph William Longmore	Rose McKeown	04 Aug 1941
Johnny Maguire	Nellie McFaul	30 Nov 1928
Patrick Maguire	Jeanie Smyth	05 Jun 1952
Gerald McAuley	Anna McFaul	08 Oct 1943
James McAuley	Eileen McFaul	27 Jun 1945
Danny McCormick	Cecelia Mc \Cullough\	21 Sep 1968
Bernard McFaul	Margaret Keenan	12 Jan 1963
Christopher McFaul	Emma Winkles	02 Sep 2000
Damien McFaul	Zoe Southgate	10 Sep 2006
Daniel McFaul	Margaret Claxton	25 Apr 1941
Daniel McFaul	Annie Hogg	20 Nov 1898

Dan Mc Faul The Weaver

Daniel McFaul	Margaret Nancy Thompson	16 Oct 1954
Daniel Joseph McFaul	Elizabeth English	20 Jun 1944
Denis McFaul	Mary Loughrane	09 Jul 1955
Denis McFaul	Ellen McAdorey	14 Mar 1864
Denis McFaul	Margaret McMullan	25 Aug 1888
Denis McFaul	Jane Purdy	05 Aug 1926
Denis McFaul	Mary Ellen Sullivan	31 Jan 1924
James McFaul	Cecilia Gribben	15 Nov 1900
Joseph McFaul	Jeanie Ramsey	27 Feb 1930
Joseph Daniel McFaul	Margaret Glover	04 Nov 1966
Patrick McFaul	Elizabeth Jane Loughran	23 Jan 1957
William John McFaul	Lily McBride	20 Oct 1931
Wm John McFaul	Ellen Hoey	13 Feb 1916
James McKeown	Ellen McFaul	25 Jul 1914
James McLean	Ellen McKay	1903
Girvan Morris	Geraldine McAuley	1965
George Murdock	Nellie Baxter	20 Dec 1963
Colin Oakes	Clare Fisher	07 Dec 2000
Michael O'Toole	Charlotte McFaul	28 Jun 1934
Bertie Pollitt	Clara Kirkbride	13 Mar 1914
Eric George Purvis	Janice Martin	23 Aug 1985
William Purvis	AnnMarie McAuley	15 Apr 1963
William Purvis	Joanne Peacock	06 Jul 2001
David Rosenthal	Eileen McFaul	1948
John Ross	Geraldine Purvis	14 Jul 1997
Chris Sneddon	Micheala Wilson	27 May 2006
Antony Stanton	Amanda Purvis	27 Jun 2009
Tony Stanton	Mary Burke	08 Jul 1961
Bernard Sullivan	Mary Ellen Crilley	1895
George Sullivan	Eileen McAllister	29 Jan 1933
Frank Sunderland	Ellen McFaul	1940
Alexander McKay Thompson	Mary Lilian Cody	24 Nov 1934
Alexander McKay Thompson	Hilda Giles	Jun 1970
Richard Thorogood	AnnaMarie McFaul	24 Mar 1973
Richard Thorogood	Svetlana Stefanovic	19 Aug 2006
Trevor Tweed	Jacqueline Purvis	25 Sep 1992
Peter Wilson	Jeanette Thompson	14 May 1966

Other McFaul marriages in Ulster.

Date	Forename	Brides/ Forename

12/09/1845 ;MCFALL ;NEAL ;PETTICREW ;ISABELLA

13/04/1850 ;MCFAUL ;ANDREW ;DOLLAR ;AGNES

16/12/1863 ;MCFALL ;DANIEL ;HOLDEN ;ELIZA

09/01/1868 ;MCFALL ;JOHN ;BRADFORD ;ELIZA

03/05/1875 ;MCFALL ;ROBERT ;PARK ;AGNES

19/08/1849 ;MCFAUL ;DANIEL ;BRENNAN ;MATILDA

08/05/1850 ;MCFAUL ;WILLIAM ;CRAWFORD ;JENNY

00/00/1855 ;MCFAUL ;JAMES ;ROWAN ;ELIZA ORR

29/05/1890 ;MCFAUL ;JAMES ;MORTON ;AGNES

3-3-1905;MCFALL ;ARCHIBALD ;HALL ;MARTHA

14/02/1888 ;MCFALL ;JOHN ;LUSK ;AGNES ;

22/06/1847 ;MCFALL ;JOHN ;PETTIGREW ;JANE

18/02/1857 ;MCFAUL ;NEAL ;MCKINLY ;ROSE

31/07/1876 ;MCFALL ;JAMES ;MONTGOMERY Marg.

26/04/1869 ;MCFAUL ;ARCHIe ;MCNEILL ; PEGGY

25/07/1873 ;MCFALL ;WILLIAM ;MCCALISTER ;

23/01/1877 ;MCFALL ;WILLIAM ;MCVEY MARGARET

30/09/1854 ;MCFALL ;MATTHEW ;MCMILLAN ;JANE ;

27/05/1869 ;MCFAUL ;JAMES ;JOHNSTON ;AGNES ;

11/06/1878 ;MCFAUL ;HUGH ;JOHNSTON ;MARY

16/04/1885 ;MCFALL ;JAMES ;MCKILLOP ;SARAH

14/04/1899 ;MCFALL ;WILLIAM ;TOPPIN ;ELIZABETH

14/03/1864 ;MCFAUL ;DENIS ;MCADORY ;ELLEN

25/08/1888 ;MCFALL ;DENIS ;MCMULLEN ;MAGGIE

24/09/1890 ;MCFALL ;DANIEL ;MCAULEY ;ANNIE ;

29/09/1896 ;MCFALL ;JAMES ;AGNEW ;MARY JANE ;

20/11/1898 ;MCFALL ;DANIEL ;HOGG ;ANNIE

16/06/1846 ;MCFALL ;Wm. DRUMMOND ;ISABELLA ;

26/11/1855 ;MCFALL ;JOHN ;MORROW ;FLORA ;

06/01/1862 ;MCFALL ;EDWARD ;LYLE ;MARGARET

04/07/1870 ;MCFALL ;WILLIAM JOHN ;BLAIR ;SARAH ;

17/09/1845 ;MCFALL ;PATRICK ;MCALLISTER ;JANE ;

02/11/1849 ;MCFALL ;HENRY MCFALL ;SARA ;

05/06/1856 ;MCFALL ;WILLIAM JOHN ;MACKAY ;JANE

15/11/1865 ;MCFALL ;WILLIAM ;APSLEY ;MARTHA

20/09/1867 ;MCFALL ;JAMES ;MCILWAIN ;MARY

27/05/1881 ;MCFALL ;DANIEL ;CARMICHAEL ;ELLEN

25/11/1881 ;MCFALL ;ANDREW ;TEMPLETON ;JANE

16/12/1898 ;MCFALL ;SAMUEL ;KELL ;MARY AGNES

17/01/1826 ;MCFALL ;JOHN ;MAGUIRE ;WILLOW

18/06/1832 ;MCFALL ;PATRICK ;MAGILL ;SARAH

02/12/1854 ;MCFALL ;JOHN ;CALLWELL ;AGNES

18/09/1855 ;MCFAUL ;DANIEL ;SAUNDERSON ;MARY

29/03/1888 ;MCFAUL ;ROBERT ;NELSON ;LIZZIE

27/06/1882 ;MCFALL ;JOSEPH ;MORRISON ;ELIZA

28/11/1882 ;MCFALL ;DAVID ;MCCORMICK ;MATILDA

02/07/1872 ;MCFALL ;Wm. ;MCCAROL ;MARGARET

20/09/1853 ;MCFALL ;JAMES ;HOUSTON ;MARY

09/02/1807 ;MCFALL ;CHARLES;DOUGHERTY ROSE;

19/11/1847 ;MCFALL ;ROBERT ;MYHTON ;ELIZA

20/11/1872 ;MCFALL ;ARCHIE ;MORRISON ;ISABELLA

03/01/1855 ;MCFALL ;ARCHIBALD ;TAYLOR ;ANNE;

01/04/1834 ;MCFAUL ;PATRICK ;MC DOWNEY ;MARY

09/03/1836 ;MCFAUL ;JAMES ;BRADLEY ;MARY ;

05/04/1836 ;MCFAUL ;JOHN ;BRADLY ;MARY ;

24/11/1837 ;MCFAUL ;CHRIS ;LOUGHRAN ;MARTHA

20/02/1852 ;MCFAUL ;PETER ;BRADLEY ;BETTY

27/01/1861 ;MCFALL ;JAMES ;GROOGAN ;MARY

28/07/1861 ;MCFALL ;JOHN ;CONNELLY ;ROSE ;

05/02/1882 ;MCFALL ;FRANCIS ;KELLY ;MARY JANE

09/01/1856 ;MCFALL ;HENRY ;KEENAN ;LUCY ;

23/01/1858 ;MCFALL ;BRIAN ;MCCREADY ;MAGGIE

07/07/1862 ;MCFALL ;JAMES ;NUGENT ;JANE ;

03/12/1876 ;MCFAUL ;HENRY ;CASSIDY ;ROSE ANN

26/05/1858 ;MCFALL ;SAMUAL ;CASSIDY ;ANNE ;

23/07/1864 ;MCFALL ;CHARLES ;MCQUILLAN ;JANE

05/02/1882 ;MCFALL ;FRANCIS ;KELLY ;MARY JEAN

23/07/1864 ;MCFALL ;CHARLES ;MCQUILLIAN ;JANE

03/12/1876 ;MCFAUL ;HENRY ;CASSIDY ;ROSANN

08/01/1894 ;MCFALL ;JOSEPH ;HAZLETT ;REBECCA

19/09/1880 ;McFALL ;DANIEL ;CONWAY ;MARY

23/03/1868 ;MCFALL ;CAMPBELL ;MCCAIG ;ROSE

01/07/1865 ;MCFAUL ;ALEXANDER ;BLACK ;ELLEN

Dan Mc Faul The Weaver

13/07/1876 ;MCFAUL ;NEAL ;BLACK ;MARY

26/02/1877 ;MCFAUL ;JOHN ;DOYLE ;JANE

21/11/1898 ;MCFAUL ;JOHN ;MCKILLOP ;MARY

27/08/1899 ;MCFALL ;DENIS ;WATSON ;SUSAN

30/03/1886 ;MCFAUL ;JOHN ;GETTY ;MARY

06/01/1882 ;MCFALL ;JAMES ;DUNLOP ;MARGRET

22/07/1890 ;MCFALL ;WILLIAM ;DUNLOP ;MARGARET

24/07/1891 ;MCFAUL ;WILLIAM ;MCCLOY ;ELLEN

21/12/1882 ;MCFALL ;WILLIAM ;MCLEAN ;ELLEN

06/02/1866 ;MCFALL ;ANDY ;MCLEAN ;MARGARET

07/11/1865 ;MCFAUL ;WILLIAM ;MCMICHAEL ;MARY

27/07/1868 ;MCFALL ;JOHN ;MCKILLOP ;ANN JANE

01/03/1854 ;MCFAUL ;JACKSON ;CURRY ;NANCY

07/07/1899 ;MCFALL ;ANDY ;MCPHERSON MAGGIE

11/09/1851 ;MCFAUL ;DAVID ;HARVEY ;MARY ;

12/08/1854 ;MCFALL ;GEORGE R ;REID ;AGNES

17/11/1895 ;MCFALL ;CHARLES ;MCLARNON ;ELIZA

29/07/1875 ;MCFALL ;ALEX ;DUNNON ;MARGARET

09/04/1855 ;MCFALL ;WILLIAM ;NEILL ;MARGARET

14/03/1880 ;MCFALL ;EDWARD ;CURTIS ;ELIZABETH

18/11/1885 ;MCFALL ;ARTHUR ;MCGAHAN ;ANNIE

02/02/1864 ;MCFALL ;CHRIS ;SPENCE ;SUSANNA

21/05/1855 ;MCFALL ;WILLIAM ;CUSHELY ;ELLEN

20/08/1858 ;MCFAUL ;JAMES ;CHURCH ;MARGARET

28/06/1890 ;MCFALL ;THOMAS ;GARDINER ;ROSETTA

20/07/1880 ;MCFAUL ;RANDAL ;OWENS ;MARGARET

26/02/1875 ;MCFALL ;GEORGE ;ELDER ;MARGARET

07/01/1876 ;MCFALL ;ANDREW ;MCKENDRY ;JANE

21/11/1861 ;MCFALL ;JOHN ; JANE ;CONNOR

19/11/1870 ;MCFALL ;JAMES ;PEPPER ;NANCY

20/12/1882 ;MCFALL ;GEORGE ;JOHNSTON ;BESSIE

14/12/1852 ;MCFALL ;SAMUEL ;HIGGINS ;MARY JANE

22/08/1857 ;MCFAUL ;ANDREW ;MOORE ;MARY

22/09/1866 ;MCFALL ;HENRY ;BARR ;ELIZA

25/05/1875 ;MCFAUL ;JOHN ;MOONEY ;JANE

21/03/1885 ;MCFALL ;JAMES ;GARDINER ;RACHAEL

21/12/1888 ;MCFALL ;HENRY ;BROWN ;MARGARET

28/12/1895 ;MCFALL ;JOHN ;CLYDE ;ELIZABETH

Dan Mc Faul The Weaver

01/02/1866 ;MCFAUL ;MICHAEL ;DOGHERTY ;AGNES

01/05/1871 ;MCFAUL ;PATRICK ;MCKENTY ;ALICE

27/10/1897 ;MCFALL ;JAMES ;KERR ;MARY

10/01/1869 ;MCFALL ;MICHAEL ;HENRY ;SARAH

17/05/1888 ;MCFALL ;CHRIS ;DOUGAN ;MARY

14/07/1871 ;MCFALL ;THOMAS ;HAUGHIAN ;ELIZA

03/03/1889 ;MCFALL ;JOHN ;HATTON ;MARTHA

22/01/1865 ;MCFALL ;CHARLES ;KENNEDY ;ESTHER

05/07/1874 ;MCFALL ;ENNES ;SCULLION ;MARY

08/03/1867 ;MCFALL ;JAMES ;LILLEY ;RACHEL

02/09/1864 ;MCFALL ;ROBERT ;CALDWELL ;LETITIA

01/06/1883 ;MCFAUL ;Wm. JAMES ;CURRY ;MAGGIE

07/03/1866 ;MCFALL ;JOHN ;CHRISTIE ;MARY

09/12/1869 ;MCFALL ;DANIEL ;MCQUIGG ;MARY

18/03/1858 ;MCFALL ;JOHN ;FULLERTON ;HANNA

22/04/1846 ;MCFAUL ;JAMES ;SLOAN ;MATILDA

30/12/1889 ;MCFALL ;DAVID ;KERR ;ANNIE ;AGNES

28/11/1892 ;MCFALL ;DAVID ;MCARTHUR ;ROSE ANN

09/04/1897 ;MCFALL ;Wm. HENRY ;JAMIESON ;SARAH

07/11/1884 ;MCFALL ;JOHN ;HOWITT ;ISABELLA

07/05/1856 ;MCFALL ;ARTHUR ;CARMICHAEL ;ROSE

12/04/1858 ;MCFALL ;JAMES ;HOUSTON ;ANN

21/08/1895 ;MCFALL ;PATRICK ;MCBURNEY ;EDITH

22/04/1867 ;MCFAUL ;WILLIAM JOHN ;DUGAN ;MARY

08/07/1883 ;MCFALL ;ROBERT ;LAWSON ;MARTHA

10/09/1864 ;MCFALL ;DANIEL ;PRITCHARD ;ELIZA

02/11/1874 ;MCFALL ;JOHN ;MORRISON ;ELIZABETH

11/11/1852 ;MCFALL ;ARCHIBALD ;GRAHAM ;MARIA

06/07/1854 ;MCFALL ;WILLIAM ;MILLER ;ANN ;

07/12/1896 ;MCFALL ;JAMES ;DONALDSON ;MARY

19-3-1921;MCFALL ;DAVID ;WARD ;JEANIE ;LYNN

15/07/1883 ;MCFALL ;MOSES ;STEWART ;HANNAH

22/06/1897 ;MCFALL ;JAMES ;CONNOR ;LETITIA

12/07/1894 ;MCFALL ;JOSEPH ;MCCORD ;MARY JANE

05/02/1876;MCFALL ;THOMAS ;HYNDMAN ; ROSE

22/04/1867 ;MCFALL ;ROBERT ;CURRAN ;MARY

14/04/1845 ;MCFALL ;JAMES ;ISLES ;JANE ;

19/03/1850 ;MCFALL ;Wm. ;MCMURRAY ;MARGARET

Dan Mc Faul The Weaver

13/04/1852 ;MCFALL ;JOHN ;CUMMINS ;MARY ;

19/02/1855 ;MCFALL ;THOMAS ;HESLIPP ;MARY ;

09/10/1855 ;MCFALL ;CHARLES ;LARGER ;SUSANNA

14/12/1863 ;MCFALL ;EDWARD ;BOOTH ;MARTHA ;

19/09/1874 ;MCFALL ;JAMES ;MCCORD ;MARGARET ;

16/04/1877 ;MCFALL ;JOHN ;HANNA ;ELIZABETH ;

14/04/1878 ;MCFALL ;WILLIAM ;MURPHY ;ESTHER ;

15/06/1879 ;MCFALL ;JOHN ;MAXWELL ;MARY ANNE

12/08/1880 ;MCFALL ;PATRICK ;HALL ;ELIZA ;

23/10/1880 ;MCFALL ;JOHN ;DUNCAN ;SUSAN ;

29/12/1884 ;MCFALL ;JAMES ;GRAY ;MATILDA ;

26/05/1889 ;MCFALL ;EDWARD ;ROWLANDS ;JANE ;

02/12/1893 ;MCFALL ;ROBERT ;MILLER ;SARAH ;

01/05/1895 ;MCFALL ; JOHN ;HAMILTON ;ELIZABETH

30/06/1765 ;MCFALL ;JAMES ;MORRISON ;ELIZABETH

20/07/1897 ;MCFALL ;THOMAS ;ARNOLD ;SARAH

13/11/1868 ;MCFALL ;JOHN ;MCFADDEN ;ANNIE ;

18/11/1892 ;MCFALL ;HENRY ;TOWNSLEY ;ELLEN

11/07/1896 ;MCFALL ;JAMES ;SMYTH ;AGNES ;

9/06/1899 ;MCFALL ;JOHN ;MCMASTER ;MARY ;

12/07/1880 ;MCFALL ;Wm. ;FORSYTHE ;ELIZABETH

05/02/1887 ;MCFALL ;THOMAS ;ARMSTRONG LETITI

02/10/1889 ;MCFALL ;JOHN ;MCILONEY ;SARAH

28/09/1890 ;MCFALL ;WILLIAM JOHN ;HAYES ;SARAH

07/07/1895 ;MCFALL ;GEORGE ;SHAW ;SARAH

11/10/1896 ;MCFALL ;PATRICK ;MCCLURE ;MARY

10/06/1899 ;MCFALL ;JOHN ;MCCLUNE ;SARAH

31/12/1899 ;MCFALL ;ROBERT ;BLAKELY ;ELLEN

11/03/1870 ;MCFALL ;WILLIAM ;DAVISON ;JANE ;

10/07/1854 ;MCFALL ;JAMES ;IRVINE ;MARGARET

14/11/1889 ;MCFALL ;JAMES ;MULRYNE ;TERESA

18/07/1872 ;MCFALL ;ALEX ;KELLY ;CATHERINE ;

03/09/1877 ;MCFALL ;WILLIAM ;LYNCH ;CATHERINE

05/02/1893 ;MCFALL ;JOHN ;FINNEGAN ;CATHERINE

12/09/1898 ;MCFALL ;ALEXANDER ;REID ;KATHY;

20/11/1887 ;MCFALL ;DAVID ;DALY ;CATHERINE

27/01/1895 ;MCFALL ;ALEXANDER ;GRANT ;MARY

06/05/1899 ;MCFALL ;ARTHUR ;CONNOR ;ISABELLA

Dan Mc Faul The Weaver

01/12/1871 ;MCFALL ;ANDREW ;SHANNON ;SARAH

09/08/1878 ;MCFALL ;WILLIAM ;MCAULEY ;REBECCA

10/05/1876 ;MCFALL ;ROBERT ;MCCUE ;JANE

15/11/1858 ;MCFALL ;HENRY ;WOODS ;JANE

25/11/1879 ;MCFAUL ;HUGH ;MCLERNON ;MARTHA

08/09/1887 ;MCFALL ;WILLIAM ;CAMERON ;AGNES ;

07/11/1892 ;MCFALL ;DAVID ;CARLISLE ;CAROLINE

18/06/1879 ;MCFALL ;THOMAS ;MCMURTY ;ELIZA

06/06/1881 ;MCFALL ;ROBERT ;LOCKHART ;MARTHA

23/12/1898 ;MCFALL ;WILLIAM JAMES ;FINLAY ;MARY

02/10/1899 ;MCFALL ;JOHN ;MCDOWELL ;SARAH

17-5-1901;MCFALL ;JOHN ;MCALLISTER ;MARY ;

31/07/1850 ;MCFALL ;JAMES ;BURLEIGH ;JANE

17/04/1884 ;MCFALL ;JAMES ;KEERS ;ELIZABETH

12-6-1903;MCFALL ;Wm. JAMES ;MCILREAVY ;LIZZIE

18/06/1859 ;MCFALL ;SAMUEL ;ANDERSON ;ANN

12/05/1890 ;MCFALL ;THOMAS ;DONNELLY ;MARY

07/05/1874 ;MCFAUL ;JOHN ;MCMATH ;MARGARET

23/02/1868 ;MCFALL ;ROBERT ;LEES ;ELLEN

19/09/1890 ;MCFALL ;ROBERT ;GLASS ;ANNIE

11/12/1890 ;MCFAUL ;WILLIAM ;REID ;ANNIE

28/06/1898 ;MCFALL ;JOSEPH ;ADAMS ;SARAH

05/10/1875 ;MCFALL ;GEORGE ;STEEN ;MARGARET

05/09/1894 ;MCFAUL ;JOHN ;MCVEIGH ;ROSEANNE

11/01/1856 ;MCFAUL ;HENERY ;KEENAN ;LUCY ;

20/06/1854 ;MCFAUL ;JOHN ;HOGAN ;NANCY

31/03/1857 ;MCFAUL ;JAMES ;MCINTYRE ;FANNY

24/04/1858 ;MCFAUL ;JAMES ;STIRLING ;PEGGY ANNE

10/11/1858 ;MCFAUL ;JOSEPH ;WARK ;RACHEL

05/09/1894 ;MCFALL ;JOHN ;MCVEY ; ROSE

08/10/1880 ;MCFALL ;JOHN ;NEVIN ;LIZZIE

08/08/1882 ;MCFAUL ;ROBERT ;DUNLOP ;MARY

31/03/1886 ;MCFALL ;EPHRAIN ;LYND ;RACHEL

21/12/1882 ;MCFALL ;WILLIAM ;MCLEAN ;ELLEN

28-11-1913;MCFALL ;DANIEL ;TODD ;MARGARET

19/09/1887 ;MCFALL ;JAMES ;MCMAGH ;MARY

16/08/1866 ;MCFALL ;JOHN ;FINNIGAN ;RACHEL

22/04/1869 ;MCFALL ;JOSEPH ;BINKS ;SARAH

19/05/1877 ;MCFALL ;JOHN ;GRAHAM ;ESTHER

23/11/1847 ;MCFALL ;NEILL ;MCCARTNEY ;ANN

25/12/1857 ;MCFALL ;MOSES ;ADAIR ;MARY ;

02/08/1880 ;MCFALL ;MOSES ;HINES ;ANN ;

12/07/1888 ;MCFALL ;JOHN ;FOY ;ANNA ;

07/02/1880 ;MCFALL ;DAVID ;MOONEY ;SARAH

25/12/1894 ;MCFALL ;THOMAS ;FINN ;JANE ;

08/11/1861 ;MCFALL ;WILLIAM ;TEDFORD ;SARAH

12/10/1872 ;MCFALL ;ISAAC ;O"NEILL ;MARTHA

24/02/1858 ;MCFALL ;JAMES ;NEAL ;ANNE ;

07/10/1888 ;MCFALL ;JOHN ;BROWN ;SUSAN

17/08/1866 ;MCFALL ;JAMES ;HEWITT ;MARY JANE

03/04/1868 ;MCFALL ;MOSES ;DAVIS ;MARY JANE

05/04/1860 ;MCFALL ;JOSEPH ;MULLEN ;JANE

19/05/1887 ;MCFALL ;DAVID JOHN ;GIBSON ;SARAH

29/01/1889 ;MCFALL ;JAMES ;MCCOMBE ;HANNAH

12/09/1899 ;MCFAUL ;JOSEPH ;HAMILTON ;ELIZA

24/07/1871 ;MCFALL ;PATRICK ;DOHERTY ;MARY

20/11/1849 ;MCFALL ;ROBERT ;EVANS ;MARY ANN

24/01/1895 ;MCFALL ;WILLIAM ;MCFALL ;MARY

05/01/1865 ;MCFALL ;EDWARD ;MCDERMOTT ;MARY

15/04/1869 ;MCFALL ;ROBERT ;MCDERMOTT ; BELLA

14/07/1874 ;MCFAUL ;JAMES ;MCDONOUGH ;SARAH

11/06/1892 ;MCFALL ;EDWARD ;O'CONNOR ;MAGGIE

23/07/1857 ;MCFAUL ;CHARLES ;O'DONNELL ;MART

14/07/1874 ;MCFALL ;JAMES ;MCDONOUGH ;SERAH

29-5-1900;MCFAUL ;DAVID ;CROCKETT ;MARGARET

13/01/1867 ;MCFALL ;JAMES ;MORAN ;BRIDGET

30/04/1867 ;MCFAUL ;JOHN ;YOUNG ;FRANCES

10/10/1880 ;MCFAUL ;MICHAEL ;DIXON ;ANNE

01/11/1888 ;MCFAUL ;CHARLES ;MCCOLGAN ;MARY

29/08/1872 ;MCFALL ;DANIEL ;MCDONNELL ;AGNES

21/02/1885 ;MCFAUL ;JOHN ;MULHOLLAND ;ELIZA

15/07/1879 ;MCFALL ;JAMES ;CROZIER ;ELIZABETH

22/05/1852 ;MCFAUL ;JOHN ;ENGLISH ;ANNE ;

Some Female McFaul marriages.

Date ;   Groom ; Forename ;Brides Name & Forename

08/08/1884 ;FINLY ;ROBERT ;MCFALL ;FANNY JANE

20/03/1846 ;GARDNER ;Wm. ;MCFALL ;ELIZABETH

18/08/1853 ;HUME ;JAMES ;MCFAUL ;ELLEN

26/06/1866 ;DONALD ;WILLIAM ;MCFALL ;ELIZA JANE

05/08/1870 ;RAINEY ;JOHN ;MCFAUL ;JANE

13/06/1871 ;HAGGAN ;HUGH ;MCFALL ;ANNIE

11/02/1872 ;MCAULEY ;HUGH ;MCFALL ;MARY ;

15/11/1892 ;MCCLURE ;SAMUEL ;MCFALL ;ANNIE

14/07/1869 ;MEHARG ;JAMES ;MCFAUL ;JANE

11/11/1870 ;JOHNSTON ;PATRICK ;MCFAUL ;ELLEN

23/06/1885 ;MOORE ;JOHN ;MCFALL ;SARAH

19/04/1897 ;BELL ;JOHN ;MCFALL ;MARGARET

18-7-1905;MCMILLAN ;JOHN ;MCFAUL ;SARAH

15/02/1848 ;MAGILL ;JOHN ;MCFALL ;MARGARET ;

14/05/1879 ;BELL ;JAMES ;MCFALL ;MARY

21/11/1884 ;HUTCHESON ;THOMAS ;MCFALL ;LIZZIE

23/11/1888 ;CARSON ;WILLIAM ;MCFALL ;JANE

13/11/1893 ;YOUNG ;DANIEL ;MCFALL ;MARTHA

27/05/1896 ;STEELE ;WILLIAM JOHN ;MCFALL ;MARY

6-7-1906;JOHNSTON ;ROBERT ;MCFALL ;JANE

11/06/1868 ;KELLY ;CHARLES ;MCFAUL ;MARGARET

30/06/1868 ;MCVEY ;STEWART ;MCFAUL ;MARGARET ;

15/06/1872 ;HAGHERTY ;CHARLES ;MCFAUL; MAGGIE

18/11/1877 ;KELLY ;ALEXANDER ;MCFALL ;ANNE

12/02/1878 ;DUNSEATH ;JOHN ;MCFALL ;MARY

01/02/1894 ;MCLOUGHLIN ;DANIEL ;MCFALL ;ANNIE

25/12/1897 ;ROGAN ;JAMES ;MCFALL ;MARGARET

30-4-1908;MCNEILL ;DANIEL ;MCFALL ;SARAH

5-5-1910;MAYBIN ;DANIEL ;MCFALL ;MARY ;

20-4-1911;MCCORMICK ; JOHN ;MCFAUL ;ELIZA

2-1-1913;ROBINSON ;CHARLES ;MCFALL ;ANN

26-11-1915;MCAULEY ;WILLIAM ;MCFALL ;MARGE

06/02/1869 ;MORRIS ;JAMES ;MCFALL ;JANE ;

30/08/1872 ;BEATTY ;WILLIAM JOHN ;MCFAUL ;ANN

13/05/1874 ;HILL ;DAVID HAY ;MCFAUL ;MARY

Dan Mc Faul The Weaver

03/06/1875 ;WILSON ;ROBERT ;MCFALL ;MARTHA

10/03/1876 ;WAUGH ;ROBERT ;MCFAUL ;ELLEN

25/01/1884 ;MCCULLOUGH ;ADAM ;MCFAUL ;MARG.

23/07/1886 ;WHARRY ;JOHN ;MCFAUL ;JANE ;

21/04/1887 ;GORDON ;ALEXANDER ;MCFALL ;JANE

03/03/1899 ;WEATHERUP ;ANDREW ;MCFAUL ;AGNES

30/03/1899 ;KIRKPATRICK ;GEORGE ;MCFALL CATHY;

19-10-1902;MARK ;DAVID ;MCFALL ;ANNIE MARIA

2-1-1904;KINEADE ;JAMES ;MCFALL ;MARTHA ;

2-3-1906;ELDER ;GORDON ;MCFALL ;AGNES ;

13-7-1906;ALLEN ;JOHN ;MCFALL ;ROSE ;

9-3-1909;REA ;GEORGE ;MCFALL ;JANE ;

9-6-1911;BURKE ;WILLIAM ;MCFALL ;ELLEN ;

14-1-1915;HOUSTON ;ROBERT ;MCFALL ;SARAH

30-11-1921;WHARRY ;HUGH ;MCFALL ;MARY ;LARNE

26/01/1865 ;MCAULEY ;BERNARD ;MCFALL ;CATHY;

25/06/1868 ;GIBSON ;JOHN ;MCFAUL ;SARAH ;

07/01/1891 ;HAYES ;ALEXANDER ;MCFALL ;ALICE

2-1-1900;BAXTER ;SAMUEL ;MCFALL ;BRIDGET

2-9-1901;COWAN ;JAMES ;MCFALL ;MARGARET

25-7-1914;MCKEOWN ;JAMES ;MCFALL ;ELLEN ;

9-6-1916;EVANS ;JAMES ;MCFALL ;MARTHA ;

4-9-1916;MCAULEY ;JAMES ;MCFAUL ;JANE ;

18-10-1918;DEEHAN ;ROBERT ;MCFAUL ;ALICE ;

3-6-1916;LOWE ;FREDERICK ;MCFAUL ;LILY ;

23/12/1864 ;ORR ;WILLIAM ;MCFALL ;JANE

3-8-1911;FRASER ;WILLIAM ;MCFALL ;ELLEN

06/08/1847 ;SHANKS ;JAMES ;MCFAUL ;MARGARET

26/05/1857 ;MCCORMICK ;JAMES ;MCFALL ;JANE

15/08/1878 ;HILL ;JOHN ;MCFALL ;MARGARET ;

3-11-1908;THOMPSON ;JAMES ;MCFALL ;MAGGIE ;

02/11/1849 ;MCFALL ;HENRY ;MCFALL ;SARA ;

18/05/1855 ;BLAIR ;WILLIAM ;MCFALL ;MARY ELIZA

02/07/1869 ;KNOX ;THOMAS ;MCFALL ;ELLEN ;

06/08/1869 ;MCALISTER ;JOHN ;MCFALL ;SARAH

11/04/1876 ;CARSON ;THOMAS ;MCFAUL ;MARY

27/11/1896 ;WOODS ;ALLAN ;MCFALL ;ROSE MARY

08/06/1897 ;COBAIN ;JAMES ;MCFALL ;SARAH JANE

19-2-1909;GILLESPIE ;JAMES ;MCFALL ;ELIZA MARY

4-2-1910;MCNEILLY ;SAMUEL ;MCFALL ;CATHERINE

20/08/1839 ;MCQUILLAN ;JAMES ;MCFALL ;JANE

22/01/1876 ;MCCAMBRIDGE ;JAMES ;MCFALL ;ELIZA ;

14/02/1878 ;MURRAY ;JOHN ;MCFALL ;ANNE

29/10/1847 ;LYLE ;WILLIAM ;MCFALL ;JANE ;

14/07/1854 ;BEGGS ;ROBERT ;MCFALL ;JANE ;

09/03/1855 ;MOORE ;WILLIAM ;MCFAUL ;ELIZABETH

31/01/1868 ;MCFERRAN ;JOHN ;MCFALL ;MATILDA

03/07/1869 ;GINGLES ;ANDREW ;MCFALL ;MARY

11-9-1916;CRAIGEN ;JAMES ;MCFALL ;ELIZA JANE

02/03/1894 ;BROWN ;CHARLES ;MCFALL ;MARGARET

02/01/1891 ;KENNEDY ;WILLIAM ;MCFALL ;JANE

02/06/1876 ;ALLISON ;THOMAS ;MCFALL ;SARAH

31/03/1891 ;WEIR ;JAMES ;MCFALL ;MAGGIE

16-6-1906;HOUSTON ;LESLIE ;MCFALL ;LIZZIE

22-10-1919;WALKER ;WILLIAM ;MCFALL ;ELIZABETH

27/08/1886 ;THOMPSON ;THOMAS ;MCFALL ;ANNIE ;

11-7-1901;GLASS ;WILLIAM J ;MCFALL ;MARY ;

5-6-1903;WRIGHT ;ANDREW ;MCFALL ;LIZZIE

16-8-1907;WOODCOCK ;ROBERT ;MCFALL ;FANNIE

1-9-1911;HOLLINGER ;JOSEPH ;MCFALL ;SUSAN

20/03/1846 ;LINN ;JAMES ;MCFALL ;ELLEN ;

04/01/1849 ;SURGINER ;WILLIAM ;MCFALL ;JANE

28/08/1857 ;MEBAN ;JOHN ;MCFALL ;MARY ;

28-8-1908;GREER ;WILLIAM ;MCFALL ;LIZZIE

9-1-1911;ROSS ;ROBERT JAMES ;MCFALL ;RACHEL

28/03/1868 ;CHRISTIE ;JOSEPH ;MCFALL ;MARY

31-10-1903;MCGUINESS ;WILLIAM J ;MCFALL ;ANNIE

16-2-1910;CLAYTON ;JAMES ;MCFALL ;ELLEN

24/01/1863 ;SEYMOUR ;ROBERT ;MCFALL ;MARY

21/09/1846 ;BLACK ;ROBERT ;MCFALL ;JANE

26/08/1851 ;MILLIKEN ;SAMUEL ;MCFALL ;MARY

01/08/1853 ;MCMANUS ;CHARLES ;MCFAUL ;MARGE

18/07/1854 ;MCILROY ;WILLIAM ;MCFAUL ;SARAH

09/12/1854 ;LEE ;WILLIAM ;MCFAUL ;ROSE

21/10/1856 ;MAWHINNEY ;JOHN ;MCFAUL

22/09/1864 ;SMYTH ;THOMAS ;MCFAUL ;ELIZABETH

I have included this table to assist those who may know some of the missing dates to include in the Notes section of the book.

Missing Data Report

Name	Birth date	Potential error.
Agnew, James		Birth Date is empty
Austin, Lee		Birth Date is empty
Baxter, Samuel		Birth Date is empty
Bonnar, Patrick		Birth Date is empty
Bonnar, Patrick		Birth Date is empty
Bradbury, Robin		Birth Date is empty
Broadfoot, John		Birth Date is empty
Brown, Jack		Birth Date is empty
Marriage Date to Kathleen McCullough is empty		
Brown, John		Birth Date is empty
Marriage Date to Kathleen Cullough is empty		
Mc Callion, Cecelia		Birth Date is empty
Marriage Date to John Gribbin is empty		
Campbell, Debrah	10 Oct 1955	
Marriage Date to Gerald McAuley is empty		

Campbell, Marie   Birth Date is empty

Marriage Date to James Mc Cullough is empty

Mc Carry, Rosetta   Birth Date is empty

Marriage Date to John Cluskey is empty

Clarke, Ellen   Birth Date is empty

Marriage Date to Joseph O'Toole is empty

Claxton, Charles   1871

Marriage Date to Annie Connell is empty

Mc Cluskey, John   Birth Date is empty

Marriage Date to Rosetta Carry is empty

Mc Cluskey, John   Birth Date is empty

Mc Cluskey, Rose   1935

Marriage Date to Joseph Longmore is empty

Mc Cluskey, Rosie   1935

Marriage Date to Joseph Longmore is empty

Mc Connell, Annie   1879

Marriage Date to Charles Claxton is empty

Connor, Anne   Birth Date is empty

Marriage Date to Marc McCormick is empty

Mc Cormick, Mary   Birth Date is empty

Craigen, James   Birth Date is empty

Craney, Rebecca   Birth Date is empty

Marriage Date to James Maguire is empty

Mc Cullough, Jackie   08 Jan 1932

Marriage Date to Teresa Lynch is empty

Mc Cullough, James   06 Feb 1934

Marriage Date to Marie Campbell is empty

Mc Cullough, Kathleen 28 Jun 1935

Marriage Date to John Brown is empty

Deckers, Chris   Birth Date is empty

Marriage Date to Liam McFaul is empty

Deehan, William   Birth Date is empty

Marriage Date to Anthony McFaul is empty

Donnelly, Joanne   Birth Date is empty

Mc Dowell, Elizabeth   Birth Date is empty

Marriage Date to William Gribbin is empty

Duffin, Sarah   Birth Date is empty

Marriage Date to Sam Hoey is empty

Edgar, Geraldine   15 Jun 1962

Marriage Date to Jim Rice is empty

Eileen Mc Faul 1923

Marriage Date to Daniel McAuley is empty

Elliot, Alex   Birth Date is empty

Evans, Robert   Birth Date is empty

Marriage Date to Mary Mc Cormick is empty

Evans, Robert   Birth Date is empty

Farrell, Margaret   Birth Date is empty

Ferguson, Isabelle   Birth Date is empty

Marriage Date to Thomas Johnson is empty

Fleck, Tommy   Birth Date is empty

Glover, Margaret   Birth Date is empty

Gribbin, John   Birth Date is empty

Marriage Date to Cecelia Mc Callion is empty

Gribbin, William   Jul 1845

Marriage Date to Elizabeth Dowell is empty

Maguire, James   Birth Date is empty

Marriage Date to Rebecca Craney is empty

Hardy, Leo Birth Date is empty

Marriage Date to Nan O'Toole is empty

Hayes, Alexander Birth Date is empty

Hilton, Neil Kenneth 27 Mar 1964

Marriage Date to Sharon Linton is empty

Hoey, Ellen Birth Date is empty

Hoey, Sam Birth Date is empty

Marriage Date to Sarah Duffin is empty

Hogg, William Birth Date is empty

Marriage Date to Sarah Martin is empty

Holroyd, Keith Birth Date is empty

Marriage Date to Marie Sunderland is empty

Holroyd, Keith Birth Date is empty

Marriage Date to Marie Sunderland is empty

Homer, Don Birth Date is empty

Marriage Date to Anne McFaul is empty

Homer, Donna 20 Feb 1970

Marriage Date to Irvine is empty

Hutchinson, Roger Birth Date is empty

Ilroy, James Mc   Birth Date is empty

Marriage Date to Nellie McFaul is empty

Ilroy, James Mc   Birth Date is empty

Irvine   Birth Date is empty

Marriage Date to Donna Homer is empty

Johnson, Thomas   Birth Date is empty

Marriage Date to Isabelle Ferguson is empty

Johnston, Hughie   Birth Date is empty

Keenan, Margaret   Birth Date is empty

Keenan, Rosie   Birth Date is empty

Marriage Date to Daniel Maguire is empty

Keenan, Rosie   Birth Date is empty

Marriage Date to Dan Maguire is empty

Kirkbride, Isaac James 16 Jan 1849

Marriage Date to Mary Howarth is empty

Larder, Susan   05 Dec 1943

Marriage Date to Robin Bradbury is empty

Linton, Denis Linton   Birth Date is empty

Longmore, Anthony   Birth Date is empty

Longmore, Bill   Birth Date is empty

Longmore, Ellen   Birth Date is empty

Longmore, Joseph   Birth Date is empty

Lynch, Teresa   Birth Date is empty

Marriage Date to Jackie Mc Cullough is empty

Lyttle, Clement   Birth Date is empty

Marriage Date to Maureen McFaul is empty

Magill, Mary   Birth Date is empty

Marriage Date to John McAuley is empty

Maguire, Dan   Birth Date is empty

Martin, Sarah   Birth Date is empty

Marriage Date to William Hogg is empty

McAllister, Eileen   Birth Date is empty

Mc Auley, Daniel   1922

Marriage Date to Eileen is empty

McAuley, Denis   Birth Date is empty

McAuley, Gerald   09 Dec 1957

Marriage Date to Debrah Campbell is empty

McAuley, Hugh   Birth Date is empty

McAuley, John   Birth Date is empty

Marriage Date to Mary Magill is empty

McAuley, John   Birth Date is empty

McAuley, Margaret   Birth Date is empty

McAuley, Mark   Birth Date is empty

McAuley, Michael   Birth Date is empty

McAuley, Naomi   Birth Date is empty

McBride, Denis   Birth Date is empty

Marriage Date to Mary Peoples is empty

McBride, Lily   Birth Date is empty

McClure, Eleanor   Birth Date is empty

McClure, Jean   Birth Date is empty

McClure, Loraine   Birth Date is empty

McClure, Patrick   Birth Date is empty

Marriage Date to Betty McFaul is empty

McCormick, Danny   Birth Date is empty

Marriage Date to Cecilia McCullough is empty

McCormick, Marc   13 Jan 1969

Marriage Date to Anne Connor is empty

McCullough, Cecilia   Birth Date is empty

Marriage Date to Danny McCormick is empty

McCullough, Donal   Birth Date is empty

McCullough, Jack   Birth Date is empty

McCullough, Jackie   Birth Date is empty

McCullough, Jimmy   Birth Date is empty

McCullough, Kathleen   Birth Date is empty

Marriage Date to Jack Brown is empty

McEvoy, Brian 08 Apr 1923

Marriage Date to Anna Sullivan is empty

McFaul, Angela   Birth Date is empty

McFaul, Anne   Birth Date is empty

Marriage Date to Neil Dent is empty

McFaul, Anne   Birth Date is empty

Marriage Date to Neil Dent is empty

McFaul, Anne 05 Oct 1945

Marriage Date to Don Homer is empty

McFaul, Annie 20 Jun 1902

Marriage Date to Tom Reid is empty

McFaul, Anthony   Birth Date is empty

Marriage Date to Joanne Donnelly is empty

McFaul, Bernadette   Birth Date is empty

Marriage Date to Danny Rowan is empty

McFaul, Betty   Birth Date is empty

Marriage Date to Patrick McClure is empty

McFaul, Bobby   Birth Date is empty

McFaul, Cecelia   20 Sep 1910

Marriage Date to James Nurse is empty

McFaul, Christopher   Birth Date is empty

McFaul, Daniel   Birth Date is empty

McFaul, Danny   Birth Date is empty

McFaul, Danny   Birth Date is empty

McFaul, Danny   Birth Date is empty

McFaul, Deidrie   Birth Date is empty

McFaul, Denis 18 Mar 1955

McFaul, Derek 1949

Marriage Date to Marie Sayers is empty

McFaul, Elizabeth   Birth Date is empty

McFaul, James   Birth Date is empty

Marriage Date to Gillian Wilson is empty

McFaul, James   Birth Date is empty

McFaul, James   06 Nov 1949

Marriage Date to Linda Williams is empty

McFaul, James Dennis   18 Oct 1923

Marriage Date to Mary McMullan is empty

McFaul, Jim   Birth Date is empty

McFaul, Joseph Daniel   21 Jul 1920

Marriage Date to Agnes McQuade is empty

McFaul, Josephine   1901

Marriage Date to Peter Meekin is empty

McFaul, Kathleen   Birth Date is empty

McFaul, Kevin   Birth Date is empty

McFaul, Kevin   Birth Date is empty

McFaul, Kevin   Birth Date is empty

McFaul, Liam   Birth Date is empty

Marriage Date to Chris Deckers is empty

McFaul, Liam Denis   Birth Date is empty

McFaul, Lily   Birth Date is empty

McFaul, Lisa Marie   Birth Date is empty

McFaul, Maureen   Birth Date is empty

Marriage Date to Clement Lyttle is empty

McFaul, Michael   Birth Date is empty

McFaul, Michael   Birth Date is empty

McFaul, Michael   Birth Date is empty

McFaul, Nellie   Birth Date is empty

Marriage Date to James Ilroy is empty

McFaul, Paddy   Birth Date is empty

McFaul, Paddy   Birth Date is empty

McFaul, Patrick   Birth Date is empty

McFaul, Robert   Birth Date is empty

McFaul, Ruby   Birth Date is empty

McFaul, Sean   Birth Date is empty

McFaul, Sean   Birth Date is empty

McFaul, Sean   Birth Date is empty

McFaul, Shamus   Birth Date is empty

McFaul, Threasa   Birth Date is empty

McFaul, Wm.John	Birth Date is empty
McKay, Ellen	Birth Date is empty
McKeown, Gerard	Birth Date is empty
McKeown, Malachy	Birth Date is empty
McKeown, Margaret	Birth Date is empty
Marriage Date to Joseph Ramsey is empty	
McKeown, Robert	Birth Date is empty
McKeown, Thomas	1844
Marriage Date to Rose Quinn is empty	
McLean, James	Birth Date is empty
McMullan, Bernadette	Birth Date is empty
Marriage Date to James McFaul is empty	
McMullan, William	Birth Date is empty
McNeill, Mary	1876
Marriage Date to John Purdy is empty	
McQuade, Agnes	Birth Date is empty
McQuade, Agnes	1915
Marriage Date to Joseph McFaul is empty	
Meekin, Eileen	Birth Date is empty

Marriage Date to David Rosental is empty

Meekin, Peter			Birth Date is empty

Meekin, Peter			Birth Date is empty

Marriage Date to Josephine McFaul is empty

Morris, Girvan			Birth Date is empty

Murdock, George			Birth Date is empty

Nurse, Bernadette		27 Sep 1947

Marriage Date to John Broadfoot is empty

Nurse, Corinne			23 Jul 1949

Marriage Date to Francis Sumner is empty

Nurse, James Collins		27 Jan 1900

Marriage Date to Cecelia McFaul is empty

Oakes, Colin			Birth Date is empty

O'Toole, Eileen			Birth Date is empty

Marriage Date to Malachy Longmore is empty

O'Toole, Eileen			Birth Date is empty

Marriage Date to Malachy Longmore is empty

O'Toole, Joseph			Birth Date is empty

Marriage Date to Ellen Clarke is empty

O'Toole, Joseph   Birth Date is empty

O'Toole, Michael   Birth Date is empty

O'Toole, Michael   Birth Date is empty

O'Toole, Nan   27 Oct 1934

Marriage Date to Leo Hardy is empty

O'Toole, Raymond   Birth Date is empty

O'Toole, Terry   Birth Date is empty

Peoples, Mary   Birth Date is empty

Marriage Date to Denis McBride is empty

Pollitt, Bertie   Birth Date is empty

Purdy, John   1853

Marriage Date to Mary McNeill is empty

Purvis, Andrew   Birth Date is empty

Marriage Date to Lavinia Taggart is empty

Quinn, Rose   1849

Marriage Date to Thomas McKeown is empty

Ramsey, Jeanie   Birth Date is empty

Ramsey, Joseph   Birth Date is empty

Marriage Date to Margaret McKeown is empty

Mc Randal, Karen	Birth Date is empty
Reid, Danny	Birth Date is empty
Reid, Margaret	Birth Date is empty
Reid, Marie	Birth Date is empty
Reid, Tom	Birth Date is empty

Marriage Date to Annie McFaul is empty

Rice, Jim	Birth Date is empty

Marriage Date to Geraldine Edgar is empty

Rosental, David	Birth Date is empty

Marriage Date to Eileen Meekin is empty

Rosenthal, David	Birth Date is empty
Ross, John	Birth Date is empty
Rowan, Barry	Birth Date is empty
Rowan, Danny	Birth Date is empty

Marriage Date to Bernadette McFaul is empty

Rowan, Danny	Birth Date is empty
Rowan, James	Birth Date is empty
Sayers, Marie	1953

Marriage Date to Derek McFaul is empty

Smith, Margaret   Birth Date is empty

Marriage Date to Paddy Maguire is empty

Smyth, Jeanie   Birth Date is empty

Southgate, Zoe   Birth Date is empty

Stanton, Tony   Birth Date is empty

Stretch, Hannah   1833

Marriage Date to John Howarth is empty

Stretch, James   Birth Date is empty

Marriage Date to Ellen is empty

Sullivan, Anna   16 Aug 1926

Marriage Date to Brian McEvoy is empty

Sullivan, Michael   04 Nov 1902

Marriage Date to Eileen Allister is empty

Sumner, Francis   Birth Date is empty

Marriage Date to Corinne Nurse is empty

Sumner, Stacey   Birth Date is empty

Sunderland, Frank   Birth Date is empty

Sunderland, Frank   Birth Date is empty

Sunderland, Jacqie   Birth Date is empty

Marriage Date to Ian Walker is empty

Sunderland, Jacqueline 28 Nov 1945

Marriage Date to Ian Walker is empty

Sunderland, Marie   Birth Date is empty

Marriage Date to Keith Holroyd is empty

Sunderland, Marie   13 Oct 1943

Marriage Date to Keith Holroyd is empty

Taggart, Lavinia   Birth Date is empty

Marriage Date to Andrew Purvis is empty

Taylor, Sharon   Birth Date is empty

Marriage Date to Andrew Linton is empty

Thorogood, Richard   Birth Date is empty

Tweedie, Ryan   Birth Date is empty

Marriage Date to Michelle Homer is empty

Walker, Ian   Birth Date is empty

Marriage Date to Jacqueline Sunderland is empty

Walker, Ian   Birth Date is empty

Marriage Date to Jacqueline Sunderland is empty

Watson, Adrienne   Birth Date is empty

Williams, Linda 06 Nov 1949

Marriage Date to James McFaul is empty

Dan Mc Faul The Weaver

Wilson, Gillian   Birth Date is empty

Marriage Date to James McFaul is empty

Winkles, Emma   Birth Date is empty

Dan Mc Faul The Weaver

Custom Report

Name	Birth date	Death date
Adrienne Watson	16 Jul 1938	
Agnes McQuade	1915	18 Dec 1965
Alex Thompson	12 May 1935	
Alexander McKay Thompson	20 Jun 1912	24 Mar 1985
Alice Baxter	15 Jan 1908	
Alice Deehan	Mar 1932	
Alice McFaul	12 Nov 1868	05 Aug 1935
Alice McFaul	10 May 1904	10 Oct 1975
Alice McFaul	1899	
Allison VanDe Langkruis	15 Jun 1968	
Amanda Purvis	12 Sep 1967	
Andrea Purvis	01 Jun 1972	
Andrew Bradbury	09 Jan 1967	
Andrew Linton	18 Jul 1966	
Angela Fisher	15 Sep 1977	
Anna McFaul	16 Aug 1926	11 Sep 1987
Anna Sullivan	16 Aug 1926	
AnnaMarie McFaul	10 Oct 1957	
Anne McFaul	05 Oct 1945	
Annie Hogg	12 Jul 1880	
Annie Mc Connell	1879	
Annie Mc Faul	18 Nov 1929	07 Jan 1999
Annie McFaul	20 Jun 1902	
AnnMarie McAuley	17 Oct 1944	
Anthony Draper	19 Mar 1975	
Antony Stanton	29 Apr 1962	
Archie Fredrick Sneddon	06 Jun 2007	
Arlene McEvoy	1963	
Barney Sullivan	11 Dec 1904	
Beau Broadfoot	Dec 2004	
Bernadette Nurse	27 Sep 1947	
Bernard McFaul	25 May 1940	
Bernard Sullivan	1864	
Bobbie Broadfoot	Jun 2006	
Brian Brown	15 Oct 1970	
Brian Edgar	11 Feb 1963	
Brian McEvoy	1947	
Brian McEvoy	08 Apr 1923	15 Jul 2007
Brian McFaul	01 Mar 1964	
Bridget Baxter	1899	
Bridget Deehan	Dec 1929	
Bridget McFaul	12 Dec 1878	12 Apr 1951
Bridget McFaul	1898	23 Sep 1957

Dan Mc Faul The Weaver

Name		
Bridget McFaul	1912	06 May 1972
Campbell Mc Cullough	08 Jan 1959	
Carol Brown	31 Oct 1965	
Cecelia Gribbin	Dec 1877	
Cecelia Mc Cullough	24 Oct 1948	
Cecelia McFaul	20 Sep 1910	20 Aug 1980
Cecelia Rose Linton	24 Jan 2007	
Cecilia Gribben	1879	11 May 1944
Charles Claxton	1871	17 Aug 1916
Charles Howarth	1853	
Charles Kirkbride	1881	
Charles McFaul	06 Jul 1942	
Charlotte McFaul	1915	29 Jan 1986
Charlotte McFaul	12 Feb 1931	
Charmaine Mc Cullough	05 Oct 1962	
Cheryl Broadfoot	24 Jul 1970	
Chloe Davidson	28 Sep 2002	
Chris Sneddon	12 Oct 1969	
Christopher Daniel McFaul	10 May 1980	
Christopher Edgar	1993	
Christopher Holroyd	09 Nov 1969	
Christopher McFaul	14 Oct 1972	
Ciara McFaul	1982	
Clara Kirkbride	Jul 1895	
Clare Fisher	21 Dec 1979	
Clare McFaul	1987	
Clare McFaul	07 Dec 1926	20 Jul 1987
Corinne Nurse	23 Jul 1949	
Courtney Natasha Purvis	14 Oct 2002	
Damien McFaul	06 Apr 1975	
Dan McFaul	1815	
Daniel James McFaul	28 Aug 1932	1932
Daniel Joseph McFaul	31 Jan 1918	30 Oct 2006
Daniel McAuley	1922	30 Jun 1989
Daniel McFaul	25 May 1934	
Daniel McFaul	07 Mar 1997	
Daniel McFaul	29 Mar 1933	29 Mar 1933
Daniel McFaul		30 Apr 1953
Daniel McFaul	12 Nov 1864	25 Jun 1869
Daniel McFaul	10 Jun 1881	06 Feb 1957
Daniel McKeown	1892	1963
Daniel Patrick O'Toole	23 Dec 1937	
Daniel Thorogood	05 Jul 2007	
Danny Mc Cluskey	1934	
Danny McCormick	04 Apr 1948	
Darren McFaul	09 Aug 1977	
David Broadfoot	14 Apr 1972	
David Brown	28 Nov 1963	

Dan Mc Faul The Weaver

Name		
David Edgar	23 Apr 1994	
David Thorogood	05 Jul 2007	
Debrah Campbell	10 Oct 1955	
Deidrie McFaul		31 Dec 2002
Denis McFaul	07 Aug 1904	28 Mar 1943
Denis McFaul	1903	23 Nov 1950
Denis McFaul	17 Dec 1866	10 Apr 1948
Denis McFaul	1840	17 Feb 1922
Denis McFaul	1912	1915
Denis McFaul	09 Feb 1930	29 Oct 1998
Denis McFaul	11 Jun 1933	01 Mar 1985
Denis McFaul	06 Aug 1944	22 Jul 2003
Denis McFaul	05 Jan 1938	
Denis McFaul	18 Mar 1955	
Denise Alexis McFaul	14 Apr 1961	
Dennis Linton	21 Feb 1938	
Derek McFaul	1949	
Desmond McFaul	12 Aug 1970	
Donald Mc Cullough	06 Feb 1933	
Donald Thompson	03 Mar 1951	15 Oct 2005
Donna Homer	20 Feb 1970	
Eileen	1923	14 Apr 1971
Eileen McFaul	10 Dec 1928	23 Aug 1978
Eileen McFaul	1928	01 Sep 1987
Elizabeth Black	1786	
Elizabeth Black	1786	
Elizabeth Claxton	1903	
Elizabeth English	04 May 1921	04 May 1993
Elizabeth Kirkbride	1834	
Elizabeth Kirkbride	1817	
Elizabeth Kirkbride	25 Dec 1842	Jul 1905
Elizabeth Kirkbride	06 Apr 1793	01 Nov 1816
Elizabeth Sunderland	1761	21 Jan 1838
Ellen Claxton	1901	
Ellen Craigen	26 May 1919	
Ellen Deehan	Sep 1923	
Ellen Gribben	1891	
Ellen Howarth	1860	
Ellen McAdorey	1840	
Ellen McFaul	1918	
Ellen McFaul	1901	1914
Ellen McFaul	16 Mar 1889	16 May 1945
Ellen McFaul	30 Aug 1873	05 Feb 1943
Eloise Linton	04 Sep 1995	
Emily Jane Linton	27 Oct 1988	
Eric George Purvis	12 Sep 1963	
Erin McCormick	10 Jul 2001	
Eve Linton	29 Jan 2004	

Dan Mc Faul The Weaver

Name		
Francis Gribben	1884	
Francis Gribbin	Jan 1855	
Francis McFaul	1900	1901
Gali Broadfoot	2001	
Gemma McFaul	04 Aug 1968	
George Sullivan	01 Aug 1906	
Gerald McAuley	23 Aug 1919	23 Nov 1963
Gerald McAuley	09 Dec 1957	
Geraldine Edgar	15 Jun 1962	
Geraldine Lorraine Morris	1972	
Geraldine Mc Cullough	26 Nov 1959	
Geraldine McAuley	1948	17 Mar 1972
Geraldine Purvis	29 Aug 1966	
Gerard Majela McKeown		02 Jan 1972
Girvin Morris	1969	
Hannah Oakes	22 Feb 2001	
Hannah Stretch	1833	
Harriet Howarth	1854	
Hayley Thorogood	29 Jun 1978	
Henry Gribbin	Jul 1842	
Hilda Giles	29 Jun 1914	07 Mar 1992
Hugh McAuley		01 Nov 1995
Hughie Johnston		01 Nov 1995
Isaac James Kirkbride	16 Jan 1849	1901
Isaac Kirkbride	23 Jan 1816	07 Feb 1873
Isaac Kirkbride	28 May 1803	16 Feb 1811
Isabele Craigen	28 Jan 1917	
Isabelle Baxter	19 Mar 1910	03 Nov 1977
Isabelle Bradbury	30 Jan 2008	
Jack Mc Cullough	23 Nov 1903	09 Aug 1987
Jack McFaul	31 Dec 2002	
Jackie Mc Cullough	08 Jan 1932	26 Apr 2000
Jacqueline Purvis	20 Dec 1964	
Jacqueline Sunderland	28 Nov 1945	
James Agnew		09 Jun 1967
James Brown	01 Nov 1975	
James Collins Nurse	27 Jan 1900	
James Craigen		20 Feb 1971
James Dennis McFaul	18 Oct 1923	
James Hayes	1892	29 May 1933
James Howarth	1859	
James Kirkbride	28 Jun 1851	19 Mar 1904
James Kirkbride	1813	1852
James Kirkbride	1882	
James Kirkbride	24 Dec 1790	1852
James Kirkbride	01 Dec 1757	22 Jul 1825
James Leo McFaul	1937	17 Jun 1981
James Linton	01 Sep 1967	

Dan Mc Faul The Weaver

Name	Date 1	Date 2
James Mc Cullough	06 Feb 1934	
James McAuley	25 May 1927	16 Oct 1975
James McFaul	06 Nov 1949	
James McFaul	03 Apr 1945	
James McFaul	05 Aug 1871	06 Jul 1944
James McKeown	10 May 1888	29 Jan 1967
Jane McFaul	19 Apr 1891	17 Nov 1959
Jane Purdy	1905	16 Jan 1948
Janette VanDe Langkruis	16 Apr 1966	
Janice Martin	19 Nov 1965	
Jeanette Thompson	08 May 1945	
Jennifer Louise McFaul	05 Oct 1985	
Joanne McFaul	1948	
Joanne McFaul	1984	
Joanne McFaul	1987	
Joanne Peacock	10 Oct 1978	
Johanne McEvoy	1961	
John Dominic Linton	28 May 1970	
John George Fisher	13 Sep 1956	
John Gribben	1877	
John Gribbin	Aug 1870	
John Gribbin	Aug 1839	
John Kirkbride	30 Dec 1786	
John Kirkbride	12 Dec 1835	
John Kirkbride	1732	
John Kirkbride	1819	
John Kirkbride	12 Dec 1835	18 Nov 1867
John Kirkbride	19 Jun 1759	
John Kirkbride	1892	
John McAuley		06 Feb 1948
John McFaul	20 Jan 1928	06 Jan 2008
John Purdy	1853	
John Sullivan	1897	1966
Johnathon Kirkbride	24 Dec 1796	Oct 1874
Johnny Maguire		30 Mar 1978
Jonathan Ross	22 Apr 1996	
Jordan Tweed	12 Oct 1995	
Joseph Daniel McFaul	21 Jul 1920	02 Mar 1994
Joseph McFaul	15 Jul 1896	12 Nov 1944
Joseph O'Toole		19 Nov 1943
Joseph Ramsey		30 Jul 1975
Joseph William Longmore		16 Apr 1993
Josephine McFaul	1901	1959
Joshua Bradbury	21 Oct 2001	
Kate Linton	30 Nov 1972	
Kathleen Mc Cullough	28 Jun 1935	20 Apr 1947
Katie Edgar	03 Jan 2003	
Kevin McAuley	1960	26 Jun 1996

Dan Mc Faul The Weaver

Name		
Kyna Broadfoot	Oct 2002	
Laura Purvis	19 Apr 1992	
Lauren McCormick	25 Sep 1995	
Leah Ross	04 Dec 2003	
Lewis Oliver Sneddon	11 Oct 2005	
Lilian Bernadette McFaul	01 Apr 1959	
Lily McBride		27 Feb 1994
Linda Purvis	28 Aug 1986	
Linda Williams	06 Nov 1949	
Lisa McFaul	1894	18 Dec 1971
Lucca Broadfoot	1991	
Luke Draper	02 Mar 2006	
Malachy Longmore		03 Sep 1984
Malachy McKeown		03 Sep 1984
Marc McCormick	13 Jan 1969	
Margaret Ann Kirkbride	24 Apr 1845	1883
Margaret Claxton	Jun 1906	06 Aug 1992
Margaret Deehan	27 Sep 1905	
Margaret Jane McAuley		30 Dec 1991
Margaret Kirkbride	02 Jan 1826	27 Jan 1906
Margaret Kirkbride	06 Jul 1785	
Margaret Kirkbride	1826	27 Jan 1906
Margaret McEvoy	1951	
Margaret McFaul	02 Apr 1943	
Margaret McKeown		27 Feb 1997
Margaret McMullan	1868	24 May 1933
Margaret Nancy Thompson	13 Sep 1936	28 Oct 1996
Marie Charlotte Kirkbride	17 Jun 1840	
Marie Charlotte Kirkbride	17 Jun 1840	18 Apr 1897
Marie Sayers	1953	
Marie Sunderland	13 Oct 1943	
Mark Walker	20 Mar 1970	
Marlene Brown	22 Oct 1955	
Marrianne Mc Cullough	08 Apr 1965	
Martha Kirkbride	21 Dec 1752	
Martha Kirkbride	07 Sep 1789	
Martha Kirkbride	04 Nov 1810	
Martine Rice	21 Jan 1994	
Mary Ann Baxter	1901	22 Nov 1982
Mary Burke	27 Dec 1934	
Mary Deehan	1902	
Mary Elizabeth Gribben	1888	
Mary Elizabeth Gribbin	May 1881	
Mary Ellen Crilley	1871	
Mary Ellen Sullivan	05 Apr 1901	05 Apr 1942
Mary Howarth	04 Jun 1857	
Mary Kirkbride	01 Sep 1761	
Mary Kirkbride	01 Sep 1761	

Dan Mc Faul The Weaver

Name		
Mary Lilian Cody	24 Apr 1911	Jun 1970
Mary Lily Kirkbride	31 Jul 1891	
Mary Mc Faul	03 Mar 1933	14 Aug 2009
Mary McAuley	12 Apr 1946	
Mary McKeown	1884	
Mary McNeill	1876	
Mary Stretch	1838	
Matthias Broadfoot	Apr 1995	
Michael Irvine	21 Feb 2002	
Michael John Davidson	31 Dec 1969	
Michael Mc Cullough	26 Oct 1963	
Michael O'Toole		27 Jan 1981
Michael Sullivan	04 Nov 1902	
Micheala Wilson	09 Sep 1970	
Michelle Homer	11 May 1967	
Mona Brown	22 Jun 1964	
Mona McEvoy	1952	
Nan O'Toole	27 Oct 1934	
Neil Kenneth Hilton	27 Mar 1964	
Nellie Baxter	31 Mar 1903	
Nellie Maguire	01 Nov 1937	
Nellie McFaul	26 Jun 1933	
Nellie McFaul	11 Mar 1909	11 May 1970
Nicholas Walker	03 May 1972	
Nicole Davidson	30 Mar 1994	
Norma Thompson	13 Aug 1946	06 Feb 1998
Patricia Cody	21 Dec 1929	
Patrick Deehan	1904	
Patrick McKeown	1894	1947
Paul Mc Cullough	18 Feb 1960	
Paul Morris	1966	
Paul Walker	25 Jun 1973	
Paula Homer	25 Jul 1973	
Peter McCormick	22 Sep 1974	
Peter Wilson	12 Apr 1938	
Phoebe McFaul	15 Dec 2005	
Rachel Irvine	08 Dec 1996	
Rebecca Hayes	1897	
Rebecca McFaul	1899	
Richard McFaul	01 Oct 1965	
Richard Purvis	12 Feb 1985	
Richard Thorogood	15 Aug 1975	
Richard Thorogood		27 Aug 2010
Rob VanDe Langkruis	08 May 1944	
Robert Brown	10 Jan 1960	
Robert Deehan	21 Aug 1921	
Robert Deehan	1897	
Robert Gribbin	Dec 1850	

Dan Mc Faul The Weaver

Name		
Robert Gribbin	Apr 1879	
Robert McKeown	1898	
Ronald Brown	21 Sep 1957	
Rose Mc Cluskey	1935	30 Jan 1990
Rose McKeown	03 Mar 1922	10 Feb 1999
Rose Quinn	1849	
Rosie Mc Cluskey	1935	30 Jan 1990
Rowen Jade Hilton	22 Dec 1995	
Ryan Tweedie	07 Apr 1993	
Sam Baxter	1880	17 Feb 1918
Sam Baxter	1905	06 Oct 1976
Sarah Hannah Kirkbride	17 Jun 1853	08 Oct 1892
Sarah Kirkbride	25 Apr 1769	Mar 1775
Sarah McFaul	10 Jun 1907	08 Jan 1974
Sarah Rome	1812	20 Mar 1883
Sean Mc Cullough	22 Nov 1958	
Sharon Linton	07 Oct 1962	
Shaun VanDe Langkruis	21 Mar 1965	
Shkiesha Broadfoot	Jan 1989	
Stephen Purvis	03 Oct 1996	
Steven Rice	12 Mar 1992	
Susan Gribben	1882	
Susan Larder	05 Dec 1943	11 Jul 2009
Susane McFaul	24 Nov 1973	
Svetlana Stefanovic	21 Nov 1981	
Teresa Mc Cullough	26 Jun 1968	
Thomas Kirkbride	27 Oct 1798	21 Feb 1837
Thomas Linton	07 May 1934	09 May 1934
Thomas Linton	12 Mar 1915	24 Oct 1942
Thomas McKeown	1844	
Tommy McKeown	1882	
Tracey Broadfoot	24 Jul 1970	
Trevor Tweed	18 Jul 1966	
Veronica Mary McFaul	11 Sep 1935	
Violet McFaul	01 Jan 2008	
William Claxton	1909	
William Cody	1880	
William Gribbin	Jul 1845	
William John McFaul	1900	26 Jan 1984
William Kirkbride	04 Jul 1847	03 Sep 1904
William Kirkbride	1818	
William Purvis	13 Dec 1943	

Dan Mc Faul The Weaver

The War was a good subject for writers and poets as there was so much going on and so many things were changing; life was not the same as before. These are my memories of dear Old Larne.

Going home to Larne:

By Danny Mc Faul.

My Childhood days often come to me and stir inside my **brain.**

So would you like to come with me as I stroll down memory **lane.**

In dreams I still return to my home **Town.**

To visit childhood haunts and walk **around.**

They start when I was a boy of **four.**

The time our country went to **war.**

The Prime Minister of the day came on the radio to **say.**

We are at war this September day we knew then dad was going **away.**

So off to the War dad had to **go.**

When he'd return we'd never **know.**

Uncles Joe, John and Cousin **Jack.**

Joined up like Dad and never came **back.**

One night before we went to **bed.**

The night sky turned a ruby **red.**

This was a night in the Belfast **blitz.**

When several people were blown to **bits.**

Dan Mc Faul The Weaver

Then one Tuesday it was the 8th.of May.

Europe got some peace they called it VE day.

It was over now after more than five long years.

What cost we'll never know in people's blood and tears.

Do you remember the town of Larne as once it used to be.

The Laharna Hotel in between the Town Hall and the Quay.

And tell me now do you recall that one line railway track.

That used to run from Station Road to Ballyclare and back.

The streets and places had names like Recreation and Waterloo.

The Old Pavilion Ballroom and the Regal Cinema too.

The Tip, the Green, the old Nut Braes they have now all gone.

Carnagie, McKenna School and a Tank from World War One.

Shipbuilding at the Harbour then Televisions there from Pye.

Were all a part of dear old Larne in days now long gone by.

The GPO in the Main Street the Fishermen in the Bay.

The Meetinghouse at Mill Street where tall flats stand there today.

The Noggy Burn the Gege Mill and on to Coopers Lane.

Were all a part of dear old Larne we'll never see again.

Can you remember Larne and then recall the scene.

When every year the Summer Fair was held at Bleach Green.

The Railway Station had two platforms yes it's true.

And in Circular Road we had a Bus Station too.

Dan Mc Faul The Weaver

*And what about the Hospital the Workhouse and Trow **Lane**.*

*The avenue in the Roddens that was once Mc Garel's **domain**.*

*The Olderfleet Hotel and the fish sold on the **Pier**.*

*These were all a part of Larne whose memory I hold **dear**.*

*So many are the memories of landmarks once I **knew**.*

*Longmore's, Dorman's and Dan Campbell's **too**.*

*Lipton Grocery Store and the Church at Black's **Lane**.*

*They were all a part of Larne we'll never see **again**.*

*The Narrow Gauge behind the green and of course Mill **Lane**.*

*Were also once a part of Larne we will never see **again**.*

*Then I left my home and Mary Burke a girl I did **adore**.*

*I never kissed her cheek again never held her hand no **more**.*

*I knew that I had lost her love no joy was there for **me**.*

*To seek my future somewhere else in a land across the **sea**.*

*I didn't have much money then misfortune was part of my **lot**.*

*And there were those who said to me "Larne's just as well **forgot**"*

*But I never forget I'm a Larne man and I'll never run **away**.*

*So I vowed that in the future I'd return again one **day**.*

*I still remember leaving England's shores **behind**.*

*Thoughts of my home coming were ever in my **mind**.*

Dan Mc Faul The Weaver

I came back to my homeland the place of my **birth**.

At last I was in Larne Lough and not the Solway **Firth**.

I wandered to my old school Yard where once I used to **play**.

But that was in the days before foreign lands called me **away**.

At that Mc Kenna School I sat on the **wall**.

I knew every stone I had walked them **all**.

That boundary wall with now no **flowers**.

The school where I spent many happy **hours**

The R.C. Church where once I knelt to **pray**.

Just looked to me the very same as on my wedding **day**.

Running home in pouring rain down the Fair Hill steps I'd **flee**.

Those were happy days in many ways in the Larne of **'43**.

I still remember from those days where I was running **to**.

It was to dear old Mill Street at number twenty **two**.

And this was just the very place where I had spent my **youth**.

But I was sad to leave it if you want to know the **truth**.

Along the Pound Street I make my **way**.

Past the old library of **yesterday**.

As I looked along the Mill Street I could only **see**.

Those tall old houses as they used to **be**.

Susan McGarel's corner shop and Jimmy Lee's, **store**.

Mossey Close's Bar with its ever open **door**.

Dan Mc Faul The Weaver

*I get at last to my old home my dream it is now **done.***

*As I look up at the window panes that reflect the setting **sun.***

Number 22 Mill Street is the house with the Chimney Breast.

Dan Mc Faul The Weaver

I would not attempt to visualise how our Victorian Ancestors lived but I know that conditions were very harsh. I do however know what it was like to live in Larne in the 1930s and 1940s during the War years. Our house in Mill Street was a three up and two down, but there were eleven people living there.

Not much privacy and with no running water inside the house, chores like washing and Bath nights were difficult times. Just about everything was rationed during the War and many things for several years after that. Things like clothes and footwear most of us had only the one set or pair.

Even if we had the money to buy more, we couldn't buy just anything without our Ration coupons; if they were used up we would have to acquire them on the "Black Market" or go without.

To give some idea of the living conditions then, I have composed a few verses that will illustrate what it was like. Though it was no laughing matter during the war years, I have tried to be as humorous as I can to accurately tell the way it was.

Dan Mc Faul The Weaver

Our House.

We didn't live in an Avenue a Close or in a Way

But in a Street where there was little room to play

Three rooms up and two down where we had to sleep and eat

And with eleven people in the house that was quite a feat

In these three bedrooms we all slept and life was very hard

More so as we only had one toilet in the yard

We never had a bath as such of this some may recall

It was six feet long and made of zinc and hung up on the wall

Bath nights for me were awful one of my worst fears

Aunt Sarah had long finger nails when washing out my ears.

She usually scrubbed my back as well it made me feel quite sick

Instead of using just a cloth I'm sure she used a brick.

We didn't have much of anything just simple things and yet

We were eternally grateful for what little we could get

We never had a wardrobe in which our clothes were kept

The shirt we wore on the day was the one in which we slept

Hand me downs that were too big and came up to our chin

With big holes in old leather boots that let the water in

Times were really hard then and no matter what anyone says

I think they must be off their heads to call them good old days.

Dan Mc Faul The Weaver

Gas Mask, Identity Card and a Midden.

We all had an identity card we had a gas mask too

Nasty horrible things they were stuck to your face like glue

It was a daily ritual to practice wearing that mask

We all hated doing it as it was quite an awkward task

The Teacher came around to see that it was fitting snug

By pulling at the head strap with a fairly hefty tug

The idea was that these would keep us all alive

But if we had to wear them long would we indeed survive

We were glad when it finally stopped as a daily routine

But still we had to carry them no matter where we'd been

We always had to carry them even to the loo

But when the War it ended they disappeared from view

Can you remember during the war when times were really hard

Ration books and gas masks and the Midden down the yard

The whole Lane had the problem it wasn't just us you know

If you had to "go" you had to trudge through the rain or snow

We would light a little candle because all lights were banned

The way to stop it blowing out was to shield it with your hand

We would set off down the garden path and then without a doubt

Just as we reached the Midden door the wind would blow it out.

Dan Mc Faul The Weaver

Larne at Christmas 1943.

No lamps shone in Larne then no lights in windows glowed

The countryside and town were dark in every street and road

But when a frost was in the air the moon and stars shone forth

The constellations all were clear with Polaris to the North

There was no rush to spend and spend as is now the fashion

For many things that we might want were strictly on the ration

So what we couldn't buy we made with great determination

Paper chains from Larne Times strips we'd paint for decoration

But some did have a Christmas tree with no electric lights

They used small coloured candles in reds and greens and whites

These candles had a real live flame with no safety regulations

Never have I heard a case of Christmas tree conflagrations

As Christmas day was approaching no presents were in sight

It wasn't safe for Santa Claus to travel during the war at night

That's what Aunt Sarah told me and my younger brother

No stockings hung for Christmas just comforting each other

The Mill Lane pump provided water for a cup of Rosie Lee

Aunt Sarah said we wouldn't survive without our Lipton's tea

My fervent hope it won't happen again to future generations

Who get on with their everyday lives no need for celebration.

Dan Mc Faul The Weaver

One night when I was a teenager I went to the Regal Cinema in Larne with some of my school pals. It was during the Blackout and an incident occurred concerning an old guy who used to live beside us in Mill Street then. The story is possibly best told like this;

It was way back in the war years in nineteen forty three

When an incident it took place that today still tickles me

Everything then was rationed and water was precious too

It had to be used very sparingly even when we used the loo

I happened to make my way home when I was just thirteen

I said Ta Ta to my young pals at the Regal where we'd been

I saw a couple who were under next door's bedroom window

The old man shouted out to them and told them where to go

But the courting got quite noisy the old man got irate

He shouted down to them "Clear off it's getting very Late"

But the couple just ignored him the old man Red he saw

"Are you going to shift" he said "Or do I call the law?"

The couple they just carried on oblivious to the old man's plea

But what then happened next was a complete surprise to me.

The old man opened his window a bucket in his hand

He tipped the contents over them just where they did stand

The couple stopped abruptly as the girl shouted out in dismay

"I'll get the law on you old man wasting water in this way

I have a mind to call the police and have you put in jail

Wasting precious water from that rusty pail"

The old man was not bothered by this menacing threat

As he waved his fist at the couple standing there all wet

"I told you twice to clear off so now you know" said he

"That wasn't water in the Pail it happens to be my Pee".

Dan Mc Faul The Weaver

My home town of Larne never suffered from any bombs or War damage, but that didn't stop me from wondering what might have been. This is how I imagine Larne heroes coping with the War.

Our Larne Town Heroes

After the War great tales were told of heroes who were unafraid

So let me tell what we befell on the night of Our Towns raid

A Tomcat growled, a tabby howled Aunt Sarah's hens had fits

The Cows bawled and mares foaled the night of our Towns blitz

A mangy old dog went streaking past which no one could pursue

A warden cried as the dog he espied "It could win the waterloo"

Out from his bed a warden sped as bombs fell round the houses

A hand he used to put out fires the other to hold up his trousers

Said Joe to Sal don't cry my love we'll be together in death or life

Light from a flare made Joe stare he was holding another man's wife

A young girl went dashing out to extinguish an incendiary's flame

Her elastic ripped down they slipped she carried on just the same

Our football goalie became a Hero at the height of five feet three

When he saw a falling land mine coming he headed it into the sea

Many other strange things went on in Larne town that night

Only the man in the moon could see and he keeps his secrets tight

So in the future years to come when I am laid to rest

My kids can tell their kids how Our Town stood the test.

Dan Mc Faul The Weaver

Our old school master was Bertie Fulton an Irish International footballer. He played for Larne FC and Belfast Celtic and gained over forty caps. He also was a member of the Great Britain Football team in the 1936 Olympic Games in Berlin. He coached our school team when we won the Irish Schools Cup. I was proud to be a member of that victorious team. This poem is to Bertie.

An Ode to Bertie Fulton.

I saw a phantom figure he was high up in the stand

He noticed I was watching him and raised a wrinkled hand

He said "Now don't worry lad, about today's big game

I helped us win the cup before and I'll do the same again"

"We'll score a goal in the second half that I'll put in off the post"

It was only then I realized that he was Bertie Fulton's ghost.

Bertie Fulton was the man who once scored a goal

In Britain's 1936 Olympic Team he'd risen from his hole

He'd haunt the pitch at Inver Park to give the team some hope

Of beating off mighty Celtic who were no foot balling joke

As Bertie said they soon slipped up then they came a cropper

Bertie smiled at me and said "We'll beat them good and proper".

On ninety minutes the Ref called time I raised my glass in toast

It was a lovely treat for me to talk with Bertie's ghost

So book your Cup final ticket we have no need to boast

There is no doubt that we will win I was told by Bertie's ghost.

Dan Mc Faul The Weaver

By the time this photograph of the teachers at McKenna Memorial was taken in 1958 only David O'Neill, Philip Wills, "Bull" McCafferty and dear old Bertie Fulton were left since my days. But I see that Father Mc Killop was still throwing his weight around in school matters.

Staff of McKenna Memorial P.E.S.
Taken a few days before the Retirement of Mr. Daniel McCafferty, Principal, 1958.
Back Row L - R: James Meehan, Joseph O'Neill, David O'Neill, Miss Winifred Houston, Edward Keenan, John Mulvenna.
Front Row L - R: Philip Willis (incoming Principal), Rev. Thomas McKillop, C.C., Daniel McCafferty, Robert Fulton.

Dan Mc Faul The Weaver

As I started this book with a dedication to our parents I think it is fitting that I end it with a dream that I had about my parents during the time that I was writing this book. I remember it started one night after a long day searching through the cemeteries from Larne to Glenariff. As it concerns my father and my mother I will title it;

I Had a Dream:

It had been a long trying day for me, but at last I was home again. The rail journey from Belfast had been the worst that I could ever remember. It was stop and start all the way with one delay after the other and precious little of anything to eat or drink on the train. Then there was the breakdown when trying to leave the platform at Carrickfergus. All the passengers had to get off while they found another train. There was also talk about ferrying the travellers to their various destinations by Bus. Three and a half hours to travel twenty five miles on what was supposed to be a modern train. But at least I had found the birthday present that I wanted for my dear wife Margaret and I had already phoned her to tell her of the delay until 7.30pm (she was under the impression that I had gone to a football match). Margaret said that she would be waiting in the car park for me at the Town Station. I would now soon be home for supper and a relaxing evening in front of the Television. I wouldn't describe myself as one of life's high flyers, I was perfectly happy to draw a month's pay for a fairly routine job that I was happy doing. Margaret and I would have liked a little more in the way of life's comforts, but we were not really struggling to make ends meet, not now that the children were off our hands. We had a little money left over at the end of each month these days, instead of the other way round. At 60 years of age, I had to retire, according to company policy. It was really to save them money.

Tomorrow was my wife's birthday Friday 13th September 2008. I had noticed the weather closing in as the journey continued to Larne where we lived at number 16 Mill Lane. The fog was ever thickening as I eventually stood in the Station at Larne watching the train pull out from the long platform number 1 on its way to the last stop at Larne Harbour. Visibility was down to about ten yards, I couldn't even see the Glar-beds. I looked around at the now dark and deserted platform and wondered why I had been the only passenger to alight from the train.

At first I wondered if I had got off at the wrong station because the surroundings seemed to somehow look different. But at the same time they were vaguely familiar. It wasn't until I approached the exit from the Station that I saw the name plate LARNE. This was definitely the correct place but I felt an eerie unease creeping through my body as I realised that I was standing on the platform of the Larne Station that had closed in 1965; and then demolished the following year.

I thought to myself, "I should know this place, I worked here as a porter, a guard and a Shunter way back in the early 1950s, but how could this be"? As the fog started to lift, the immediate area became clearer and to my amazement the Market Place outside the station to my left had disappeared and was replaced by the Regal Cinema which had closed its doors for the last time in 1961.

By this time, I was now pretty sure of where I was, the only question was, what year was this? I was thinking that I needed to find a shop or something familiar and if memory served me right there used to be a Fish and Chip shop on the right, at the top of Station Road, near the corner with Bridge Street. I looked at my watch the time was 7.35 pm just five minutes after the time that I should have been meeting my wife Margaret. (She would be waiting for me in the car park). But of course there was no car park there.

I walked up Station Road, turned into Bridge Street, over the bridge and realization appeared, there it was the Thatch pub. Across the road was Dan Campbell's Store, with the usual array of advertising boards and stuff hanging on racks outside the shop. I couldn't resist having a peek up Mill Street and I recognized The Mourne Clothing Company building. But what I really needed was a newspaper and a fresh packet of cigarettes. I walked down Dunluce Street and into the Larne Times Newspaper shop, next door to their Office. The doorbell tinkled as I entered and an elderly man came through from the back room. The man smiled and asked if he could be of help. I asked him for a newspaper and twenty Superking cigarettes. The man looked at me as if I was mad. "What?" he said. "A newspaper and twenty Superking cigarettes please", I repeated. "We've got Park Drive, Woodbines, or Gallagher Blue, take your pick".

I opted for the Woodbines, then fiddled around amongst the change in my pocket and selected a couple of twenty pence pieces and passed them to the shopkeeper who picked up the coins and looked at them. He glanced back at me and said; "What's this?" "What's what?" I said. "This" the man said, holding the coins up in front of my face. "Oh, I'm sorry" I replied fumbling in my pocket for some more money. "Daft twit, you've given me too much. What price are fags where you come from?" He handed back to me, one of the twenty pence pieces together with the change from the other one. I heaved a sigh of relief and apologised again. The shopkeeper smiled and slowly shook his head. I looked at my watch again, 7.45 pm and still a little shaken I left the shop and looked at the top of the newspaper. The date was Thursday 25th of March 1947, just two years after the end of World War Two in Europe. My first thoughts were about how I am going to get back to 2008. Margaret would be at the station waiting for me and wondering where I had got to after the train departed. But where on Earth can I go for help. I had to think fast. Then I had a brainwave;

Quay Lane of course; If this was really 1947 then my Grandparents would be living in Quay Lane with my father and it was only a ten minute walk away. There was no time to lose, and at least it would give me time to think as I walked and to work out what my next move was going to be. This would need some thought. I could pass myself off as a relative, if they asked me questions, because my dad had told me stories of life at Quay Lane.

Stories like when Granddad and his brothers were able to take their fishing boat out into Larne Lough from the back yard when the tide was right. My Grandfather Daniel McFaul was regarded locally as something of a 'free spirit' and he was easily identified by his Hitler moustache. He would, in later years, be regarded by some as a bit of an odd ball. Still, that didn't make me feel any easier as I walked up the street and knocked on the old "Property Brown" coloured front door of number 4 Quay Lane. A blonde woman in her thirties opened it, and it was all I could do to prevent myself wrapping my arms around her. This was my aunt Sarah Alice, my father's sister and if I had a favourite, she was it.

Dan Mc Faul The Weaver

"I'm sorry to bother you" I said "But could I speak to Denis McFaul, please?" I was asked to wait for a moment, and after a brief conversation inside, a man in his sixties appeared at the door. I had only ever seen photographs of my grandfather before; and it was now rather strange and emotional to meet him face to face. I knew it was my Grandfather as he still had that Hitler moustache He had an air of dignity about him but working as a docker at Larne Harbour all his life, had clearly taken its toll. I explained to him that I was a relative and that I was trying to trace Denis McFaul, as I had something to give to him. If this conversation had taken place in 2008 the door would probably have been shut in my face, but back in 1947 people were inclined to be more trusting towards strangers after the upheaval of the war and the displacement of large numbers of the population. I was invited inside and offered refreshments when I explained that I had come all the way from Belfast. The house was as I remembered it when I had been there with my Grandmother, when my Grandfather was at work. I felt strangely out of place even in these familiar and yet somehow strange surroundings. I recognised the old Grandfather clock against the wall, except it wasn't so old, the time was 7.55pm. My Grandfather gave me a slip of paper with an address on it, and told me that his son Denis had been married for several years and was living at that address with his wife, Mary Ellen.

I breathed a huge sigh of relief as I realised that I had not yet been born. What would have happened if I had bumped into myself? I dared not think about it. I gratefully accepted the cup of tea offered to me and smiled as I saw the Organ in the corner, an old friend from past years. My Grandmother used to let me bang on the keyboard to keep me out of mischief. Grandfather noticed my glance. "Do you play the organ?" he said. "Not for many years, would you mind if I tried?" I ask.

"Not at all" said my Grandfather. "There's some sheet music in the stool seat". I spent a further quarter of an hour with the old Organ and found all the old times coming back to me. I finished my second cup of tea and prepared to leave. It was nearly 9.00pm and it would take me about fifteen minutes to get to my father's address. I managed to gloss over one or two of my Grandfather's probing questions about my connection to the family. I thanked my Grandfather for his hospitality and set out for my father's house. My main priority was getting back home in the correct year and a plan was developing in my brain. This was 1947 and I was the possessor of a considerable amount of information not available to anyone in this time. I wondered about the possibility of maybe just persuading my father to have a bet on the horses, or the Football Pools or maybe the FA Cup Final.

My father Denis McFaul had never, to the best of my knowledge, been a betting man, apart from the usual small weekly flutter on the football pools. Of course, that was it. I couldn't possibly remember or predict enough draws to enable my father to hit the jackpot with Littlewoods or any of the other operators, but my sporting knowledge is quite good and I did know the result of the FA Cup Final that was taking place in 32 days time between Charlton Athletic and Burnley. I was also pretty sure that I knew the winner of the Grand National which was taking place in 4 days time on Saturday March 29th 1947. The Winner CAUGHOO won at 100/1.

I stopped at the War Memorial outside the Laharna Hotel and sat down on the step there. Taking a piece of paper from my wallet and a pen from my top pocket, I wrote the information down, ready to hand over to my father. I was now ready for another strange encounter as I knocked at a very familiar door, number 19 Ronald Street where I was born. It was opened by my father. I explained that I had travelled from Belfast and that I had some important information which he must not give to anyone else. We went into the back parlour where the list was produced and instructions given for its use. Denis, unlike his father, was suspicious and asked what the catch was. "No catch, I told him, just put any winnings into a building society. Keep the book somewhere safe, like under a loose floor board on the stairs, and don't tell anyone where it is." My father looked at me brow furrowed, but took the piece of paper and after giving it a cursory glance put it in his pocket. As far as I was concerned, only time would tell now; and I really had to leave. I made my excuses, saying that I had a train to catch and left. At the end of Ronald Street I turned around and saw my dad standing under the street lamp close to the house watching me. It was now 10.00pm and very soon I was hurrying past the Thatch Pub in Bridge Street on my way back to the station only to find it closed for the night. I had figured that as the station had 'brought' me to 1947, maybe catching a train there would take me back to 2008.

It seemed the only chance I would have, but now there was the need for somewhere to sleep for the night. I decided to use the Laharna Hotel. I had a little money from the change given to me by the newsagent, but had no other money with me. I decided to face that problem when it arose. The Hotel was not too expensive and I could also get a meal. It seemed ages since I had eaten and I felt as though time had stood still.

I explained to the manager of the Hotel about my financial position and he said that my Seiko watch would suffice as full payment. People were inclined to barter in those days when money was in short supply. The accommodation was comfortable and shortly after dinner I retired to bed and was soon sound asleep. A knock at the bedroom door the following morning confirmed to me that it had not all been a dream and I went down to a full breakfast. I was now nearer to Larne Harbour Station so I decided to get the train from there to the town station where Margaret was to meet me.

The Station Master at the Harbour was just arriving as I approached the ticket office and I accepted the offer of a cup of tea while I waited for the early morning train to depart. Getting into the first carriage I thought that I would simply travel back up the line and get off at the first stop. Looking out of the window I noticed that a dense fog had started to form again as the train passed the Glarbeds and the sky had become very dark. This was nothing new for Larne Harbour, where the wind frequently reached gale force and the mist came in from the sea. The train halted at the first stop Larne; and like before, I was the only passenger to alight, it wasn't until the carriages had cleared the platform that I recognised where I was. I was back at the modern station at 7.35pm and presumably in 2008. I stood for a moment as the fog cleared and I was diverted from my thoughts by the tooting of a car horn. Turning around I was relieved to see Margaret waving at me from the car park.

I tried to explain to her what had happened and asked if she had been worried that I hadn't been on the platform the previous day. She gave me an odd kind of look and asked me what day I thought it was. There had been no loss in time whilst I had "been in 1947" and nothing unusual had happened.

However, when I saw an entry in the Properties section of the Larne Times some weeks later, my interest was awakened. My parent's old home in Ronald Street was up for sale. They had died some years earlier and the council had sold the property to a private purchaser. But this person had now moved on, leaving the house vacant and in the hands of a local estate agent.

A telephone call got me the keys to the house and an uninterrupted viewing. This was my chance to see if my dad had carried out the scheme which I had suggested. Taking a few tools along in a carrier bag, I set off. There was no one about when I got there towards lunchtime, and letting myself in I made for the stairs. Thinking back to my childhood I remembered that the stair riser next to the top had always been loose and dad had never got around to fixing it. Taking a screwdriver out of the bag I levered it to one side to find a brown envelope behind it.

With trembling hands I opened it and a building society deposit book fell out. I took a deep breath, opened it at the last page and sat back in amazement. The date of the last deposit was listed as 1971 and the balance stood at £754, 254 and 65 pence. This was the inheritance; and since I was the only child left it was mine. It wasn't until my head had cleared and my eyes refocused, that I saw a little stamp at the bottom of the page:

Account Closed - 26th May 1972

There was a neatly folded piece of notepaper on the stair and this had clearly fallen out of the book when I opened it. I unfolded it and immediately recognised my mother's handwriting.

My mother's message to my father was brief and to the point;

Dan Mc Faul The Weaver

25 May 1972

Dear Denis,

Thanks for the gift. I'll make sure that I find a good use for it after all the years that I have spent penny pinching with you. Don't bother looking for me I will be long gone by the time you read this.

Mary Ellen.

I had to smile, when I woke up, you see, in 'real life' mum and dad had stayed happily together, but evidently my actions in 1947 had completely changed the whole course of our McFaul family history.

Now, is it any wonder that I have so much trouble trying to trace people from my Family Tree.

NOTES

NOTES